The Navigation Quartet

2: Setting a New Course

Chris Cheek

83 Latimer Road
Eastbourne
East Sussex, BN22 7EL
Tel: 01729 840756
Email: admin@two-fm.co.uk

This is a work of fiction. Names, characters, businesses, places, events, locales, and incidents are either the products of the author's imagination or used in a fictitious manner. Any resemblance to actual persons, living or dead, or actual events is purely coincidental.

Warning: This book includes material that is intended for a mature adult audience, including scenes featuring explicit sexual content, some graphic language and adult situations.

Cover images: Shutterstock, David Burrell

A CIP catalogue record for this book is available from the British Library

ISBN 978-1-9996479-8-8

For Michael

"Journeys end in lovers' meeting,
    Every wise man's son doth know.

What is love, 'tis not hereafter,
Present mirth, hath present laughter:
    What's to come, is still unsure."

Twelfth Night
William Shakespeare.

The Navigation Quartet

2: Setting a New Course

Chapter 1

David

The sun was high when David awoke. He felt disoriented for a moment, wondering where he was, then he recognised his surroundings: Alan's flat in London. Staring out of the bedroom window into a clear blue sky marked only by vapour trails, the events of the previous day flashed across his mind's eye like episodes from a badly edited film.

It was an odd sensation, leaving him feeling detached from reality: an observer in his own drama. For that was what it had been yesterday, a right kerfuffle. Outed as bisexual to his wife and family by his own union chairman, thrown out by his wife without even being allowed to say goodbye to his two sons, and finally rejected by his own father for not honouring the promises he had made when he'd married six years earlier.

Faced with this triple whammy, he'd done the only logical thing – headed back to Alan's arms, to the sanctuary provided by his best friend and lover, with all possible speed. Getting from Yorkshire to London late on an August Saturday night was easier said than done, but David had been incredibly fortunate to hitch a lift from a

London-based photographer who had brought him safely to the end of the road.

He'd remember the guy, Gavin, for the rest of his life – not only for the lift, but also for the words of comfort and wisdom he'd offered during the two-hundred-mile journey down the motorway. The other thing he'd never forget was being wrapped in Alan's arms, the feelings of comfort, warmth and protection that he gave. Even now, lying in bed on his own, David wriggled with joy at the sensations. They made him feel as if he'd arrived home, literally and metaphorically, and it had felt glorious both on the doorstep and later in this bed.

It had all started back in February, the day when Alan, his closest friend since the age of nine, had boarded his bus in Leeds bus station. They'd not set eyes on each other for six years until that gloomy winter's morning seven short months ago. David had been so glad to see him again, little realising that his life was about to be turned upside down completely and shaken to bits.

At the age of nineteen, Alan had buggered off to London in search of fame and fortune. Suddenly there he'd been, as large as life and twice as natural, paying his fare on the bus that David drove for a living, then riding to Sedgethwaite, the West Yorkshire town where they'd grown up.

The sight of Alan that day had reminded David of his own cowardice in not following his friend to London. Instead, he had stayed put, avoiding risk and marrying Mona, another friend from school. 'Settling down' and playing safe had been a mistake. Deep down, David had always known it but had refused to admit it even to himself – at least until that February morning. When Alan bounced back into his life, he realised how big an error he had made. A single night out and a few drinks, that's all it had taken. It had been such a powerful reminder of what he'd been missing – companionship, a shared sense of humour, a common history, just being able to goof about.

Then there'd been the other thing. David had been convinced that he'd shut and locked the door on the feelings he'd experienced as a nineteen year old during one night spent in Alan's arms. That door had been wrenched open after Alan's return, but the real key to unlocking it permanently had been delivered by his employer. The company had offered David the chance to swap local bus driving for work on an express coach service to London. This involved overnight stays in the capital every eight days or so, and for several months these had been spent happily in Alan's arms.

He'd quickly realised that something would have to give, that he'd have to act if he wanted to spend the rest of his life with Alan. But he had hesitated, somehow unable to find the words to announce his intentions to his wife. Instead, he and Alan had created a little world of their own for a few weeks, a small bubble to which David returned each week for twelve short hours.

The bubble had certainly burst on Friday night when Douggie Thorpe, union chairman and Sedgethwaite bus depot's resident homophobe, had spotted him holding hands with Alan and kissing his friend Simon on the cheek outside the Salisbury pub in the heart of London. All the joy of having just seen his first West End musical had melted away, dissolved by the acid of Douggie's sneer.

Now, less than two days later, David was contemplating

the wreck of his home life and his career. He realised with sickening clarity exactly how much this meant. He was going to lose everything he had taken for granted for the last few years – friends and acquaintances, his parents and siblings, the routine of life at the depot, the house he and Mona had shared for the last five years, his marriage and his kids. He might have grown apart from her in the last few months but she'd still represented something in his life. He'd felt secure, even though he'd sometimes chafed against it. It had been familiar. Comfortable.

All gone.

There were the boys, too. David might not have been particularly demonstrative – it was not in his nature, or at least it hadn't been until Alan reappeared in his life – but he loved Tommy and Kevin with all his heart. He still remembered the wonder of holding them in his arms as newly born babies, and the silent vow he'd made each time to love and protect them.

That hadn't gone well, had it? In the brilliant light of this hot August morning, he realised how the boys would feel losing their father so suddenly and without notice. They'd be bound to think that he didn't love them any more. He knew from last night's experience with his own father how awful that could feel; it had resembled a physical sensation, as if part of his insides had shrivelled up. Even now, it made him want to curl up as if to ward off a punch in the stomach.

On a more practical level, he worried about what his enforced departure and future absence would do to the boys' lives. He was abandoning them to single parenthood and the influence of his mother-in-law with all her false gentility and social climbing. Now she was free to feed them intolerance and hatred of their father. Christ!

He turned away from the window, suddenly unable to cope with the brightness of the sunshine. Instead, he stared at the wall on the other side of the bed so closely that he could pick out faint brush marks in the emulsion. Tears sprang to his eyes born as much from frustration with himself as sadness or regret. God, he'd been such a fool!

If only he'd manned up and told the truth. It might not have made that much difference –his marriage breaking up had probably been inevitable – but at least it might have been less confrontational. It might have been possible to make better arrangements for the boys. But not after this weekend: at best he'd be mired in arguments that could end up in court; at worst, he might never see them again.

His reverie was interrupted when Alan came into the room and placed a mug of coffee on the bedside table. "Oh, good. You're awake. How are you feeling, Davy?"

David turned to face him, revealing his tear-streaked face. He tried to speak but his throat was constricted. He felt the mattress dip as Alan got onto the bed next to him, and immediately found himself wrapped into a tight hug.

The feelings of comfort and warmth took over once again, and David was able to let go of his emotions. His body was wracked with sobs. Alan held him, rubbing his back gently, whispering words of comfort. Eventually, the sobs faded away and he felt calmer, surrounded by the warmth of Alan's embrace and grounded by his calmness.

Alan released him for a moment and reached across to the bedside table. David felt the brush of paper as his cheeks were wiped gently before the tissue was placed in his hands.

"Good blow," Alan murmured with a gentle smile. David had a sudden memory of being ten years old again, being comforted by his friend after falling over and grazing his knee. He realised how secure and contented he felt when Alan took care of him. It was a timely reminder of why he was here, this special feeling of loving and being loved back unconditionally.

He did as he was bidden and blew his nose. That made him feel better too.

"There. Better?"

David nodded. "Thanks."

"Do you want some of this coffee?"

Another nod. "Please."

Alan helped him to sit up then passed him the mug but remained glued to David's side, arm still round his shoulders. David rested his head on Alan's shoulder and sipped quietly, eyes still stinging and feeling slightly headachy.

"Did you manage much sleep?" Alan asked.

"Yeah, about six hours all told, I think. You?"

"Bit less, I think. Woke up a little before eight, saw the sunshine and knew that I wasn't going to drop off again, so I got up and left you in peace."

"Thanks."

"Talked to Simon, who sends his love by the way, and to Tris, ditto. Ian sent you a big hug too."

"Thanks." David momentarily felt overwhelmed by their kindness and concern. He was sure he didn't deserve it. "I... er... I'm sorry about imposing on you. I never dreamed…"

"Hush now, none of that. You mustn't start blaming yourself for what happened, okay?"

Alan's words shocked David. "How can I not, Al? It's all my fault…"

"It's not *all* your fault, Davy. Mona didn't have to throw you out bag and baggage. That was her decision…"

"More like her mother's," David responded bitterly.

"That's as maybe. Anyway, the point is that *she* threw *you* out. You didn't desert her or walk out on her without a word."

"But the boys…"

"Same applies, Davy. Mona and her mother took them away from home and refused to allow you to see them. What choice did you have?"

"None, I agree. But…"

"But nothing. And us, down here? You can't possibly take sole responsibility for this… It takes two to tango. And I've no doubt whatever that even now there'll be people in Sedgethwaite saying that this is all my fault, leading you astray with my fancy London ways."

"Even if that was true – and it isn't, by the way – I could still have said no, Al. I was a married man with responsibilities. As my dad said, I made promises to Mona six years ago and I should've stuck to them."

Even as he uttered the words, David knew how impossible that would have been. Once he'd met Alan again and they had talked, he could no more have sent him packing than flown to the moon. How could he have spent the rest of his life stuck in Sedgethwaite knowing that Alan loved him and wanted him? It was inconceivable that he could have acted out the role of respectable family man for the next twenty or thirty years knowing what he had thrown away. It would have driven him round the bend. However, recognising the inevitability of what had happened did not make it right, nor did it ease his conscience.

They were silent for a moment or two. David was still encased in Alan's embrace and revelled in the feeling of security it gave him. Eventually he broke the silence; his instinct told him that the attempt to alleviate his suffering should be acknowledged even if he didn't feel that he deserved such comfort. "Anyway, thanks, Al."

"Whatever for?"

"Trying to help. Being here. Loving me. Putting up with me."

David felt Alan squeeze his shoulder in response. "Anything for my Davy."

Chapter 2

Alan

Alan sat on the bed for a few minutes longer, luxuriating in the feel of David in his arms. Despite all the trauma of the last forty-eight hours, he felt enormously happy that his old friend and lover was here.

The rekindling of their relationship after such a long gap had brought him a happiness that he hadn't experienced for a very long time, if ever. He had high hopes that what they had now would prove durable – but he also recognised that the next few weeks and months would be hard.

He looked down and saw the look of peace that had descended on David's face. His breathing had become calmer and more even in the last few minutes: he was asleep again. Good. He needed the rest. Alan smiled. He'd have to move soon and get on with his day, but meanwhile he would enjoy this moment.

But his brain refused to shut down and he couldn't help thinking about what they might be facing. First, there were the legal ramifications of a divorce and access dispute. Given what he'd been told about Mona's behaviour and attitude last night, he knew there'd be a battle and it would not be pretty. There was also the question of a job for David and what he wanted to do with his career. Not least of the challenges would be coming to terms with life in London – the sheer pace of the place, the cultural differences, and the enormous social gap that had opened up between them since Alan's departure from Yorkshire.

They'd had glimpses of that problem at Simon's dinner party the other week when the conversation had gone completely over David's head and left him feeling extremely uncomfortable. There'd been the incident at Tris and Ian's party as well, when two of the guests had referred to David as Alan's "rough trade". Alan still burned with anger when he recalled the incident. The snobbery and pure bitchiness on display that night – didn't the gay community have enough to deal with without being so judgemental of each other? It was like a self-inflicted wound. Sad though it was, he was sure there'd be more of it to come.

No, it wouldn't be easy but he couldn't think of any challenge he would rather face. Meeting up with Davy again, Alan had realised that something had been missing for the six years they'd spent apart. Life in London had seemed so exciting at first – his career, meeting Tris and through him discovering so much about music, theatre and the arts. Now he realised that he'd been like an incomplete jigsaw puzzle the whole time, almost all there but with one crucial piece missing. David. Now that he'd found his missing piece, he never wanted to lose it again.

David stirred, bringing him back to the present. The most immediate concern was the three-day course that Alan had to go on, which meant leaving for a remote venue in Shropshire this evening. It was clear that David was in no state to be left on his own. Alan desperately wanted to pull out but he knew how much importance his boss attached to this social media business and what it might mean in future. Non-attendance would seriously damage his career, so he had to go. Being unemployed now would do neither him nor David any good.

Tris's partner Ian, who was also Alan's co-worker, was attending the course too and they'd planned to travel together. He'd spoken to Tris earlier this morning to float the idea of David staying with him for a few days and the answer had been an enthusiastic yes. All Alan now had to do was to persuade David that it would be a good idea.

David seemed a bit wary of Tris, perhaps because of the closeness of Alan's friendship with him and the fact that they'd once been lovers. There was also the fact that Tris was a bit of a toff; he was amazingly well-off and lived in a rather grand house in one of the poshest parts of London. David had only met him once at Tris and Ian's engagement party, but Tris had liked David on sight and immediately taken him under his wing. Alan hoped that everything would be okay.

David stirred again. "I must have fallen sleep again. Sorry."

"It's alright. I'm sure you need the rest."

"True, but I can't stay here all day."

"It wouldn't do you any harm to rest and relax a bit."

David wriggled slightly, pressing himself closer to Alan. "Mebbe so – specially if you're with me, cuddling, like."

"I'd love to, sweetheart, but unfortunately I've got to go on this bloody course."

"Oh hell, aye. I'd forgotten about that."

"Believe me, Davy, I'd get out of it if I could. But I'm giving Ian a lift, and my boss would have my guts for garters if I didn't go."

"I know, Al. I do understand. I'll be okay here. It'll do me good to chill for a couple of days. Simon and Peter are downstairs if I need some company."

"They're away too, I'm afraid. They fly off to Italy tomorrow for a couple of weeks. So, Tris wondered whether you'd like to go over to his place and keep him company as Ian's away too."

As he'd half-expected, Alan felt David's body tense up. He wouldn't meet Alan's eyes.

"I'll be all right on my own, honestly," came the predictable reply. "I couldn't put Tris to any trouble."

"I'm sure it'd be no trouble. I thought it would be nice for you to have a bit of luxury – and some company, if you wanted it."

"Really, Al, I'll be all right. I don't feel much like company at present."

This was not going the way that Alan had hoped. He hated the idea of leaving David on his own, especially as he was clearly in such an emotional state. "I get that, Davy, totally. But you've had an awful time the last three days. To be honest, I'd be happier if there was somebody around to look after you."

David huffed a short laugh. "I'm not going to top myself or anything, you know."

"I know you're not." Alan tried to keep his slight irritation out of his tone. "That's not the point at all. It's about having somebody who's there for you..."

"But he hardly knows me. He met me once at his engagement party – what can he know about me?"

"He knows what I've told him."

"Oh, been gossiping about me behind my back, have you? Talking about your 'rough trade'?"

"Davy, that's hardly fair. Just because one distant acquaintance made a snobby remark at Tris's party, you can't blame him for what happened that night. And he is my best friend. I needed to talk about ... what was happening."

"I thought I was your best friend."

Alan felt that he was being trapped into an unnecessary argument and tried to keep calm, but the irritation in his voice remained. "Davy, you know fine well that you're far more than that to me."

Suddenly the tension left David's body. "I know, Al. I'm sorry. That was a daft thing to say. Of course I'll stay with Tris. It'll be a good chance to get to know him a bit better."

Inwardly, Alan breathed a sigh of relief. "That's what I thought, too."

"Yeah. I just wish everything was a bit less fraught, that's all."

"Tris will help. He's got a heart of gold. You can say anything to him and if there's anything he can do for you, he will. Believe me."

David grinned up at him. "Thanks. It might be good to get another view, you know."

"I'm sure it will."

"Only trouble is, I haven't actually got any clothes. I've only got what was in my overnight bag from Friday and what I was stood up in last night."

"Ah. Hadn't thought of that. I'm not sure that my stuff will fit you, either. We'd better nip out and get you something to wear, then."

Chapter 3

David

As he lay in bed, David heard Tris's grandfather clock strike the hour. It was now seven o'clock on Sunday evening, and he was in the process of waking up after a rest and another sleep.

The earlier part of the day had passed so quickly – waking up in Alan's bed, a quick cup of coffee with Simon and Peter who were frantically busy packing for their holiday. Afterwards there was a brisk shopping trip for clothes and other essentials to get him through the next few days, plus a quick burger, before Alan had to get ready and pack for his course. Before he'd known it, it was time to head over the river for Alan to drop him off and collect Ian for their drive to the Midlands. Now David found himself in this fantastically posh house with a man he'd only met once – and he was totally out of his comfort zone.

All the activity earlier had done little to end the sense of detachment he'd felt as soon as he'd woken up this morning. He felt like something between a social work client and a parcel, shepherded about and dropped off so that yet another concerned pair of eyes could pat his hand, express sympathy for his predicament and pass him on to the next office.

The welcome he'd received from Tris and Ian had been as warm as Alan had predicted. There were big hugs from both of them before Ian disappeared off with Alan to the wilds of Shropshire and their training course.

He'd been brought up to the room he was in now, the same one that he and Alan had shared on the night of the party. It had also been Alan's room when he'd shared the house with Tris a few years previously.

"I'll leave you to get settled," Tris said. "No pressure – take your time and have a rest if you want one. I don't want to crowd you or overwhelm you with sympathy or unwelcome advice. Chill is the operative word for the next few days, I think."

David smiled at that. "Thanks, Tris. A rest would be grand."

"Fine. I'll make us some supper about eight. You happy with pasta?"

"Definitely – specially if it's as good as Al's."

Tris laughed and headed for the door. "My dear, trust me. I taught him all he knows. See you later."

David unpacked and lay down on the bed: it looked so comfy, he had to try it. He leant back on the soft pillows, cuddling one of the scatter cushions to his chest. He was on his back and he stared at the ceiling, reflecting how high it seemed and how spacious it made the room feel. He closed his eyes for a moment to rest them. Next thing he knew, two hours had passed and the clock was striking seven. He still felt drained but in a better frame of mind than earlier, less detached from reality.

After a few moments luxuriating, he roused himself, gave his face a quick rinse and headed downstairs. He found Tris in the basement kitchen preparing their supper. He looked up and smiled. "Good rest?"

"Grand, thanks. That bed is wonderful."

"Good. Drink? There's beer or wine, or something soft if you'd prefer."

"White wine would be lovely, thanks." David had noticed a glass next to Trist's chopping board and thought it would be a good choice. He accepted a glass and lifted it. "Cheers." He took a sip and savoured the cold sharpness. "You know, Al's given me quite a taste for this since I started on the London run."

"Yes, he likes his drop of vino. That's my fault, I suspect."

David laughed. "He was definitely a beer man when he left Yorkshire, I can tell you. He could drink me under the table anytime when we were younger. I couldn't put it away like him – two pints has always been my limit."

"Me too. Ian can sink a few, as well. I suppose it's because he's a cricketer – he got used to it during all those post-match boozing sessions."

"Have you always preferred wine?"

Tris nodded. "It was always around the house when I was growing up. I was allowed a sip at Christmas from when I was quite young, and it went on from there."

"There was never any wine in our house. Dad was never keen on drink at all – could manage the odd half in the pub, if pressed. Mum liked the occasional sweet sherry – you know, Christmas, birthdays. She once gave me a taste when I was about fourteen: brown, thick and sticky, it was." David grinned. "It looked like sweet cough medicine and tasted like treacle." He shuddered at the memory.

Tris laughed. "I remember it too. My gran used to drink it – God, it was awful stuff."

David took another sip of his wine. "Not like this. This is great."

"Glad you like it. Now take a pew and I'll dish this lot up."

"Smells amazing. It's made me realise how hungry I am."

As they sat down to eat, both their phones buzzed with text messages. Alan and Ian had arrived safely at their hotel. "Good," remarked David. "Didn't envy them that trip on the M6 on a busy summer Sunday."

"Me neither. Why on earth their boss insisted on a Sunday night start, I don't know. Because he's a workaholic, he thinks everybody else should be the same."

"Al said that he's very demanding."

"You're not kidding. I know I work crazy hours sometimes, but really… Anyway, enough of that. They've both heard me moan about him often enough."

"Has Ian worked there as long as Al?"

Tris shook his head. "No, he only joined about three years ago. He became friends with Alan and that's how he and I met – he came here for supper one night and *kapow*!"

David smiled. "That quick, eh?"

"Absolutely. Bit like you two in February, I gather."

"Yeah, I suppose you're right. I hadn't thought of it like that." He gave a short laugh. "I know I had a hell of a shock when Al got on my bus in Leeds that morning."

"I can imagine. Out of the blue like that."

"I was chuffed to bits about seeing him again, but to tell the truth I was frightened to death too."

"How come?"

"I'd been feeling a bit unsettled. Then Al turns up and stirs it all up good and proper. We'd only got as far as sharing a quick coffee and I realised how much I'd missed him, how boring my life was compared with his, how I could have gone too. And, of course, there was that business on his last night in Sedgethwaite – how it had felt just to hold him, you know?" David felt his eyes fill again as he remembered his walk back from Alan's hotel after their reunion drink, and the conflict that had been going through his mind.

Tris noticed his distress and reached across the table to lay his hand over David's. It felt comfortable and warm. "You must have been absolutely terrified."

David looked up and smiled wanly, noticing the warmth and sympathy in his host's eyes. "Yep. And I was right to be, given what's gone on."

Tris nodded. He lifted his hand from David's and topped up their wine. "And now? How do you feel now?"

That was exactly the question that David hoped Tris wouldn't ask. But he'd known all along that he would have to face it at some point.

Tris noticed his hesitation and spoke again. "It's okay if you'd rather not talk about it."

"No, it's fine. I need to, I know. So... I'm okay, I think. It all still seems so unreal, Tris. As if it was all on the telly, happening to somebody else. If I start to think or talk about it, it becomes too real and then I can't cope. I had a meltdown with Al this morning, and I've avoided thinking about anything since."

"What prompted the meltdown?"

David sighed. "Guilt, mainly. Mona, obviously – the way I cheated on her. The boys, mainly. How they must be feeling. And there's the future – divorce, I assume. Mona'll keep the boys and will try to keep them away from me. And my life. Will my dad ever come round? And what about Al? Will he still want me after this drama? What about my job? Should I quit? Do I move down here? Where am I going to get a job and how am I going to manage ... and... what about money... and..." The longer David talked the shorter his sentences became. He found himself becoming short of breath.

Tris moved round the table to sit next to him and put his arm round his shoulders. "Hey, slow down, old chap. Take some deep breaths. Come on now, breathe with me..."

David followed Tris's instructions and took several deep breaths, immediately feeling better and coming out of what had clearly been shaping up to be a panic attack. He smiled wistfully. "See? That's what happens every time I think about what's going on."

Tris kept his arm in place for a few more moments before moving away and reaching for his wine. "I can understand how you feel. It is a pretty formidable list of unknowns."

David smiled. "Yeah, that's the problem, I suppose. Nothing is certain."

"So, I think the best thing we can do for the next couple of days is try to remove some of the uncertainty. And I think you should start with Alan."

"How do you mean?"

"You can be certain of him. I'm sure you know that in

your heart of hearts. But believe me his love for you is rock solid, as much as mine is for Ian."

"But…"

"No buts, David. If you'd seen how much he's changed since meeting up with you again in February, you'd understand. He'll stand by you, whatever it takes. So, cross that off your list to worry about."

David took a deep breath and exhaled slowly, closing his eyes for a moment. Deep down, he knew that Tris was right and that his future with Alan was the least of his worries right now. "Yeah, you're right, of course."

"Good. So, what else on your list can we cross off, I wonder? Job?"

"Possibly. But how? What?"

"You're a qualified and experienced PSV driver, with an excellent record I've no doubt."

David nodded.

"I don't think there'll be a problem. Judging by all the ads I see on the backs of buses and in the evening paper, the world and his wife seem to be crying out for bus and coach drivers down here. You'd have no trouble getting that sort of job if that's what you want." Tris grinned at him. "Bloody hard in London traffic, though."

"You're not kidding. I've seen a bit of it coming into Victoria from the M1."

"If not that, what else might you want to do?"

David shook his head. "I … I'm not sure. I had wondered about going back to college, doing something with my maths. Al reminded me the other week that I was good at figures and stuff when we were at school. But if I've got Mona and the kids to support…"

"Hmm. There might be some grants about, or you might be able to do a day-release course. Might be best to get a driving job to tide you over while you work it all out."

David nodded. "I think you're right, you know. It'll take a few months to sort this lot out anyway, so it'd be October next year before I could do much about that."

"You could start making enquiries about driving jobs this week."

"I ought to resign at Sedgethwaite, too. I've got some holiday due, so that can be my notice. Wouldn't want to get a name as a 'bad leaver'."

Tris nodded. "Sooner the better, I would have thought. I guess it won't come as a shock."

"Definitely not. The depot inspector has already covered my duties for this week. In any case, I was scheduled for rest days today and tomorrow, so they wouldn't expect to see me till Tuesday."

"Great. You can get out with your record intact."

David laughed. "Hardly that, Tris. Not with all the poison Douggie Thorpe and his cronies will be spreading."

Tris shook his head. "I don't think that matters. Union men don't give references, the bosses do – and they wouldn't mention this. Besides, people down here are hardly likely to worry about you being gay or bi or whatever."

Knowing what the bus industry's grapevine could be like, David wasn't convinced but he thought Tris was probably right about London companies not caring about his sexuality. "That's true, I hadn't thought of that."

Tris grinned at him. "See? You must always listen to your Uncle Tristan."

"Promise."

"And the family? We ought to have a plan there too, you know."

David sighed. He didn't want to think about Mona and the boys tonight, but he knew the question had to be faced and that he hadn't got the first idea about what to do. "Divorce, I suppose," he replied. "I assume that's what she'll want now. She can claim adultery."

"Er, no, actually. Legally, to commit adultery you have to do with a person of the opposite sex."

David began to laugh. For some reason, this revelation struck him as incredibly funny. He was free of the sin of adultery because he'd done it with a man and not a woman. Eventually he recovered himself and managed to speak. "That's crazy."

"Quite so, quite so. I think that, as things stand, the only grounds either of you have are what they call 'unreasonable behaviour'. I think she could claim that because of your affair with Alan. I'm no divorce expert, but I reckon you could probably agree on that as the grounds."

"I see. Do we have to agree on everything? Can't we simply do it through lawyers?"

"It makes life simpler if you can reach agreement on the kids, money and what they call the 'irretrievable breakdown' of the marriage."

"I can't imagine her agreeing to anything in her current mood."

"No, I'm sure you're right. But I suspect that she'll calm down eventually and I'm sure she'll get the same advice from her own lawyer, assuming she goes to one."

"She'll do that, all right. Mummy will insist. I think

they're both determined to keep me away from the kids."

"What, for ever?"

"That's what she said on Saturday night."

"Hmm. I don't think she'll get away with that. She'll have to allow you some access."

"But how, Tris? That's the problem. If I'm living down here, two hundred miles away?"

"You could agree visitation rights. You could go up once a month and see the boys at your mum's house or somewhere. But she can't stop you seeing them, I'm sure of that."

"Jen's husband said I should avoid going to court."

"I think he's right. Much better try to reach agreement, if you can – though I know how difficult that must seem."

"Would a court be sympathetic to me?"

Tris shook his head. "I'm not going to lie, David. Attitudes to being gay have improved greatly, and the law has changed a huge amount, but I'm not sure that a family court is ever going to look kindly on a guy in your situation."

"You mean leaving his family to become a queer?" David laughed bitterly. "Not good anywhere, I guess. But especially not in a place like Sedgethwaite."

"You know your own people better than I do, old son," Tris responded diplomatically. "But I don't think you'd be flavour of the month in any family court. Which is why it would be better to stay clear of them, if you can."

"Aye, I think you're right. So what do I do next?"

"Normally the first thing to try would be mediation. But if you're right and she's gone straight to a solicitor, you'd better get one too. I know a guy who's a great family lawyer and would be very sympathetic. Just say the word and I'll put you in touch with him."

"That would be great, Tris. Thanks. But I don't know how I'm going to pay for it all."

"You can cross that bridge when you come to it, though it does bring me to one thing I wanted to say, which you might not like."

"Oh?"

"Yes. About money."

David couldn't help it. He found himself bridling. "And?"

"You must be prepared to accept help if you need it. Especially from Alan."

"But..."

Tris held both up hands palm outwards. "No buts, David. I know how difficult it can be – you Yorkshiremen are so bloody independent-minded. God knows, I shared a house with one for three years."

David couldn't help smiling. "Go on."

"It's simply this. Alan has a good job, as does Ian, so neither is short of a bob or two. And me, I have more money than I know what to do with. So helping is not a problem – and you must *not* get stressed about money."

"I can't be a sponger, Tris."

"I understand that, David. Absolutely. But don't forget that you and Alan are planning to be in a relationship, and that implies sharing and working together. A bit like you've done with your wife for the last six years."

"Aye. I suppose you're right."

"Yeah, you're a team, you and Alan, and I suspect a bloody good one. If you remember that, you'll be all right.

Now, let's clear these pots up and settle down to watch a film."

Tris's film choice was *Beautiful Thing,* a gay romance set in London in the late nineties. David and Mona had never been big cinemagoers, especially after the boys were born, and in any case this was not the sort of thing she would ever watch.

David watched entranced as the adventures of Jamie and Ste unfolded, and he cried a little at the happy ending. He found that he could identify with the gay characters in a working-class environment, albeit London rather than Yorkshire. It was liberating and he enjoyed the feeling that he was not alone; other ordinary guys could be gay too.

He thanked Tris warmly for the evening and headed upstairs, suddenly exhausted once more.

"I've got one early conference on a forthcoming case tomorrow, but I should be back here by eleven and we can go somewhere nice for lunch. You know where everything is in the kitchen so you can rustle up some breakfast, I think."

"I'll be fine, Tris, thanks. Goodnight."

"Sleep well, old chap. See you in the morning."

As David got upstairs, a text message arrived from Alan asking if he was free. He replied that he was and undressed quickly, waiting for Alan's call. After chatting for a few minutes it became clear that they were both very tired so David, in particular, was keen to shoo Alan away. "I had a couple of hours' rest this afternoon. You had a stressful drive for two-and-a-half hours. And you've got to be all bright-eyed and bushy-tailed in the morning. Time for bed, love."

As if to confirm David's statement, Alan let out a loud and long yawn.

"See? Told you. Now good night … and thanks for bringing me here, Al. Tris has been wonderful tonight, so kind and helpful."

"Oh, I am glad. I knew he would be. Talk tomorrow sometime. 'Night."

David disconnected and lay back on his pillows. Talking to Alan had made him crave his presence, especially the warm feeling of being held securely in his arms. At the moment it was about the only place that offered him any certainty.

He felt a good deal better, though. His talk with Tris had certainly helped, and his host had been right to try to tackle some of the issues bothering him. David felt less at sea and could begin to look forwards again. It was a welcome sensation that left him with a small smile on his face as he drifted off.

With Tris's help, the next couple of days saw some movement in the process of untangling David's life.

The first task on Monday was to send a formal written resignation from his job. After he'd posted it, he spoke to his depot inspector on the phone to tell him it was on the way. He'd always got on well with Jack Davis, and this was no exception. Jack said he would be sorry to lose David and wished him all the best for the future. "If you need a reference for another bus company, tell 'em to ring me, lad," he said. "I'll put 'em right."

Jack also updated him on latest news from the depot; apparently Douggie Thorpe's actions had not been appreciated by the younger guys on the staff. Several had told him to stop making homophobic remarks and one had even pointed out that, apart from anything else, such intolerance was against union policy. David snorted – Douggie wouldn't have appreciated that at all.

He also began looking for a job in London. As Tris had predicted, there were certainly no lack of vacancies. He wanted to talk to Alan before making any decisions about the sort of job he wanted. He could go back to local bus work, or try to stick with express work. He could branch into one of the tourist coach companies, where there were plenty of opportunities at this time of year, though his lack of experience and limited knowledge of the capital's streets would be a big disadvantage initially.

The big issue was the hours; whichever sort of driving job he did, it would involve some unsocial hours and working at weekends. David wanted to make sure that Alan was okay with that because he knew from his experience with his wife that it took some getting used to. His absences had caused some problems in the early days of their marriage before they'd settled into a routine. He didn't want the same thing to happen with Al. In that sense, driving local buses might be better because schedules and rotas made life predictable, whereas he'd been told that tourist and charter coach drivers rarely knew what jobs they were doing from one day to the next. On the other hand, he felt he'd outgrown local buses in Sedgethwaite, and there'd be even less interaction with the public here in London.

So many different options, each one with arguments in its favour. His head began to spin as he tried to think through the choices and he could feel his breath getting shorter again. It was easier to stop thinking about it.

At the back of his mind, he was nervous about his apparent inability to think about pretty much anything without getting into a bit of a state – like his mini panic attack with Tris the previous evening. He'd never felt like this before, except possibly that one time when they were nineteen when Alan had asked him to go to London with him. He knew now that it was panic that night that had led him to say no. Look what a good decision that had been.

Feeling so anxious at the slightest thing rather frightened him. Where had that had come from? Best thing to do was switch off, not think too much, take life as it came. He'd talk to Al when they were back home together.

Chapter 4

Alan

Alan and Ian arrived back from their course late on Thursday evening in an exuberant mood. They had enjoyed their four days and were full of enthusiasm about what they'd learned. Like their boss, they were now convinced that the burgeoning of social media programs on the internet promised to be the next big thing to transform the marketing business.

Warned of their arrival, Tris had prepared supper. The four friends sat in the basement kitchen, drinking wine and chatting while he put the finishing touches to the meal. The room was full of laughter and it warmed Alan's heart to see David fully involved.

After *Beautiful Thing* on Sunday night, David and Tris had been watching other notable LGBT films all week. Judging by his comments, David had enjoyed Monday and Tuesday nights' offerings, *Torch Song Trilogy* and *Maurice*, but the one he'd loved most – and the cause of the current hilarity – was the original 1978 version of *La Cage aux Folles*.

"I tell you," he was busy telling Ian, "I'd never actually

seen a foreign film before, so I was a bit worried. I was so glad of the subtitles. I was laughing so hard I'd have missed half the jokes if the words hadn't been on the screen."

Alan laughed, delighted to see David so animated. He remembered the first time he'd seen the film. "I thought Jacob the maid was so marvellous – hilarious, as well as hot as anything."

"You're not kidding," Tris responded. "It's a while since I'd watched it and I'd forgotten how wonderful it is. It must have seemed so outrageous when it came out. It was a bit of a shock when I first saw it ten years ago."

As the meal progressed, they created a steadily lengthening list of films for David to watch in order to bring him up to speed on gay culture, the upshot being a plan for an LGBT film night for the four of them once a week.

By the time they'd progressed to coffee, the discussion had moved from film to books. Early gay authors such as Gore Vidal, Fritz Peters and Michael Campbell cropped up, but Tris counselled against them at present. "Too depressing," he warned. "They were all written in an era when 'happily ever after' was not considered a possibility for gay men."

"Forster's *Maurice* is the first novel I read where a happy ending was envisaged for a gay love affair," added Ian. "But of course he's been lambasted ever since for refusing to publish it till after his death."

"Why?" David asked.

"It's a generational thing, I suppose," Tris replied. "For somebody of Forster's age, being gay was a matter of deep shame, as you saw in the film the other night. Not to mention the danger of prosecution and imprisonment. After all, he was a teenager during the Oscar Wilde scandal and we'd only been legal for a couple of years when he died."

"Aye, we forget that," David said. "And I know a bit about the shame after last weekend."

"Yeah, sorry to remind you of that," Tris said. "We should talk about something a bit more cheerful."

"No, no. It's okay, honestly," David said. "I loved the film, thought it was grand. Especially the happy ending."

"Except somehow you know they'll all be in the First World War and won't survive it," Ian interrupted gloomily.

Alan laughed. "Thanks for putting a dampener on it!"

"I know, but it's true," Ian responded. "I always think about that for all those guys in Forster's novels. They simply don't know what the world's got in store for them."

"Ultimately, none of us does, do we?" David asked. "Look at me last February. Cruising along living a nice quiet life, then along comes this one and immediately turns everything upside down."

"You're right, Davy," Alan agreed with a small laugh. "We can't know the future – that's why so many of us live for the day. And on that cheerful note, I'm going to take you home. It's getting late and Ian and I have got to be on parade again in the morning."

While David disappeared upstairs to collect his bag. Alan turned to Tris. "Was he okay?"

Tris nodded and smiled reassuringly. "Fine. I'm sure everything will be all right eventually, though I think he's in for a tough few months. But we've got your backs. If you need anything, just ask."

David reappeared and he and Alan said their goodnights. David gave Tris a special hug. "Thanks for everything. It's been grand – more helpful than you can ever know."

Once back at Alan's flat, the first job was to open all the windows. It had been very hot while the place was empty and all the windows were closed, so the rooms were like an oven. Fortunately a breeze had sprung up during the evening, so it didn't take long for them to cool down.

"Do you want a quick cuppa before we turn in, Davy?"

"I'd love one, thanks. I'll do it while you unpack and sort yourself out."

He pottered off to the kitchen to put the kettle on and Alan smiled to himself at this pleasantly domestic scene. He'd enjoyed having David stay during his overnights in London for those few weeks before his life had blown up, but one night in eight had only made him crave more of his friend's company on the other seven. Now that his wish had been granted, he hoped everything would be okay.

Alan busied himself unpacking until he heard David's utter the magic words, "Tea's up." He joined him on the sofa in the sitting room and they sat close together, bodies pressed against one another.

"Hmm, this is nice," Alan said after a few moments. "I missed you this week. Kept wondering how you were."

David seemed surprised. "Straight up? No kidding? I'd have thought you were too busy."

"Nope, no kidding. I know life's difficult, Davy, and that it's probably going to get worse before it gets better.

But I'm still so glad you're here."

"Thanks, love. To answer your question, I'm okay ... I think. Lots to worry about, lots to do, but Tris has been so helpful these last few days, you wouldn't believe it."

Alan laughed. "You forget I've known Tris for a long time. I told you he'd want to help."

"He certainly has – legal advice, employment advice, helping with jobs, you name it."

"Good, I'm glad. I was worried about you on Sunday. You seemed so overwhelmed."

"I was. Worried about imposing myself on you, my job, the boys, my dad, the future..."

Alan's stomach dipped violently at David's words. "Imposing yourself? You surely don't think that?"

"No, love, no, I don't. Not now. But it must have come as a bit of a shock. There's a big difference between somebody staying for the odd night and having somebody with you twenty-four-seven."

"But we'd talked about this, Davy. You knew I wanted you in my life. We discussed it the other week."

"Yes, I know, but as a possibility some way down the road. Not in the middle of the night on Sunday with no notice at all."

Alan shook his head. "It doesn't matter how or when or where, Davy. I want you in my life and never want to let you go. Is that understood?"

David snuggled even closer. "Bless you, Al. I knew it really, but I was so unsure about everything on Sunday. Tris told me not to worry, so hearing you say that now makes me feel even better." He reached up and kissed Alan. "Thanks."

"Don't be daft, lad. But I also wanted to mention another thought I had, about Aunty Mary's house."

"Oh? It's up for sale, isn't it?"

"Not any more. It struck me the other day that we might need a base in Sedgethwaite, so I rang the agents and took it off the market."

"Christ, Al! You shouldn't have done that."

"It wasn't selling anyway, so I'm no worse off. You're going to need somewhere up there if you're going to spend some time with the boys, so I'm happy to keep it for the time being."

"Ee, lad. I don't know what to say. I mean all that money tied up, just for me. You can't do that."

Alan shook his head. "It's no problem, believe me, Davy. With the promotion I got at the end of last year, the current value of the house is less than a year's salary. The place is worth much more to us to stay in and as a base for you. Please don't worry about it."

David stared at him for a moment in disbelief but quickly saw that arguing would be futile. "All right, then. Thank you. It's a bloody brilliant idea, Al, and I'm more grateful than I can say."

"You can take the key with you next time you go and assess what we'll need to do to get the place habitable again."

"I need to go up there at the end of this week, I think. Try and sort a few things out."

Alan nodded. He'd expected this, but was concerned about how it might play out. David obviously couldn't stay at his own home nor with his parents, given his dad's current mood. Jen had a houseful with her kids, so there weren't many options. In fact, it had been that exact train of thought on Sunday night that had led to Alan's decision to cancel the house sale, and to make the call before the course had started on Monday morning. By keeping the house they would have a refuge, somewhere safe to go when the family stuff got too tough. It would be a sanctuary full of happy memories into which David could retreat when Alan couldn't be there with him.

"I know you need to go and I'd love to come with you, but I can't get away from the office on Friday and I've got an important client meeting next Monday afternoon."

"You mustn't worry, Al. I'll be okay, especially if I can stay at the house. I don't think there's a lot you could do, to be honest."

"Just to have your back, I think. But if you're sure, Davy. Anyway, we'll need to warn Hilda Rodgerson that you're coming."

"Oh, hell, aye. If she's in next door and hears me moving about, she'll have a fit. Don't want her thinking I'm a criminal and screaming the place down."

"When will you go?"

"Thursday morning, I was thinking. Only for a couple of days. I'll come back Saturday."

"That would be good. At least we'd have Sunday together."

"That's what I thought."

Alan swallowed the last of his tea, and stood up, holding his hand out to haul David up. "Come on, Davy, past our bedtime, I think. I'm knackered."

"I'm sure you are, too. I'm certainly ready for bed," David replied, breaking into a mischievous grin.

Setting a New Course

Chapter 5

David

As planned, David travelled north on Thursday morning, arriving in Leeds shortly after lunch. Despite knowing the city all his life, it still felt slightly strange. He'd only been away a week, but now it seemed part of another life.

He walked from the railway station to the bus station to pick up the Sedgethwaite bus, his head full of memories of childhood shopping trips and teenage trips to the 'big' cinema, which got blockbuster films way before they arrived at their local fleapit. Later, there'd been all those journeys along the Sedgethwaite road in his bus – almost six years of seeing the same streets and the buildings in different lights and in all sorts of weather.

Boarding the bus was the first hurdle he faced. His stomach tightened and his breath grew slightly shorter as he neared the terminal building and made for the Sedgethwaite stand. He wondered who would be driving. Would he be acknowledged or ignored? The most extreme reaction would be for the driver to refuse to carry him. But surely nobody he knew would do that, would they?

He reached the stand to find the next departure already there, the driver busy taking fares and checking passes as he got ready to depart. David recognised him as a regular, but he was one of the younger guys with whom David had been on nodding terms but little else. An occasional "na then" might have crossed their lips, but so far as he could remember that had been the extent of their conversation.

David still had his staff pass, so technically could have travelled free, but he didn't feel comfortable using it given that he'd resigned. He boarded and asked for a single to Sedgethwaite.

The reply was a brief smile, a wink and, "Don't be daft, lad. Get on with you."

David breathed a sigh of relief, gave a small smile in return and fled upstairs, his cheeks burning with embarrassment. But at least he'd jumped the first hurdle.

He got off the bus short of the town centre at the end of the road where Alan's Auntie Mary had lived. He gave the driver a nod and a thanks as he alighted, relieved to have got this far without incident.

The street was attractive, tree-lined, sloping gently upwards in a northerly direction from the town centre. The house was on an Edwardian terrace like so many built in the early years of the twentieth century. Stone-built and standing slightly above the road, it had a large ground-floor bay window overlooking a small front garden and a short flight of steps leading up to the front door. On the ground floor there were three receptions rooms and a small kitchen to the rear, together with three bedrooms and a bathroom on the first floor.

It was full of memories for David, who'd spent a huge

amount of time here with Alan from the age of nine through to nineteen. Like his friend, he had often been on the receiving end of the owner's gruff affection. Alan's aunt had been an austere woman with a sharp tongue, but she'd had a big heart which she expressed through deeds rather than words. She'd been an excellent, if traditional, cook, an expert baker and a terrific seamstress.

As he let himself into the house, he could still detect the familiar smells of pine and eucalyptus, though they were fading now. The house had been empty for several months awaiting a purchaser that never came. Alan had cleared out a lot of his aunt's personal possessions earlier in the spring but the furniture was still in place, covered with dust and looking decidedly forlorn.

David took his bag upstairs to Alan's old room. His first job was to locate the central heating boiler and get it going again so that he would have some hot water for washing and cleaning. Once he'd done that, the airing cupboard would warm up a bit, airing the bedding he would use later.

His next job was to phone his sister Jen and let her know he'd arrived safely. He'd warned her that he was coming, and she'd insisted on feeding him that night. That was good; he wanted to see her again, to thank her for all her efforts at peace making the other Saturday night. She and her husband Mark had been the first people he'd told about his burgeoning relationship with Alan, and they'd been so helpful and supportive.

Jen had made no secret of her view that David was wasting his potential when he'd chosen not to follow Alan to London but elected to stay in Sedgethwaite, drive buses for a living and marry his childhood friend.

"Hi, sis. Thought I'd let you know that I arrived safely."

"Oh, great. Good journey?"

"Yeah, fine. I was a bit nervous about getting the bus to here, but it was fine in the end."

"Good. Now you are still coming for your tea tonight, aren't you?"

"Yes, Jen. I promised."

"Good. Mark's taking the kids bowling so we can have a good natter while they're out."

"Bless you, love. See you around five?"

"Grand. I'll look forward to it. And Mum's expecting you in the morning."

"Oh?"

"Yes, Dad's out all day tomorrow – going to the races with a gang from his bowls club, apparently. So she wants to see you. You will go, David, won't you?"

"Promise. Now I need to clean this place up a bit. See you at teatime."

He rang off, feeling better for the human contact.

"So, talk to me, little brother. What's happening?"

As Jen had promised, Mark had taken the kids off ten-pin bowling so David was left alone with his sister for a couple of hours. He had enjoyed eating with the family; the babble of chatter and laughter that filled the room reminded him of his own home life before recent events.

There had been one awkward moment when Marcus, Jen's eldest boy, asked after his cousins Tommy and Kevin and whether they'd be coming for tea again soon.

The innocent question from an eight year old completely floored David. He could do little more than gape at his nephew as his eyes filled up. Fortunately, Mark intervened quickly to tell Marcus that Uncle David had been away for a few days, so he hadn't seen the boys. He'd promised that they would see their cousins soon. Mark shot David a look of silent apology and the moment passed, but it was a sharp reminder of his own two sons and how much he was missing them.

He didn't know how to respond to his sister's question. "The short answer is 'too much'. I don't know where to begin."

"Start with the basic facts – we can take it from there."

"The basic facts are that Alan has asked me to move in with him and I've agreed, so I suppose that makes us boyfriends or partners. He's taken his Auntie Mary's house off the market so that we'll have a base up here. And I've chucked my job with the bus company."

"The one about the house is a bit of a stunner – that's very generous of him."

"I know, Jen. I was staggered when he told me. So much money tied up – I couldn't believe that he'd do that."

"It's also very practical of him, I think. You'll need somewhere once you sort out access to the boys."

"That's what he said. It had never even occurred to me, I'm afraid."

"Hardly surprising in the circumstances."

"True. That's my real problem, I think. Everything seems so huge... I can't think clearly about anything. I feel a bit like a rabbit caught in the headlights."

"The only way is to take one issue at a time, break it

down into manageable chunks."

David gave a short laugh. "Why does that remind me of tinned pineapple?"

"Oh God, yes," his sister replied. "Sunday teas with Grandma!"

"Exactly what I was thinking. Fish-paste sandwiches and tinned pineapple with evaporated milk."

"And getting home in time to hear the end of *Pick of the Pops* on the radio."

They laughed about their childhood Sundays for a moment longer before returning to the subject in hand.

"So, manageable chunks, David," Jen advised.

"Yes. You're right. That's what Alan's friend Tris said last week. I think I told you, he's the guy I stayed with while Alan was on that course."

"Yes. Didn't you say he lives in Kensington?"

"That's right – real posh, he is. But he's so kind – a lovely man."

"What's first on the list?"

"A job, I think. I've got to be able to support Mona and the boys and I can't live off Alan, it wouldn't be fair. I shouldn't have a problem getting a driving job. Most operators in London seem to have vacancies pretty much all the time."

"That's good, but is that what you really want to do?"

"Maybe not, eventually. But it'd a good start. It's what I know, Jen."

"I can see that. You've got enough changes to cope with, so sticking to what you know is probably for the best." She paused to look him in the eye. "And what about Mona?"

David shook his head. "That's the big unknown. If

she's still in the same mood as last weekend, getting an agreement out is going to be a bit of a bugger."

"She's feeling angry and betrayed, David."

"I understand – but surely she'll get over it? She's young enough to find somebody else, and it's not as if I was much good as a husband."

Jen laughed. "How like I man! I'm sorry to disappoint you, David, but I suspect your performance in bed is the last thing on her mind at the moment."

David frowned. "I didn't mean that. I get that she probably still loved me in her own way and she'll be feeling betrayed."

"Yes, but it's more than that. Being a married woman with a nice home and a couple of kids gave her status, especially up on that estate. You were saving for a deposit on a house, weren't you?"

He nodded.

"And you had prospects of promotion."

"True."

"So she's lost the status of a full-time mum, having her own home and being married to a junior manager with prospects, all the things her mother taught her to aspire to. All gone, suddenly, without any notice. Of course she's angry and upset. She's lost far, far more than an inadequate husband, love."

"Oh my God, Jen. I hadn't thought of it like that."

Jen smiled. "Well you wouldn't, lovey, because none of those things were important to you. And I'll tell you another thing that'll make her even more upset: she was about to prove her mother wrong about you."

"How do you mean?"

"Cheryl regards you as beneath her beloved daughter, a no-hoper with a manual job. Not the thing she wanted for her Mona at all. Everything that Mona thought was about to happen would have vindicated her decision to marry you. Instead, you've gone and proved her mother right. And if I know Cheryl Spensley, she won't have wasted much time in saying 'I told you so'."

"Crikey. Poor old Mona."

"Quite. So now she faces a bleak future as another single mum on an estate full of them, potentially another number in the deprivation statistics, and at the mercy of her mother. Tommy and Kevin will be another two fatherless kids amongst hundreds of others with no prospects and at risk of drugs and God knows what else."

"Christ, Jen. Make me feel even more guilty!"

"I'm not saying it will end up like that. It's not inevitable, and I know you'll do your best to make the outcome different – we all will. But I'm trying to make you understand that your defection means more to her than losing somebody she slept with."

"When you put it like that, I can see what you mean. Even so, she won't be calling me anything I haven't called myself over the last week or so. I *am* sorry and I *do* want to make amends, as far as I can. But I can't undo any of it. And anyway, she wouldn't have me back now even if I wanted to go, which I don't."

"Apparently she and her mother have been bad-mouthing you to anyone who'll listen this week. Mum's had her on the phone several times and Mona even rang here on Sunday to see where you were."

David sighed. "I'd better give her a ring, see how the

land lies. I'd like to collect some of my stuff, and see what she wants to do about a divorce and custody. Tris says that we should reach an agreement if possible, and stay out of court. Maybe go to arbitration."

"Mark also said you needed to make a deal with her, didn't he? A few weeks ago."

"Yeah. I wish I'd taken more notice of what you both said that day. If I could have plucked up the courage to talk to Mona then, things might have turned out better." He paused. "Something else to feel guilty about."

"Poor David, you're not used to being anybody's villain, are you?"

He frowned. Was that the reason this whole business felt so awful? His sister was right, though; he'd rarely caused pain to anyone before. Maybe that was why he'd been so reluctant to own up to his wife about his feelings for Alan throughout the summer.

Jen started to speak again and he forced his attention back to her. "But do you honestly think the outcome would have been that different?" she asked. "If you'd told her, I mean. Knowing Mona, she'd still have told you to sling your hook."

"You're probably right. But somehow I'd have felt better."

"I can understand that. So what's the deal? What will you offer her?"

"An agreed divorce on the grounds of irretrievable breakdown. Tris says we can't do adultery 'cos doing it with a fella doesn't count, apparently. With that goes a deal on access rights for me to see the boys and me paying her maintenance money."

"Sounds reasonable to me. Do you think she'll go for it?"

David shrugged. "She'll want to keep me away from the boys if she can. Leastways, that's what she said on Saturday night. That'll be her mother's doing, I reckon. She's hugely anti-gay, especially since she started going to that bloke's church. What's he called?"

"Oh, you mean the Rev Archie? Appears on all those local radio shows?"

"That's him."

"Oh my God, he's awful! Mark turns the radio off every time he comes on. How on earth did Mona's mother get in with him?"

"Through one of her friends. She was on about it to us one night earlier in the year. All gays are going to hell in a handcart, apparently."

Jen shuddered. "I do hate that sort of thing."

"Me too, but she was all in favour of it and Mona seemed to be following her."

"Which might explain why she's reacting like this now."

"Could be, but there's more to it. All the stuff you said just now, I'd never thought of it like that."

"And you can't really blame Mona, can you?"

"No, you're right."

Jen heaved a big sigh. "So what if she turns you down?"

David shrugged. "Dunno. I suppose she doesn't get any money from me until she grants access."

"Couldn't she force the issue through that Child Support Agency thing?"

"Possibly. I don't know the ins and outs of it. All I know is that I want it resolved as soon as possible. I don't want the boys to forget me or think I don't love them It's going to be difficult enough to reconnect with them as it is, and it'll only get worse as the months go by, especially if Mona and her mother are poisoning their minds against me. It's that more than anything else that's stressing me out at the moment."

"I can see that. And I suppose Dad isn't helping either."

"No. Him throwing me out last week was a bit of a stunner."

Jen shook her head. "I was staggered when he said that to me about you keeping your wedding vows. I tried to talk him round but he can be so stubborn sometimes. Mum's so upset."

"I can see where he's coming from but I didn't walk out on Mona, she threw me out. What's more, she wouldn't have me back now at any price, so how can I keep my vows? I don't see what I can do to make Dad see that."

"I think you've got to give him time, love. It all came as a big shock. He was so proud of you and your little family and he thinks the world of the boys, like he does all his grandchildren. Without warning, his son's ideal life blows up in everybody's faces. He was bound to be pissed off about it."

David gave a long sigh. "I understand that, Jen. I just wish he'd try to understand my point of view, that's all. Be more like Mum."

"He'll come round, you wait. And as for Mum, I think it was less of a surprise to her."

David frowned, puzzled by his sister's remark. "What do you mean?"

"Mums know a lot more about their boys than you think. From what she's said this week, she remembered how close you were to Alan before he left for London. Like me, she was a bit surprised when you didn't go with him. So when she heard that you two had met up again, well... I don't think what followed came as a total shock."

"That's amazing. I'd no idea." He laughed uncertainly.

"We always tend to underestimate our parents."

"You may be right. Anyway, thanks for that. It'll help when I talk to her in the morning."

"And try to be patient – give Dad a bit more time, all right?"

He nodded and smiled.

"So tell me about this posh place in Kensington. What's it like?"

David found himself grinning as he talked about Tris's house and what a warm welcome he'd received. He told her the story of how Tris and Alan had met when Tris tripped over him in a London pub, which had her in stitches. He told her about Alan's flat and the view over the Common, and about his new friend Gavin, who'd given him a lift to London. Jen was fascinated; most importantly, it distracted David from thinking about his difficult day tomorrow. As he talked, he felt excited about his new life in London; it was beginning to seem like part of his new normal.

Before they knew it, Mark and the kids were back. Mayhem followed as the bedtime routines got under way for the younger ones. It reminded David of his own kids and he was filled with sadness and guilt all over again. Retreat seemed the best policy, so he thanked his sister and her husband and returned to his base.

As he walked up the road, it occurred to him that they'd have to stop calling it Auntie Mary's house. "Our Yorkshire home" sounded way too posh. Using the street address – "are we going to Edward Street this weekend?" – might seem a bit pretentious too. There was always the number – forty-nine. Maybe they should call it that: Number Forty-nine. He'd have to talk to Al about that when he got back. Edward Street sounded better, though.

These thoughts occupied him happily until he reached the front door. He'd enjoyed seeing his sister and her family, but watching them together had been a powerful reminder of what he had given up. He let himself into the house; it was less unkempt and a good deal cleaner and fresher thanks to his efforts earlier in the afternoon, but it still seemed cheerless. The warmth that he remembered from when Alan's aunt had been alive was lacking, as if it had left with her.

In the kitchen, he glanced at his watch. He had half an hour before the time he'd arranged to call Alan, so he decided to try Mona. Hands shaking slightly, he sat down at the table and dialled the number. She picked up on the third ring. "Mona? Hello, it's David."

"Oh, hello." Her voice was cold. "Where are you?"

"Here in Sedgethwaite. I arrived this afternoon."

"So you've been with him, in London, since..."

"Yes. I have. I'm ... er ... moving in with him."

"I see. So you'll be in London. What about us?"

"I'll keep supporting you and the boys, Mona, like I promised."

She snorted. "Great. So you're two hundred miles away living it up with your boyfriend and I get to look after the kids. Thanks a bunch, David."

His hands were still shaking but he forced himself to stay

calm. He knew she was right. It wasn't fair on her. "I'll still be able to help. Alan's taking his Auntie Mary's house off the market, so we'll have somewhere up here. I can see the boys regularly and help."

"Oh, no. I'm not letting the boys anywhere near you, especially if *he's* there. Mum says..."

"I'm not interested in what your mother says, Mona. And do you seriously believe that I – or either of us, for that matter – would do anything to harm the boys? They're my sons, too. I love them just as much as I did before last week."

"You've got a funny way of showing it, that's all I can say."

"You threw me out, Mona. Remember? You and your precious mother took the boys away from me and didn't even let me say goodbye."

"Was it any wonder? With you cavorting about with several men openly on the streets of London. It's disgusting!"

"Mona, I don't know what lies Douggie Thorpe told you last week but I was not cavorting. I was with Alan's friends and we were leaving a pub when he saw me."

"That's as may be, David Edgeley, but the fact remains that you're a bloody queer and I don't want anything more to do with you."

"Mona, listen to me. If you keep talking like that and don't let me see the boys, you'll not see a single penny piece from me."

"Oh yes, I will. I'll chase you through every court in the land. My lawyer says..."

"Ho-ho! Got a lawyer already, have we? You didn't

waste much time."

"What was I supposed to do? You take off and I've no idea whether you're alive or dead, much less where you are."

"I took off because you told me to. You said you hated me and never wanted to see me again. What was I supposed to do? Sit on the doorstep in case you calmed down?"

"Your father's on my side, any road. I hear he told you to sling your hook. Quite right too."

David closed his eyes and took a deep breath. This was getting them nowhere. He forced himself to calm down.

"David? Are you still there?"

"Yes, Mona, I'm still here." He was calm now; his voice was several tones lower and sounded cold, even to him. "I don't see the point of continuing this discussion. I would like to collect some of my stuff tomorrow. If you don't want to see me or let me see the boys, perhaps you'd arrange to be out for a while so that I can come into the house."

Something in his tone must have resonated with his wife because she also sounded calmer. "Okay. I'll get Dad to come round and be here. I'm not letting you in the house on your own. And anyway, Mother made me change the locks. I'll text you a time."

"And about a deal? Between us?"

"Send me some money and I might talk about it."

"Let me see the boys and I might send you some."

"Fuck off, David. Don't phone here again. Talk to my lawyer." She slammed down the phone.

David sighed deeply as he replaced the receiver. He was still trembling, angry with his wife for her attitude and especially her foul-mouthed prejudices, but the feeling was laced with guilt and frustration that he couldn't see a way of fixing any of it.

He felt his eyes filling. He forced himself to sit still and concentrate on breathing, making his mind go blank until eventually he calmed down. Thinking back to what Jen had said, he may never have played the villain before but he was certainly getting plenty of practice now.

Chapter 6

Alan

It was after nine when Alan got home. It had been a long day, ending with a client meeting that adjourned to a West End wine bar. He was exhausted and feeling the consumption of a fair amount of red wine over a fairly short period of time. At least somebody had ordered some tapas, so his stomach hadn't been entirely empty.

He'd still felt hungry on the Tube so had called in for some Chinese takeaway on the way from the station. It was the first time for more than a week that he'd come home to an empty flat, and with Simon and Peter still away he couldn't pour out his woes to them.

He knew David would be ringing soon and he couldn't wait to hear his voice and find out how he'd got on. It would have been difficult for sure, and Alan was worried about his state of mind. He rather regretted not insisting that the trip be postponed until they could make the journey together. He recognised, though, that David would have to face some aspects of the situation alone. His own intervention would be counterproductive.

This was especially true of Mona. She'd already be blaming him as much than David for what had happened, if not more. Alan understood why – but that didn't make the situation any easier to deal with.

He sat in the kitchen and ate his takeaway, rinsed his plate and disposed of the containers then moved upstairs to the sitting room. As he sat down on the sofa, the phone began to ring. He was delighted to hear David's voice. "Hey, bang on time, Davy. How've you got on?"

"Not too badly." David's flat, lacklustre tone gave away his mood.

"Hey, you're upset, love. Tell me what's been going on."

"I was doing okay. I cleaned the house up a bit this afternoon before going over to see Jen and Mark. He took the kids bowling so that Jen and I could talk." He relayed the headlines of his chat with Jen and explained that they'd agreed he should phone Mona. "But it was a mistake."

"Hmm. I suppose you had to face it some time, Davy."

"I know, and at least I know where we stand. But I don't know how I can fix this. I can't face the idea of a long-drawn-out fight, having to expose our private lives to a whole bunch of people in a courtroom."

"It would be pretty shitty, I agree. But maybe in the end that's what she wants, her day in court. Maybe she feels humiliated and wants to give you a taste of your own medicine, so to speak."

"She's so inconsistent. One minute, she's complaining about having to raise the boys on her own, but when I offer to help she starts calling me all the names under the sun."

"That's not surprising. Like your Jen said, she's angry and hurt. She's probably not thinking straight."

"I don't know, Al. You may be right. Mona might calm down eventually but she can be so obstinate at times. Once she makes up her mind about something, it's very difficult to shift her."

Alan couldn't help his short bark of laughter. "She certainly made up her mind about me a long time ago."

"Aye, and I dare say that won't help. But her biggest issue seems to be about us harming the boys and I'm sure that's coming from her bloody mother. Mona was never like this about gay people before. We knew two or three gay couples on the estate and through work, and she always got on okay with them."

"Yes, but that was all in the abstract. It didn't threaten her like this situation does. It must feel very different now when it's turning her life upside down."

"You sound almost as if you're on her side."

"Don't be daft, Davy. I'm simply trying to understand her point of view. If we're going to get her to calm down and be more reasonable, we have to try and understand where she's coming from."

"You're right. Jen said more or less the same thing. Give her time, she said."

"Which is all very fine and nice, Davy, but you've still got to deal with it in the meantime. I think we need to start the process of getting you a lawyer."

"You're probably right. What makes it worse is that this is all my fault. I should never have married her in the first place. It wasn't fair."

"You may be right, but it doesn't get you anywhere. What's passed is done, and you can't undo it. What matters now is the future – *our* future together."

"I know that, Al and I can think more like that when we're together. But here on my own it's more difficult, especially here, in this house. It's so full of memories of us when we were boys. I wish you'd never gone away, Al."

Alan detected a tremor in David's voice and wracked his brains for way to shift his lover's mood. He hated the thought of his Davy being alone, traumatised by everything that was going on. But Alan had to get him through this phase if they were going to have a future as a couple.

"Come on now, don't go all nostalgic on me. We're still young and we've got our whole lives in front of us. This is no time to start living in the past."

David sighed then was silent for a moment. When he spoke again, his voice was firmer. "No, you're right, Al. There *is* a lot to look forward to, more than there ever was when I was living here in Sedgethwaite."

"That's the spirit, Davy," Alan responded. "So what's the plan for tomorrow?"

"I'm going round to see Mum in the morning. Dad's going out for the day, so he'll be out of the way. After that, I'm hoping to go and get some of my stuff from home. Mona said she'd get her dad to let me in. She said her mother's made her change the locks."

"Christ. The old bat."

"No doubt she had divine inspiration. I don't think she ever liked me. I wasn't good enough for her daughter, only being a bus driver. With any luck, she'll remember that soon and decide that her Mona's had a lucky escape."

"If she thinks that, she's a fool. You were a bloody good catch, and don't you ever think otherwise, David Edgeley."

David laughed a little at Alan's vehemence which eased

their tension a little.

"Anyway, like you said, Al, that's all in the past. I promise to try and look forwards."

"Good. That's what I like to hear, Davy."

They chatted for a few minutes more, Alan telling stories of his day at the office and making David laugh with his imitation of the pompous client he'd had to entertain earlier in the evening. Then it was time to say good night. The earlier wistful tone returned to their conversation but they managed to remain positive. David promised to text Alan to let him know about his visit to his mum, and they arranged to speak at the same time the following night.

"Night, love. Miss you, Davy. See you Saturday."

"Night, Al. And thanks. Feel better now."

"Good. Sleep tight."

Alan put down the phone with a sigh. God, that had been hard, especially as he was already so tired. But at least David had seemed more cheerful by the end of it. That had to be an achievement. Quite what tomorrow would bring, he wasn't sure; all he could do was hope that David would get through it. It would be such a relief to get him back home on Saturday.

He sat back on the sofa for a few minutes but couldn't settle. Despite his tiredness, he couldn't relax. The conversation with David had unsettled him.

He longed to hold David in his arms and make him feel better, and he was on edge and frustrated that he couldn't. But he realised that it was also about his own needs. Even though it had only been a few days, David's presence in his life seemed so natural. They had picked up from where they had left off six years earlier. The shared history, the jokes, the turns of phrase, all seemed comfortable and familiar. They didn't need to get to know each other because they already did in so many ways.

The new parts were the physical affection and making love but those didn't feel strange either; they simply added another dimension to what was already there. Alan had no idea that he'd be so addicted to the idea of physical contact with his partner. He'd never felt the need to touch another person so much, nor had he realised how much comfort and joy could be experienced by being in someone's arms.

In the weeks since he and David had reconnected, he had become addicted to that side of their relationship. Fortunately, David seemed to relish their physical contact too. Tonight, not having the warmth of David's skin next to his own left Alan with a sense of aching loss.

Eventually he decided to go to bed. He might still be restless but there was a chance that he would drop off to sleep. Fortunately, that was exactly what happened.

Chapter 7

David

David woke suddenly from a deep sleep, panicking. He was puzzled because he was on his own, couldn't work out where he was, and did not know what had disturbed him. He heard a loud bang from immediately outside the bedroom window, signalling that the dustbin lorry was in the vicinity, upending 'wheelie' bins as it moved along the street.

He sat up and rubbed his eyes then recognised his surroundings in Alan's old bedroom at Auntie Mary's house. It had obviously been the bin lorry that had woken him up, and he was on his own because Alan had been forced to stay in London for a work thing.

Properly oriented, he forced himself to face the day. He was due at his mum's for ten-thirty, before going to get some of his belongings from home. He corrected himself quickly: not home any more. Mona's house now. He'd have to get used to that.

He glanced at his phone; it was only eight forty-five, so he had plenty of time. He noticed that there were a couple of text messages. His wife's came first, giving him a time of two-thirty for when her dad would be at the house to admit him. His heart sank at the thought of having to face his father-in-law, but he'd always got on okay with him and it might be easier than confronting Mona in her current mood.

The other message was from Alan, sending him best wishes for the day. The fact that he had sent the message gave David goose bumps, made him feel cherished. It might only be five words – *Good luck today, Love You* – but the fact that Alan had found time to send it on a busy morning while getting ready for work increased its value beyond measure. David hadn't used texting a lot yet – he'd only been able to afford a mobile phone in the middle of the previous year – but he was beginning to understand how powerful it was.

He lay back on his pillow and smiled, basking in the memory of their phone conversation the night before. It felt good to know that he had somebody on his side who was so intent on keeping up his morale. It made him feel wanted in a way that his marriage never had. The old firm was back up and running – it truly was Al and Davy against the world.

He sent a quick thank you text back to Alan, plus a brief okay to Mona, then got up to prepare for the day.

David's childhood home lay on the other side of the town from Auntie Mary's house. When he was young, the ten-minute bus journey to and from Alan's house had been part of the excitement of the visit. Today, it was an ordeal. As with the journey from Leeds the previous day, he was uncertain of the reception he would receive from the driver. He briefly considered getting a cab but he'd probably need one later to get back from Mona's house if he collected any of his stuff, and he wasn't that well off for cash. Better stick to the bus.

He gathered his courage and walked down to the stop nearest the house. He didn't have long to wait and, when the bus drew up, he recognised Andy Clegg, one of Douggie Thorpe's cronies, behind the wheel. David's heart sank and his hands began to shake.

The doors opened and David boarded, asking for a day ticket. Andy's eyes widened and his lip curled but he only nodded, took the proffered note and put the change and the ticket in the tray. Still shaking, David nodded, thanked him and went to find a seat. He caught a muttered remark, which sounded distinctly like "Fucking shirt lifter". He ignored it and sat down, careful to stay out of Andy's line of sight, but he couldn't prevent the heat suffusing his face or his stomach churning with embarrassment and shame.

A few minutes later, as they were approaching the stop for his parents' house, David noticed to his intense relief that he was not the only passenger planning to get off. A couple stood up and moved towards the front of the bus. David stayed where he was until the bus slowed, then moved to the edge of his seat. As the doors opened, he rose and quickly followed on the heels of his fellow passengers. He averted his eyes as he passed the cab, alighting so quickly that Andy was deprived of the opportunity to say anything else.

David made it safely on to the pavement and walked away, keeping his head turned. He heard the swish of the closing doors followed by rhe revving of the engine as the bus set off again. Breathing more easily now, but still shaking a little, he moved towards his turning. With the bus gone, he could look up and take in his surroundings. He noticed that he was passing the spot where Gavin had picked him up the other Saturday for his heaven-sent lift to London. It somehow made him feel that he had come full circle.

He turned the corner and started along the street he'd known his entire life. It was a long road, running east–west for about three-quarters of a mile; it sloped gently downwards until it reached the bottom of a dip, before rising up again to a junction with the Huddersfield road at the other end of the shallow valley. The road was also built on a gentle north–south slope, so the houses on one side were slightly above street level whereas those opposite were either at or slightly below it. David's parents lived on the side above the road.

As with Alan's boyhood home with his Auntie Mary, the houses were Edwardian, built between 1907 and 1909. These were also stone built, but slightly larger and posher. The original residents had been attracted up the hill by the fresher air away from the densely packed housing around the mills in the valley. In those days, they'd been able to commute easily aboard the brand-new electric tramway.

It was still quite a pleasant place to live, even if the once-spacious road was now filled with parked cars and wheelie bins. Some houses had been divided into flats and sub-let to student nurses at the nearby Sedgethwaite Royal

Infirmary. They looked slightly faded compared with the owner-occupied properties.

David's mother had often hinted about moving "to a nice bungalow somewhere", especially now that they were retired, but his father refused to budge. He was content with the surroundings that had been part of his life since they'd moved into the house as newly-wed tenants in 1958. They'd managed to buy the property from their landlord in the late sixties on the back of Dad's promotion, firstly to foreman and later to junior manager.

Walking down the street, David was once again struck by the strange feeling of alienation that he'd experienced when he'd arrived in town the previous afternoon. The surroundings were familiar – comforting even – but were no longer an integral part of his life. Instead they felt like part of his history. He'd always been popping round, bringing the kids to see their nan and gramps, coming for Sunday dinner or tea, or attending family celebrations such as birthdays and Christmas. Now his life was going to be two hundred miles away with a completely fresh group of people, developing totally different attitudes, tastes and aspirations.

It was scary but he couldn't bring himself to regret the fact, and he was excited by the opportunities ahead. This street and the house he was about to enter, in defiance of his father's wishes, would always be important to him and carry happy memories but they would never again be a part of his everyday existence.

His mum was at the door. She must have been watching for him from the front room. She smiled as he climbed the half-dozen steps to greet her then opened her arms to embrace him.

David was very close to his mother and immensely proud of her. A strongly-built, extremely capable woman, she was now in her late sixties. She was highly intelligent despite having had little formal education. Leaving school in Coronation Year at the age of fifteen, she'd spent fifteen years in domestic service in an era when such an occupation was extremely unfashionable. As a boy, David had loved her stories of her life in those days. After being promoted several times, she had risen to be assistant housekeeper with a local aristocratic family before she had met George and married him when she was thirty.

Her years in service had given her all sorts of interests and aspirations for herself and for her kids. She had built a wide circle of friends in Sedgethwaite and developed interests in art, music and theatre. Cultural opportunities were limited in a Yorkshire mill town, but she had done as much as she could and more than most.

Her three children, Jen, Robert and David had all turned out to be intelligent and interesting people. David, being the youngest by six years, had been the baby of the family and always seemed to get the most attention, especially after Robert had emigrated to Australia ten years previously.

David had mostly revelled in the attention, though he was keenly aware that in some ways he had been his mother's biggest disappointment – bright and able at school, yet limited in his horizons with an unambitious wife and a relatively unskilled job. Like her daughter Jen, Marion had thought that David was capable of so much more and she had sometimes found it difficult to disguise her feelings. She'd recognised early on, though, that he'd inherited a good deal of his father's obstinacy, so had largely given up trying to push him to do more.

The two of them were of a height so always fitted together nicely, and David had always been a big one for his mum's hugs. It was probably why he loved cuddling up with Alan so much. Mona had been much more stand-offish and called him a soft bugger when he'd asked for a hug from her.

"Oh, David lad, it's so good to see you, love. I've been so worried."

"Nay, Mum, I'm fine," he replied, pulling back slightly to give her a big grin. "You mustn't worry so much."

"How could I not, you silly devil? Taking off like that when your dad said what he did."

"Yeah, well. It seemed the right thing to do at the time."

"No, it's all right. I understand, love. You must have felt bloody awful that Saturday. Not surprising that you'd want to be with Alan. He always looked out for you."

"Jen says you always knew."

His mother nodded and gave him a wistful smile. "She's right, I did. You were so close, the pair of you. Soul mates, I think they call it. You could have knocked me down with a feather when he went off to London and you stayed."

"Yes, I was a bloody coward. I should have gone with him."

"Aye, lad. And what on earth possessed you to turn round and marry Mona, I've no idea."

"I was scared, Mum. I didn't want … I didn't want to be like *that*. Even if it meant saying goodbye to Alan."

"Well, it's certainly landed you in a mess now, that's for sure."

"I wish you'd said something at the time."

His mum laughed. "As if you'd have listened! You were so fixed on the idea, love. You went round that spring until the wedding with your jaw all set and determined. I'd known that look since you were little, so I knew that there'd be no shifting you. You're just like your father sometimes."

David smiled at that. It wasn't the first time she'd said that. "How is he?"

"Bloody obstinate, as ever," she replied, cross but still with a look of deep affection on her face for the man she'd married all those years ago. "I can't shift him over this business, at least not yet. And it's stupid, because I know he misses you. Every time your name is mentioned, he blinks and looks askance in that silly way of his when anything upsets him."

It was David's turn to laugh. "God, does he know that you can read him like a book?"

"How else would I be after nearly forty years? Oblivious? I don't think so, David."

"True. Anyway, I'm sorry he's so upset. I know he blames me – what he said the other Saturday about 'giving in to my urges' – but it's not that simple, Mum. And honestly, I couldn't live a lie for the rest of my life. I know countless others like me have done so in the past, but that's not me."

"I understand that, love. And I think your dad will eventually. I've told him that the next time Mona rings, he can listen to one of her tirades. Then he might understand."

"Oh, God. Has she been a nuisance?"

"A bit. She rang on the Sunday and was clearly still upset, but she was sympathising with me while she thought I was on her side. As soon as I suggested that she might have been a bit previous in throwing you out, she changed her tune. She ranted on at me as if it was all my fault."

"Oh, Mum. Has she rung again since?"

His mother nodded. "Twice. More in the same vein, demanding to know where you are and what was happening. Anyway, come through and I'll make us a nice cup of coffee."

They went into the kitchen and David sorted out cups and teaspoons while his mother put the kettle on.

"Have you spoken to her?" Marion asked.

David nodded. "Aye, and much good did it do me. She launched into another rant about me leaving her with the kids to bring up, but adamantly refused to let me anywhere near them. I told her she wasn't getting a divorce or any money until we'd made a deal about access."

"Can you make that stick?"

David shrugged. "I honestly haven't a clue, Mum. Al's friend Tris knows a good lawyer and has promised to put me in touch when the time's right, so I'll know more then. But I do know we have to reach a deal for the divorce to go through quickly."

"Good. And there's no chance of you getting back together?"

He wasn't quite sure whether that was a statement or a question, but nevertheless he shook his head vehemently. "No, Mum. I can't now, even if she was prepared to have me, which she certainly isn't."

"For what it's worth, I think you're right. But I am worried about the boys."

"You and me both. I left so abruptly, so they won't

know what's going on. God knows what nonsense Mona's mother is filling their heads with. I don't want to leave them with their mother bringing them up on her own, but at the moment I don't have a lot of choice."

"I'm sure you don't," Marion replied with a sigh. "You know that we'll do whatever we can to help. She might let me see the boys, I suppose. I could try, anyway."

"That would be grand. It'd take a whole weight off my mind if I knew they were okay."

"I'll let you know. Are you going to see her? Get some of your belongings?"

"I'm going round this afternoon, but she won't be there. She's arranged for her dad to let me in. She's changed the locks, apparently."

"That was a bit sharp, wasn't it? What did she think you were going to do, steal all the furniture?"

"Keep me away from the boys, I think. She said her mother had pushed her to do it."

His mother shook her head. "Poor Cheryl. Such an angry, disappointed woman."

David chuckled. "She was certainly disappointed when Mona agreed to marry me."

"I remember," Marion replied, echoing his laughter. "If looks could have killed at your wedding, you'd have been an orphan that day. But it's more than that, love. I'm afraid she's one of those people whose glass is always half-empty. I've noticed on all the occasions we've met that she finds something to be disappointed about or disapprove of."

"I bet she's in her element over this."

"Oh, I expect so. Between slating you, telling Mona 'I

told you so' and railing against 'all those homosexuals', she'll be having a fine old time." His mother had always been a good mimic, and her imitation of Cheryl Spensley's false, refined accent had David chuckling again.

"I like her dad, though. Always got on with him."

"Yes," Marion responded. "Brian's a nice man. How he's put up with Cheryl all these years, I'll never know."

"I've always wondered. Resignation, I suppose. I think he tunes her out most of the time."

"It's the only way to survive, I expect. Anyway, enough of them. Tell me about London. How do you like it?"

David found himself describing Alan's flat and his friends, Simon and Peter from downstairs, and Tris and Ian. He described going to a West End musical for the first time. That trip to *The Producers* at Drury Lane had taken place on the Friday night almost two weeks ago, a couple of hours before everything had blown up in his face.

"It was amazing, Mum. Took my breath away," he enthused. "It was funny and stylish and touching, all at once."

His mother smiled at his enthusiasm. This was so like the David she remembered as a boy, not the rather serious, almost dour young man he'd become since his marriage. "I know how you feel, David. The West End does have a magical quality. It's years since I saw a show down there."

"I'll never forget it, despite what happened afterwards."

"What do you mean, love? Was that when the union man saw you?"

"Yes. We were on our way for supper after the show when Douggie spotted us."

"Such a shame it happened that way. It would have been

much better if you could have told Mona, given her some warning."

"I know. But to be honest, Mum, I'm not sure I'd ever have had the courage to tell her. I tried several times, you know, but I couldn't find the words."

"I can understand that, but it's still a shame. Anyway, it is what it is." She sighed and stood up. "What time are you due at the house?"

"Half-past two."

"Right. Your dad won't be home till teatime, so you'll be all right. How about some lunch?"

After feasting on a bowl of his favourite home-made soup with some home-baked bread, David was spared the ordeal of more bus journeys by his mum's insistence on giving him a lift to his marital home. Not keen to see Mona's father, she dropped him at the end of the road, leaving him with a short walk to the house.

For the six years of his marriage, this had been such a familiar route down the hill to the bus stop for his journeys to work and requiring a slog up again at the end of his shifts. As with the other parts of this visit to his home town, he again felt a curious sense of detachment, almost as if he were watching a documentary about his past life rather than living his present one.

It occurred to him that he might be erecting some sort of defensive shield to deflect any feelings of regret. Perhaps he ought to feel some degree of sadness about leaving his old life behind, but sorrow was the last thing he felt.

Indeed, the conversation with his mother had, if anything, reinforced his enthusiasm about his new life. She'd obviously spotted the change in him too, as evidenced by her parting words. "It's great to see that you've got some of your old spark back again, David. Try not to lose it again during the divorce business."

That was all very fine and nice, he reflected as he reached his old home, but there wasn't going to be much joy in his next encounter. Trembling slightly, he opened the gate and walked up the path. His sense of detachment resurfaced, so much so that he could hardly believe that this had been his home until two and a half weeks ago.

As he'd told his mother before lunch, David had always liked his father-in-law. Brian was a kind man, well-meaning and liberal. Unlike his wife, he was a person who saw the best in everybody and would do anything to help people. Nevertheless, David was nervous about the reception he'd get, and dreaded another confrontation along the lines of the ones he'd had with Mona.

Arriving on the front step, he paused for a moment before reaching out and ringing the doorbell. There was a pause before the door opened then Brian's gentle face appeared. He blinked behind his thick pebble lenses and gave a nod of recognition. "You'd best come in."

"Thanks."

Brian stepped back and David walked into the house. For a moment, the sight of the interior and the familiar smells – Mona's perfume, baby shampoo, damp washing – combined to overwhelm him. Glancing to his left, he noticed the boys' toys scattered over the floor in the front room and he half-expected to hear their voices as they raced out to greet him. Instead, all he heard as he moved down the hall was the click of the front door shutting behind him.

As he got to the foot of the stairs, he turned to face his father-in-law. Managing to overcome the lump in his throat, he spoke. "Thanks for agreeing to be here, Brian. I'm sorry about what's happened."

"I should hope you are," his father-in-law replied tartly. "But it's a bit late now, isn't it? Better that you hadn't married at all, given your secret."

"I get that you must be angry, Brian, and hate me for what's happened. But there was no secret and I wasn't hiding anything. I loved Mona when I married her, and I never lied to her about this."

Brian scoffed, "Pull the other one."

David shrugged. "I'm sorry that you don't know me better than that after all these years. I would never do that to anybody. Once and for all, I did not use Mona as some sort of disguise for being bi or gay or whatever. I genuinely didn't know about that ... that side of me until the start of this year. I know Mona won't believe me when I say that, but I'm telling the truth."

Brian looked at him hard, straight in the eye. After a moment or two, he nodded. "All right, lad, I believe you."

"I suppose it doesn't really change anything," David added. "We're still where we are, but I hated how Mona immediately assumed that our marriage was a sham from the start."

"That'll be her mother, I expect. Playing it up, as usual."

"Anyway, I'm sorry. I never meant for this to happen and I never meant to hurt anybody, least of all the boys."

"Okay, I understand. But it doesn't get us much farther forward, does it?"

"No, I agree. And I understand that Mona's upset and angry – she's got every right to be. I do want to help, both with the boys and the money, but I can't do that if she won't let me see them."

"I understand, lad. But you know what they're like. Cheryl's the irresistible force and Mona's the immovable object."

Brian's allusions made David smile. "Yeah, something's gotta give."

"We'll see. You've got to give it time as much as anything."

"You're probably right. I certainly hope so."

"Mona said you were moving to London permanently, so I don't suppose you'll have much time for the boys anyway."

David shook his head. "No, that's why we're keeping the house."

Brian looked genuinely puzzled. "What house?"

"Alan's auntie's place in Edward Street. Didn't Moira tell you?"

There was a shake of the head in response. "Who's Alan?"

David clenched his fists in frustration. "You see, this is what I'm up against. She's not even telling you half the story." He paused, making a conscious effort to relax again. There was no point in getting cross with his father-in-law; he might turn out to be very helpful. "Alan is Alan Foreshaw – Mona and I both went to school with him. He was my best friend until he moved to London six years ago."

"Yes, I remember him. He was quite a nice lad, as I recall."

"His Auntie Mary, who brought him up, died in February. That's what brought him back here and how we met again. He inherited her house and he's been trying to sell it, but when all this blew up a fortnight ago, he took it off the market. He plans to keep it as a base for me – for us – to visit regularly."

"Ah, right. I understand now. So the guys you were seen with in London were..."

"Alan Foreshaw and his neighbours from the flat downstairs."

"Right. So not random strangers that you'd met when you were staying over."

"No. This is all about Alan and me. I don't think any of this would have happened if I hadn't met up with him again."

"No, Mona hasn't said any of that. Only that you were qu— gay and had been seen kissing another man in London."

"Christ. She's hasn't told you much, has she?"

Brian smiled ruefully. "Less than that, I reckon. Even when she was little, she always knew how to dress things up so that she'd be seen in the best light. Gets it from her mother, I think."

"I suppose she'd argue that the effect is the same. She still threw me out."

"Yes, but it isn't, is it, David? The story you've told me is a bit more understandable, going to be with someone you've been close to most of your life. And this house business tells me he must think a lot of you."

David blushed but remained silent for a moment, unsure how or whether to respond. In the end, he muttered his thanks.

"Anyway, I shall have words with her,' Brian said. 'Telling lies or making stuff up isn't going to help this situation, however angry she is."

"No, you're right there. I hope you understand that I know I'm to blame, that this is my fault. I'm determined to do what I can to make everything right – at least as far as she'll let me."

Brian nodded. "I understand, David lad. And thanks for being so frank with me. Now, let's sort out your stuff and get you on your way."

Packing up his belongings took about an hour, but in the end they all fitted into the one suitcase that Mona had left for him and a couple of bin bags. He wasn't interested in any of their CDs or DVDs, and his teenage record collection was still in his parents' loft, so the load comprised mostly clothes and a few books. He called a cab to return to Edward Street. As he waited for it to arrive, he reflected that it was a pretty poor do that, at the age of twenty-five, his entire life could fit into one suitcase and three black dustbin liners.

He wondered how long it would be, if ever, until he saw this house again. It was an odd feeling. He'd never been *un*happy here; he'd felt unfulfilled sometimes, and frustrated with some aspects of their life at other times, but he'd never been so miserable that he'd wanted to leave. Now, the boys aside, he wasn't sorry to be going. The way Mona had behaved that Saturday night and again the other night – plus the revelation that she'd lied to her parents – had pretty much finished off any affection he felt for her.

The cab arrived and Brian gave David a helping hand with his stuff. Once it had been loaded, the two of them shook hands. David got into the front seat next to the driver and confirmed his destination. He did not look back as the vehicle sped away.

Back at Edward Street, David dropped his bags in the hall and went straight into the kitchen to make a hot drink.

The day had left him physically and emotionally exhausted. There had been some positive aspects – he'd enjoyed seeing his mum, and it had felt good to bathe in her affection and her belief in him. He still felt sad about his dad but he was resigned to waiting for a change of heart; there was no point in trying to push him.

His meeting with his father-in-law could have been a whole lot worse, especially given the distortions and half-truths Mona had been feeding her parents. David couldn't help but reflect that Mona's self-serving behaviour would do her harm in the long run. The stupid part was that it was so unnecessary; she already had a first-class claim to the role of wronged wife – why weaken her case by gilding the lily? He'd have to think about sending her a letter when he got back to London. If she was going to distort the facts, it would probably be a good idea to put stuff in writing.

He finished his tea and glanced at his watch – five-thirty. Time he roused himself from the kitchen table and got on with things. There was his stuff to sort out: he had to decide what, if any, of the things he'd collected should go to London with him the next day. The rest could stay here either permanently, or until he and Alan had a car with them. Then there was a meal to be cooked and eaten before his call with Alan.

"Come along, David," he said to himself as he stood up, "let's be up and at 'em."

Setting a New Course

Chapter 8

Alan

Looking back on his working day, Alan couldn't remember a better one in all his time in London. In the morning he'd led a pitch to a potential new client who had liked what he heard so much that he'd given them a three-year contract on the spot. After lunch came a crucial session with one of their biggest existing clients who needed a new campaign. Alan and his team had presented their first creative ideas and, not to put too fine a point on it, the meeting had been a triumph.

Most of the team had once again retreated to their local wine bar to celebrate, ordering champagne all round. Conscious that he wanted to be on form when he talked to David, Alan had restricted himself to two glasses. The party was in full swing by the time he left at eight-fifteen. He'd arranged to talk to David around nine and he was determined to be ready on time.

He was anxious to find out how matters stood, given everything that had happened today. He was sure that David's visit to his mum and confrontation with his father-in-law would each have been traumatic in their own way, and he expected to find an exhausted young man on the other end of the line. Consequently, he was surprised – but pleased – when David sounded calm and even quite cheerful. The accounts of the two meetings both sounded positive and it took a massive weight off Alan's mind. He shared David's anger about Mona's distortions of the truth; she'd never been one of his favourite people, and the latest story seemed to be entirely in character with the girl he remembered from school.

The discussion turned to more practical matters. "So you collected your stuff from the house okay?" Alan asked.

"Thanks, yes. When it came down to it, there wasn't that much – and to be honest after going through it tonight, a lot of it wants to go to a charity shop or in the bin."

"Wow. That's a bit of a surprise. You were a bit of a natty dresser in the old days."

David laughed. "Never thought of myself as natty anything. But what with having my uniform for work and not going out much after the boys came along, I've not really had much cause to buy many clothes. I lived mainly in jeans and tee-shirts."

"I can understand that – and I expect the boys always came first."

David laughed. "Aye, you're right there. Always needing something."

Alan realised that they were straying onto dangerous ground in talking about the kids, especially when he detected a slight wavering in David's voice. Time for a change of subject. "About tomorrow, Davy. Are you still coming on the train that gets in at four o'clock?"

"That's the one. I'm going to get a cab into Leeds. There's a lot to carry and getting from the bus station would be a bit of a pain."

"Have you had any hassle on the buses?"

"A bit this morning. But it was okay. One of Douggie Thorpe's pals made a crack about shirt lifters, but I ignored him."

Alan winced, but was relieved that David had brushed it aside as being of no consequence. "Good. Listen, I'll pick you up at King's Cross. Parking is a bit difficult but if you can get out into York Way – that's the road on the left as you come off the platform – I'll be somewhere around there."

"If you're sure, that would be great."

"No problem, Davy. Can't wait to have you back here."

"Yeah. I've missed you terribly, Al. Can't stop thinking about you."

Again, Alan spotted the tell-tale crack in the voice that showed that David was still on the edge. His own eyes filled and he closed them against the tears, curling the fingers of his free hand into a fist to control his own emotions. The miles that separated them suddenly seemed so much more. They would both have benefited so much from a hug at that moment.

"Hey, I didn't tell you about my brilliant day, did I?"

"No. What happened, Al?"

Alan launched into the story of his double triumph and they chatted happily about that for a few minutes, bringing the atmosphere down a notch or two. Eventually David betrayed his exhaustion with a loud yawn, and they said their goodbyes.

After replacing the receiver, Alan restarted the CD that he'd paused when the phone rang. His favourite Mozart concerto started to play and he released a deep sigh. He sat back and stared into space, letting the music wash over him. The combination of his long day, the effort of trying to keep up David's morale and keeping his own reactions under control had left him utterly exhausted. He could barely think, let alone move.

As the music finished, his brain began to work again. Thank God it was Friday. He could relax for most of tomorrow, and there was lots to look forward to; as well as David's return from Yorkshire, Simon and Peter were due back from their two weeks in Italy. The building had been so quiet without them, and he suspected that their support would be very welcome over the next few weeks.

Eventually he summoned up the energy to take himself to the bathroom to brush his teeth. A few minutes later he fell into bed and was asleep as soon as his head hit the pillow.

When he awoke, it was to one of those golden late September mornings when the low sun shone out of a clear blue sky, throwing everything into sharp relief. He loved the way the light from his bedroom window caught the spectacular reds and golds of the leaves on the trees, whilst the angle of the sun highlighted virtually every bump on the Common. It reminded him how lucky he was to have such a view and how much he loved London's green spaces.

He felt refreshed from a long, dreamless sleep but he

couldn't help feeling slightly guilty that he'd been able to have such a night despite David's absence and all that was going on around him. On the other hand, he felt much more able to cope with whatever the day brought. It occurred to him that a shower would improve things even more.

Shaved and showered, he enjoyed a leisurely breakfast and several cups of his favourite coffee as he read the paper and a couple of marketing trade magazines. After the third cup, he realised that he needed to get a move on. There was the flat to clean, groceries to buy, and he needed to leave around three-fifteen to collect David. He could hardly wait, and kept a close eye on his phone all morning in case of a message. He wasn't expecting one until David's text to confirm that he was safely on the train, but that wouldn't be until after two.

His brain started to play tricks with him, though. As he was cleaning the bathroom, a random thought popped into his head, completely out of the blue: "What if he tells you he's not coming back?" He dismissed it almost immediately, but not before it sent a shiver of fear down his spine.

Don't be daft, Alan, he wouldn't do that to you.

"Bet Mona thought the same until two weeks ago." Alan had to acknowledge that was a fair point, but he was confident in David's feelings and his determination to make a new life in London. "Anyway he'll leave you eventually. People always do."

Oh, shut the fuck up.

"That's a weak response to what you've got to admit is a strong point." He had to acknowledge that too. His parents getting killed, David refusing to come to London with him... Look at Tris, his closest friend and flatmate for three years, meeting and falling in love with Ian. Finally his aunt had upped and died. Everybody he'd ever cared for had left him at some point.

Stop feeling sorry for yourself – it isn't even true. Tris is still your best friend and David's back in your life.

His phone buzzed with a text. He grabbed it to read the message. It was Simon: they were home and inviting him down for a coffee. Welcoming the distraction from his internal arguments, Alan sent a quick acknowledgement and prepared to pop downstairs.

Judging by their relaxed mood, the deep suntans and their ecstatic accounts of the guest house in which they'd stayed, the holiday has been a success. Situated in Lombardy in the hills above Florence, it sounded idyllic. In Simon's view, the surroundings had been improved greatly by the regular appearance of an extremely handsome gardener/pool boy.

"My dear, the view was spectacular! And I'm not talking about the hills, although they were lovely too. I kid you not – that smile! It was like all your Hollywood heroes rolled into one."

"He was pretty awesome," agreed Peter. "The sight of him bending down to weed the flower beds or clean the pool definitely improved our mood every morning."

"The food was amazing, too. It was barely worth driving into the village for dinner though we went a couple of times. Did you ever see that TV film *Enchanted April*?”

“The one with Josie Lawrence and Michael Kitchen?”

“Yes, that one. Our place was just like that. You should definitely take David some time. We’ll give you the details.”

“Sounds heavenly, Si.”

“It is, believe me – even without Giovanni the gardener.”

Alan laughed. “First name terms, eh?”

To his credit, Simon blushed a little. “I had to practise my Italian on somebody.”

“You never did find out what the Italian for ‘threesome’ was, did you, Si?” Peter asked with a laugh.

“Oh, shut up,” replied his husband, punching his arm but unable the stop a blush rising across his face. “You know I don’t share you with anybody, ever.”

Peter laughed. “Only kidding. Anyway, I Googled it last night before we left. It’s *terzetto*. So now you know.”

“And are you sure you didn’t get to see Giovanni’s room?” Alan enquired.

“Oh, ha ha. A literary joke on a Saturday morning. Very good, Foreshaw,” Simon responded with a big grin. “Enough about Giovanni – what about you and the boy David?”

“I’m okay, I think. Not so sure about the boy, though.”

“That’s hardly surprising, I suppose, in all the circs. Tell me more.”

“After you’d gone, I had that bloody course so Davy stayed with Tris for a few days. After a few days back here, David thought he should go up to Sedgethwaite to get some of his stuff and see how the land lies. He went up on Thursday and will be back this afternoon, thank God. He’s still shell-shocked, I think, but he’s begun to come to terms with everything."

"Do I infer that you might possibly have missed him the teeniest little bit?" Simon asked with a smirk.

"You might be right. But we've kept in touch. His wife's being a bitch, I'm afraid, and his dad still won't speak to him. Oh, and one of his former colleagues gave him some homophobic abuse – but apart from that everything's going swimmingly."

"Oh my love. Poor lad!"

"He's held it together remarkably well, and others have been kind. He's seen his sister Jen and his mum, who were fine, and apparently even his father-in-law was quite sympathetic, so it's not all bad. But I got the distinct impression he was hanging on by his finger ends last night. I'll be so relieved when he gets home."

"I'm not surprised, love. I'd have been *frantic*. I still get extremely twitchy every time Peter goes to see Mother, and we've been coping with her for fifteen years!"

Alan laughed. Peter's mother was famously stuck up and difficult. She disliked Simon with a passion only matched by his dislike of her.

Simon shuddered. "She's a terrible woman," he added, rolling the 'r' sounds. He giggled. "Anyway mustn't go on about *her*. You've got enough to worry about with your boy, sweetheart."

"I know. I'm so frightened that he'll decide that he's made a terrible mistake and bugger off back to Yorkshire."

"And if I know anything, old love," interjected Peter, "that says more about you than him."

"You're probably right, but it doesn't make the fear any less real."

"I get that, lovey. I really do," Simon said. "But you've got to be a bit patient. After all, think what he's been through since the turn of the year – seeing you again, facing up to being bi or gay, coping with rejection by Mona and his dad *on the same night*, and not seeing the boys. It's enough to give anybody a bad case of PTSD."

"True. But it all seemed so right before all the drama blew up," Alan responded.

"And it will again. Trust Aunty Si. I'm sure of it. He just needs some time and space to get himself settled."

"I suppose so. One thing you could always say about Davy, even when he was only eleven, was that he was determined and persistent. He was cautious, too, and took ages to make up his mind sometimes – but once he did there was no stopping him." Alan couldn't help but smile at the memory of the early days of their friendship. David had been so determined to draw Alan out of the shell into which he'd retreated after his parents' death. "I don't know whether you've noticed, but his chin sticks out and his jaw goes rigid when he's being determined about something."

Peter and Simon exchanged a quick glance, noting Alan's softer tone when he spoke about David. "I don't know him well enough yet," Simon replied, "but I certainly plan to. And I'm already sure there's one thing he *is* determined about, and that's you."

Alan felt warmed by Simon's confidence. He only wished he could share it.

Setting a New Course

Setting a New Course

Chapter 9

David

David woke early on Saturday with a sense of excitement akin to the feeling he used to have Christmas morning. He was puzzled for a moment but quickly remembered: he was going home today, back to Al. He still found it slightly odd to be thinking of London as home but it certainly felt that way. If anything, the last two days had only served to confirm it.

After a shower in the old-fashioned bathroom, he dressed and packed his belongings. He put the rest of his stuff away in the airing cupboard on the landing. He planned to spend the last couple of hours cleaning, and compiling a list of what they'd need to do to bring the house up to modern standards.

He focussed on the front room, which he hadn't yet touched. It was still furnished with an elderly moquette three-piece suite. There was an old-fashioned bureau in the corner of the room by the bay window. Seeing it now reminded him of his idea of writing to Mona. His discussion with her father the previous day had made the idea of getting his side of the story down on paper even more important. Writing it now, whilst everything was fresh in his mind, would be a good idea.

Opening the bureau, he found a stock of writing paper. He'd always done quite well at English at school but had not written much since. He felt rusty and ill at ease during the first couple of paragraphs, and scrapped two versions before his thoughts came together. He recalled some of the disciplines he'd learned about essay writing: beginning, middle, end – state your proposition, set out your case in full and write a conclusion. He could hear the voice of Mr Forsyth, his English master, "Tell the buggers what you're going to say, say it, and then tell 'em what you've said." So that was what he did.

He said he was sorry for what had happened and explained once again that he had married Mona in good faith and not as a disguise for his sexuality. He had not seen or contacted Alan between his friend's departure from Sedgethwaite six years earlier and the day in February when he had boarded his bus in Leeds. He repeated his offer of help to bring up and financially support the boys. He hoped they could agree a divorce based on irretrievable breakdown but stated again that was conditional on him being granted reasonable access to see his children.

After an hour of writing, and without too many crossings out, he reached his conclusion. He signed the letter and added Alan's address at the bottom, in case Mona wanted to reply. On the whole, he was proud of his efforts. He took a picture of the finished pages with his phone, sealed the envelope, found a stamp and set out for the postbox on the corner. With the letter safely on its way, he had half an hour before his cab arrived.

As he brought his bags down to the hall, he felt better than he'd done for the two weeks since his life had fallen apart. Writing everything down had helped to clarify matters and to clear his brain. He could only hope that Mona would gain a similar benefit from reading it.

The journey south was uneventful. The taxi turned up on time and the train was punctual, too. David thought how sleek it looked in the late summer sunshine and was impressed by how smart the GNER staff were in their uniforms. He wished he could have an outfit as smart as that.

Emerging at King's Cross into the humid air of a late summer heatwave, he was once again struck by the bustle of life in the capital. Everybody seemed to walk faster, exuding a vibe that said "get out of my way, I'm in a hurry". He followed his instructions about getting into York Way and recognised Alan's sleek BMW waiting on the other side of the road.

Alan leapt out of the car to greet him and was nearly run over by a passing taxi, which honked loudly whilst the driver shouted some choice words. Distracted by the incident, David lost track of where Alan was so he was surprised to be enveloped in a huge hug. Not that he minded. Far from it, in fact.

God, it felt so good to be in Alan's arms again; the warmth of his body against his own was almost overwhelming. David had only been away for two days but it seemed a lifetime, leaving him with a sense of being adrift and untethered like a hot air balloon out of control. The embrace brought him back to earth, to a solid reality, somewhere he could be himself.

They stood there for what seemed like ages, not speaking but simply holding on to each other. They were completely unaware of their surroundings until they were brought back to reality by a wolf whistle from another passing taxi driver, followed by an invitation to "get a fucking room, mate".

Alan flipped him off but the moment was broken. "God, it's good to see you."

"Me too." David grinned. "It's good to be back, even if it is like a bloody oven."

"Tell me about it – going to last most of next week, they say." They stowed David's luggage in the boot, got into the car and set off back to Clapham.

David looked across as Alan negotiated the traffic on Euston Road. It was so good to see him looking cool and sexy in a trendy linen shirt and trousers, complete with his Rayban sunglasses. How on earth he could have let his friend leave six years ago? He must have been mad.

The drive home passed quickly. Alan asked him about his journey and what he'd done before he'd left. David explained about the cleaning and his list of tasks for the house, and also about his decision to write to Mona.

"Well done, Davy. That can't have been easy."

"It wasn't. Lots of pen chewing and staring into space. Took me three goes to get started."

"Still, it's all done now."

"Yeah, I needed to do it. I felt a lot better afterwards."

"Good. Let's see what she says in reply."

"Hmm – that worries me a bit. But I needed to get it all down in writing."

"Great stuff. By the way, I spoke to Tris about a solicitor for you. He's recommended a guy called Tom Parkes. Tris gave me his number. I've met Tom and his boyfriend Hugo. I think he'd be great."

"That's grand. I'll ring him next week. What about Simon and Peter?" David asked, suddenly anxious to change the subject for some reason he couldn't fathom. "Are they home yet?"

"Early this morning. I had a coffee with them before I came to pick you up. They had a terrific time. The place they stayed sounds fabulous – and seem to have come complete with a rather sexy gardener."

David laughed, feeling more of the tension of the last two days draining away. Back at the flat, their hug was resumed. He found himself with his back against the front door as Alan added a passionate welcome home kiss. Their bodies moved in sync, pressing together, and David shuddered with pleasure as Alan moved his hips slightly, allowing their crotches to brush together before he brought his leg up between David's.

Eventually, they broke the kiss, gasping for air. "Take me to bed, Al. Now. Please."

They stumbled up the stairs to the bedroom, breathless and grinning at each other. Their grins were quickly swallowed by kisses as they tried to undress and keep their lips locked together. They parted for a moment to finish undressing each other.

Once naked, David almost swooned with the joyous

sensation of Alan's body against his. They battled good naturedly for dominance, rolling first one way and then the other, lips locked. Eventually, David ended up beneath Alan and opened his legs so that they fitted together. They both shivered with pleasure at the contact. They began to thrust into one another.

Alan moved slightly, kissing David's neck and collar bone before moving to his nipples, leaving him squirming and arching his back. Then Alan paused, drawing breath and looking down into his lover's eyes.

David melted under Alan's gaze and his eyes filled with tears. If he'd been asked, he couldn't have said whether they were happy tears or sad ones – it was pure emotion.

"Tell me what you want, Davy. Anything, my sweet."

David moved against him and wrapped his legs around Alan's back. "Just this, Al. Hold me and keep me safe. I want to come like this, in your arms. I always want to be in your arms."

Alan smiled and began to move, his hips undulating gently. David revelled in the sensation but he needed more. He started to thrust back, his legs crossed at the ankles behind Alan's back to urge him on. After a few moments, Alan reached between them and grasped their two cocks, holding them together as they moved.

David closed his eyes. He knew he wouldn't last long. After a few more thrusts, he gasped, "I'm gonna come, Al. Oh God, this feels so wonderf—" The rest of the word was cut off as he uttered a strangled cry and shot copiously between their bodies. Alan echoed his shout and followed immediately afterwards.

They lay there for a few moments, recovering their

breath, their bodies slick with their own release and the sweat of a hot, humid afternoon. Lying on their sides facing each other, legs still entangled, David brushed a strand of Alan's hair away from where it had stuck to his forehead. The love he saw in Alan's eyes overwhelmed him again. In that moment, he understood why he was going through the hell of his marriage break-up and everything that flowed from it. For moments like these, it was worth it.

Life seemed to settle a little during the next couple of weeks. At the beginning of October Alan's classes for his marketing degree started again, so he was out one night a week and studying hard on another couple. David hugely admired his lover's drive and ambition. He enjoyed the quiet evenings as he sat on the sofa reading, classical music playing softly in the background while Alan studied.

One thing that pleased David was that he reconnected with Gavin. When they first chatted over the phone the week after his Yorkshire trip, it was the first time they had spoken since the night when Gavin had driven him down to London. They'd promised to keep in touch before parting in the early hours of that Sunday morning, and David was delighted to get Gavin's call.

They agreed to meet for a drink one evening when Alan was at class. Gavin's partner, Ben, was occupied with a parents' evening, so they arranged to meet in a gay pub in Clapham High Street. It was only about ten minutes' walk from the flat so it didn't challenge David's knowledge of

London's geography, which was still very limited.

David arrived first just before seven. It was his first time alone in a London pub, let alone a gay one; he felt more than a little intimidated when he saw the imposing Victorian building and its impressive entrance. He steeled himself and walked into a large, richly decorated room lit in rainbow colours. Rock music was playing softly. Despite there being no more than half a dozen regulars grouped at one end of the bar, the atmosphere seemed warm. The attractive young barman was welcoming as David bought a pint. He was conscious of the regulars following his every move and it made him a little nervous. He gave them a small nod and a smile, then headed to a quiet table away from prying eyes.

He was delighted to see Gavin's warm smile and friendly brown eyes a couple of minutes later. Those were the eyes he'd first seen properly at Leicester services on the night of his flight south. They'd struck him as kind and understanding, and so Gavin had proved to be during the rest of their journey.

Gavin got a drink and settled down at the table. "So, then, old son," he asked. "How's London? How are you coping?"

"It's grand. I like it down here – a lot. I'm trying to get the family stuff sorted. That's the worst bit."

"What's the news on the job front?"

"Good, I think. There's plenty of jobs around for drivers. I've made enquiries with several firms. It's a question of deciding what I want – to go back on the service buses or go for coaching. If I went for coaching, there's a possibility of tourist stuff or the express work I've been doing for the last few months.”

"Wow, you're spoilt for choice by the sound of it.”

"Yeah, I ought to get on with it. Make some decisions.”

"Yes, but I wouldn't rush it, David. It's been a turbulent few months. A bit of a rest won't do you any harm.”

"That's exactly what Alan says, that there's no hurry. But I can't help worrying about it. I can't keep sponging off him. I need to pay my way.”

"But you're a couple now, aren't you?" Gavin pointed out. "You're not just friends or flatmates, old son. This is about sharing, isn't it?”

David thought for a moment before replying. "I suppose you're right. I hadn't really thought of it like that. It seems such a big change. I'm used to being the breadwinner, to providing for Mona and the boys.”

"I don't think that's the right way to look at it. You're a household now and one day soon you might even be able to make it legal. You have a household income between you, which you share.”

David sighed. "You're right, I suppose. It all takes a bit of getting used to, especially since I'm not allowed to look after the boys any more.”

"Oh? That bad, eh?”

"Let's just say that she's still pissed off with me in a big way. I tried talking to her over the phone when I was up in Yorkshire the other week. I wanted to see her, but she wouldn't. I've tried writing, but she hasn't replied.”

"Have you seen the boys?”

David shook his head. "No. She's adamant about that. Won't let me near them.”

"Crikey, that must be hard.”

"It is."

"Got yourself a lawyer?"

"I was hoping it wouldn't be necessary." David sighed. "But we're sorting it. Al's ex-flatmate is in the law and he's recommended a guy. Unfortunately, he's away at the moment, but at least it's under way."

"Good. Sounds as if you'll need one. My older brother went through a messy divorce, so I know a bit of what it's like."

David felt himself tensing up and needed a change of subject. "So how's Ben?"

"Doing fine. It's half-term in a couple of weeks so he'll get a break. He's starting to look as though he needs it."

"Are you going away?"

Gavin nodded. "Canaries, as always. Get some sun for a few days before the onslaught of winter."

"Sounds glorious. And work? Are you busy?"

"Frantic, thank Gawd," Gavin replied with a grin. "I even had to refuse a couple of jobs last week – and, believe me, that's rare for me."

They chatted away through another round of drinks. David felt relaxed with his new friend and with the pub; being with other gay people was a new sensation, and he realised how good it was not to worry about what you did or said.

With both their partners due home, they left the pub around nine, hugged and headed their separate ways. Gavin was taking the tube for a couple of stops back to Balham. David conveyed Alan's suggestion that the four of them should have supper some time, and they fixed a date.

David strolled happily back to the flat, forgetting his

family troubles for a while and revelling in this glimpse of the new life that could await him.

The next morning, Mona's reply to his letter arrived. It was the day that David had promised himself he would start to get on with the rest of his life, decide what sort of driving work he wanted to do and apply to some firms.

Alan had already left for work. David was in the kitchen drinking a second cup of coffee when he heard the rattle of the ground-floor letterbox. He went downstairs to investigate. Most of the mail was for Simon or Peter but then he saw it: a pale lavender envelope with his name on it.

He recognised the handwriting straight away. Back in the flat, he tore open the envelope. Maybe the fact that she'd bothered to reply was a sign that she was coming round. Maybe he'd get to see his sons again.

The opening paragraphs gave him some hope: she started in the same reasonable tone that he'd tried to use in his own letter. But halfway down the second page, it was as if a switch had been thrown. The tone changed completely, back to the sort of language she'd used during their phone conversation. The attitude was exactly the same: no hint of compromise and an adamant refusal to grant him any access to the boys. She ended with a torrent of homophobic abuse.

His hopes extinguished, David stared miserably out of the kitchen window, oblivious to the bright sunshine and the trees of the Common floating in the light breeze.

Eventually, he stirred himself. It was now lunchtime and he needed to eat.

He had to keep himself together for Al's sake; Al didn't need to be distracted by David's problems, what with it being his busy time at work and now his studies. That view was vindicated that evening when Alan arrived home almost grey with fatigue. David made him eat some supper and they watched TV for an hour before falling into bed.

He stuck to his resolve not to mention the letter, though a voice inside him kept telling him that he was a fool not to share the burden of his disappointment. He dismissed it; this whole business was his own fault and he needed to face up to it and sort it out himself.

Chapter 10

Alan

The autumn sun streamed through the tall windows of the restaurant where Alan sat over lunch with his best friend Tris, making the glassware and cutlery sparkle. They grinned at each other. What with one thing and another, they had not seen each other for several weeks, keeping in touch with texts and messages via Ian, Tris's partner and Alan's close colleague at work.

With a few days between court appearances, Tris had seized the opportunity to make a lunch date for the two of them. "Do you realise we haven't done this since that Saturday in Richmond?"

Alan shook his head. "That was when? June?" He ran his hand through his hair. "God, a lot's happened since then."

Tris grinned at him. "Yes, indeed. Paul Foot died. And Bernard Levin. And Brian Clough. Oh, and we've had the Olympics and two by-elections to add to the fun. And Warwickshire won the county championship. Have I missed anything?"

"Idiot. You know what I mean."

"This wouldn't have anything to do with a handsome young bus driver from Yorkshire by any chance, would it?"

"I'm glad you think he's handsome, 'cos I think he's bloody gorgeous."

"I think Ian and I might have been able to work that out."

Alan beamed at him. "I suppose it is moderately obvious that I'm crazy about him."

Tris nodded. "Just a tad. Not that I'm complaining, mind you. And you won't find any criticism from this man who still goes gooey at the sight of his boyfriend after three years together."

Alan laughed. "Gooey, eh? Is that cheesy gooey or melted chocolate gooey?"

"Oh, I'd have to own up to cheesy, I suppose – in all senses of the word. Mind you, the substance is immaterial. It's the hotness that counts."

Alan guffawed, causing heads to turn in the restaurant. He blushed and murmured, "Sorry. Got carried away."

"Don't be daft. It's lovely to see you so relaxed. Do I take it that things are going well in the romance department?"

"Thanks. And yes, it's really good. I love having him with me full time, and he seems to be settling down here. All we need to do is to get the family stuff sorted."

"The missus still being difficult?"

"Yup. No change there."

Tris sighed. "You can't blame her, I suppose. He was a bad lad."

"I know. That's what makes it harder, I suppose. If she

wasn't somehow the injured party, it would be easier to be angry over her intransigence."

"Anything I can do?"

Alan nodded. "I don't think so. Thanks for suggesting Tom Parkes, I really liked him when we met."

"Me too. Tom'll be perfect – being gay will help him to understand what David's going through, and I've got a soft spot for the pair of them... Plus Tom's a bloody good family lawyer into the bargain."

"And Hugo's great too – and so talented. I got him a couple of commissions from our place recently."

"That's good. He's getting well established – from what I've seen of his graphics, he should go far."

"Agreed. David said that Tom's away?"

"Yes, he and Hugo are in Sicily at the moment. They'll be back at the end of next week. I'll talk to him as soon as he gets back."

"That's great. David and I are both floundering a bit at the moment. It would be good to have a professional who's got our back."

The conversation was interrupted by the arrival of their first course and then moved on to more mundane subjects. Over coffee, they returned to the subject of Tris's and Ian's future. "So will you be at the head of the queue next year?" Alan asked.

Tris frowned for a moment then his face cleared. "Oh, the civil partnership business, you mean?"

Alan nodded. "The Bill's going to go through now, right?"

"Definitely. Royal Assent is expected next month, with implementation late next year. And, yes, we're planning to be what the marketing people call 'early adopters'."

"Good. That's something to look forward to. I'm so pleased for both of you."

Tris looked at his watch. "Is that the time? I'd better move. I have a conference in chambers in half an hour."

They split the bill and parted with hugs. "Now don't forget to keep an eye on young David. I've an idea that he seems stronger than he actually is at the moment. Don't let him get broken amidst all the drama."

"I won't. Promise."

Mindful of Simon's advice earlier in the year about the need for joy in their lives, especially during this phase of uncertainty and doubt, Alan decided to arrange another visit to a West End theatre.

Their first trip, to see the Mel Brooks' musical *The Producers* at Drury Lane, had been a tremendous success. Alan could still see David almost bouncing in his seat with excitement as the curtain went up, and the look of joy on his face throughout the show. The evening might have been ruined by their chance meeting with the union man from Sedgethwaite, but the occasion remained a happy memory for Alan.

David had said he wanted to see more theatre, and so he would. Alan consulted Simon, who suggested *Les Misérables.* It was a musical, he said, with a good strong story line which had some funny moments as well as being very moving. Most of all, he argued, it was a long-running show which everybody loved.

"If you do go, we'll come with you," Simon added. "We haven't seen the new version at the Queen's yet, so it'll be a good excuse to see it again. I can't get enough of it."

"Okay, *Les Mis* it is," Alan replied. "I'll organise the tickets. I think Ian at work knows somebody who might help."

"Super. We'll book supper at Joe's afterwards. It's time David was introduced to the delights of my favourite restaurant."

"It's a deal, Si. What are your diaries like?"

They sorted out a couple of possible dates and Ian's contact was able to get them seats for the Tuesday of the following week.

On the night of the planned trip, it was almost inevitable that Alan would be delayed at the office because of a last-minute panic over some advertising copy. As the minutes ticked by, it was clear that he wouldn't have time to get home and change before the show. He texted David to warn him and asked him to travel into the West End with Simon and Peter. Tris and Ian had also decided to join the party, so they arranged to meet in the Duke of Wellington pub off Shaftesbury Avenue, round the corner from the theatre.

In the event, Alan arrived a few minutes early, having disposed of his problem in time to freshen up before leaving the office. Fortunately, he hadn't been too formally dressed since he'd not been scheduled for a client meeting, so he didn't have to spend the evening stuck in a suit.

He bought a drink and a sandwich. The pub was not as busy as it would be later, so he secured a table and sat back to eat and do some people watching. It was one of his favourite occupations, especially in a gay-friendly pub; after six years in the capital, he was still sometimes taken aback by London's relaxed atmosphere. He still remembered the feeling of wonder during his first few weeks that he could be amongst people of his own kind – and that there were so many of them. After years of isolation in his Yorkshire home town, scared even to tell his best friend David that he liked boys, life in London had felt like a fresh start. The city might be smelly and noisy and too full of people sometimes, but he loved the life and wouldn't dream of giving it up.

In here, he loved the mix of cultures. In one corner, a Chinese boy sat holding hands with a large Afro-Caribbean guy who was twice his size. The table next to Alan was occupied by a boy of South Asian origin – India, or Sri Lanka perhaps – alongside his Caucasian boyfriend who, judging by his lilting tones, was born on the other side of the Irish Sea. Alan could hear an American accent from across the bar, and several seriously hot boys clearly hailed from Eastern Europe.

He was exhilarated by it all. When his friends found him ten minutes later, he was sitting with a smile on his face that broadened when he caught sight of them all, especially David.

There was something different about David tonight – he seemed brighter and more alive. He was obviously fascinated by being in the West End again, as well as finding himself in a gay pub for only the second or third time in his life. His eyes were bright and he could barely keep his head still as his eyes darted about, taking in his surroundings and his fellow drinkers.

Alan stood up to greet them all and gave David a quick peck on the cheek. "Hey. You okay?" he asked. "Sorry I couldn't get away to come home first."

If he were honest, Alan would say that *Les Mis* was not his favourite show. He'd seen it a couple of times when it had been at the much larger Palace Theatre and found it impressive rather than lovable. He could see that the show was clever in inducing an emotional reaction from the audience but he didn't experience the emotions himself.

His companions, on the other hand, were in raptures. Simon, Peter, Ian and Tris were devoted fans, having been at least half a dozen times, and David was bowled over. From almost the first bar to the last curtain call, his eyes glistened, overflowing with tears more than once. As at Drury Lane, he seized Alan's hand at the start and, apart from going to the bar at the interval, only let go as they rose to leave the auditorium.

As the finale 'Do You Hear the People Sing?' ended and the theatre rang to the cheers of the audience, David leaned across, tears pouring down his face, and whispered, "Thank you, thank you, thank you. Al, that was totally amazing. I'll never forget tonight."

Alan leaned into his shoulder then turned and beamed at him. "My pleasure, Davy. Glad you liked it."

They stayed in their seats until the last chords from the

orchestra died away, then filed out into the still warm air of a muggy London night. The six of them gathered on the pavement in Shaftesbury Avenue, surrounded by milling crowds and flanked by slow-moving traffic negotiating the post-theatre congestion.

"No need to ask whether you enjoyed that," Simon said to David.

"Certainly did! Wow, Si. It were reet grand, as they'd say at home. What about you?"

Simon nodded vigorously. "Absolutely. I was a bit worried what it would be like in a smaller theatre, but I thought it was every bit as good."

"Me too," said Tris. "Loved it. Now, I'm starved. How are we going to get to Joe's? We'll need two cabs, won't we?"

Even in the chaos, they managed to flag down a couple of taxis without too long a wait and were soon outside the restaurant. They were in a dimly lit, narrow street. Alan smiled as he saw David looking a little puzzled at the unassuming door they were heading towards. There was a narrow awning above it but, other than that, the entrance was unadorned. Going through the front door, there was a sharp turn to the right followed by a flight of stairs heading downwards.

Alan smiled as David looked more than a little nervous. "Trust us, Davy. You'll love it."

Chapter 11

David

"Trust us, Davy. You'll love it."

David shrugged and followed their friends down the stairs, with Alan close behind. As they neared the bottom, the noise grew louder: loud voices, laughter and the notes of a piano. There was another sharp turn, this time to the left, which brought them to a red velvet curtain.

Once they had passed through it, David's eyes widened as Joe Allen's restaurant opened out before him. To the right, a long, highly polished bar ran almost the full length of the huge room. To the left were tables covered with white paper cloths, mostly laid for two or four, in rows either side of a semi-open partition that divided the space into two. The walls were bare brick but covered almost completely by framed theatrical posters.

As David looked round, Simon and Peter were receiving a hug from the maître d', whilst Tris and Ian greeted the pianist, Jimmy, a small elderly guy with a big smile and twinkling eyes. He managed to say hello without missing a beat, morphing seamlessly into a medley of the songs from

Les Mis as soon he learned which show they'd seen that night.

The maître d' hugged Alan next. When he learned that David was a "Joe Allen Virgin", the welcome was as warm for him, too.

The six of them were whisked off to a round table at the far end of the room, menus were produced closely followed by a bottle of Prosecco and six glasses. David was wide-eyed and fascinated. The place was cheerful and informal, buzzing with chatter and laughter. It was beyond anything he'd ever imagined and so different from what he'd expected a famous London restaurant would be like: there were no starched tablecloths, hushed voices or snooty waiters.

The Prosecco went down easily and was followed by a couple of bottles of red wine. By the end of the main course, they were all relaxed and mellow, chatting about favourite shows they'd each seen over the years before returning to that evening's performance.

For the most part David remained quiet, smiling as he listened to their anecdotes and opinions. He wanted to know more about everything. "So has Victor Yugo written any other shows?" he asked.

There was a momentary silence before Simon emitted a hastily supressed giggle. Tris smiled gently. "He only wrote the novel, David. Tonight's show was written by two guys called Boublil and Schönberg."

"Oh, I see," David responded, his heart sinking as he realised that he'd shown his ignorance.

Alan chipped in. "Yes, Davy. Victor Hugo was a nineteenth-century French novelist."

"Right," he snapped. "I'm ignorant. No need to labour the point." There was an embarrassed silence for a second or two before Simon intervened.

"It's an easy mistake to make, Alan," he said. "*Les Mis* is probably more famous as a show than it ever was as a book. I bet more people have seen the musical and the film than have ever read the novel."

"That's probably true," Ian added. "After all, it's still one of the longest ever written."

"God, yes," said Simon. "I tried to read it once – but 650,000 words ... come on."

"Did you manage *War and Peace*?" asked Tris.

"Yeah, but it took me months..." They were off again, chatting animatedly about another book that David knew nothing about. He dimly remembered watching the film with his mum when he was younger and thinking it would go on for ever. Anyway, that was the extent of his knowledge.

The evening had gone rather flat for him. He enjoyed it but he regretted snapping at Alan. Would he ever truly fit in with these friends? Alan noticed his mood shifting and squeezed his hand under the table. David squeezed back and mouthed "Sorry" to him. Alan winked in return, before trying to suppress a yawn.

It was time to go. They summoned the bill, split it three ways and emerged once more into London's humid air. Ian and Tris said goodnight and went to find a taxi back to Kensington, leaving the other four to return to Clapham. Alan and Peter set off to lead the search, leaving Simon and David standing together.

David felt Simon step close to him and link his arm. "You

mustn't worry, sweetheart," he said. "Nobody cares, you know."

"I know that deep down," David replied sadly. "But *I* care."

The next morning, another letter arrived from his wife.

When he awoke, he felt calmer about the incident in Joe Allen's and was determined not to let the stupidity of his own question spoil the otherwise golden memory of the evening. Simon had understood and been kind; somehow, that had meant more than Alan's similar but more flippant reassurances when they'd got back to the flat.

He knew he was being a little unfair to Alan; they'd always taken the mickey out of each other, and it was only right that there'd been some ribbing before bed. When David had snapped at him, telling him to shut up, Alan had quickly let the subject drop and given him a big hug. That made him feel a bit better but his mind kept looping back to the incident and how stupid he'd felt.

Still not in the best of moods, his heart sank even further when he saw the familiar envelope lying on the front door mat. The theme for this letter was all about what a useless husband he'd been, especially in bed. She was surprised that David had had enough "lead in his pencil" to father two children. In a particularly spiteful paragraph, she claimed that he had never satisfied her sexually, making her put up with his lack of interest in sex, having perfunctory intercourse and always ejaculated prematurely.

He knew in his heart of hearts that some of what she

said was true, but he hadn't meant it to be. His failure to perform had never implied a lack of affection for her, or ingratitude for how hard she worked in keeping house and mothering the boys. It was … simply the way he was. Until Al had come back into his life, he hadn't understood it. He had thought that his life with Mona was all he had and he'd have to put up with it. He felt so sad, so ashamed, so fucking inadequate. *Again.*

He sat at the kitchen table, tears pouring down his cheeks, reliving his marriage in a nightmarish kaleidoscope of scenes.

As luck would have it, it was Alan's night for classes, so David was on his own all day and well into the evening. He made himself eat some lunch, but he didn't have the inclination or the willpower to do anything during the afternoon. When he heard Alan's key in the door, he realised that he'd spent virtually the entire day sitting at the kitchen table, staring into space.

David sprang into action, getting out the ingredients for the supper he had planned. He schooled his expression carefully as he turned to greet his boyfriend. For a moment he was overwhelmed by the sight of Alan, rumpled and tired but still absolutely beautiful. The moment passed quickly, and they greeted each other with a more mundane brush of the lips.

David longed to be drawn into Alan's arms and to stay there for ever, but recognised that if he allowed himself to do that he would fall apart. All the stuff about Mona's letters would come spilling out. Still convinced that it would be unfair to burden Alan at this time, he settled for the brief greeting and busied himself with supper, telling Alan to shower while he cooked.

As he defrosted and reheated his favourite homemade pasta sauce, the voice inside him started up once more, pointing out how wrong he was. Alan had a right to know; he would want to help. He ignored it again, acknowledging the argument but telling himself that tonight was not the time.

The result was that more days passed without anything being said; somehow the time never seemed right and the longer he left it, the more difficult it became to find the right words. He debated responding to his wife's latest letter but decided that there was no point. It would only upset him more – and nothing would change her mind about him.

It was the Friday when Gavin and his partner Ben were coming for supper. The evening was especially important to David because this was a friendship that *he* was bringing to the table. He and Gavin had chatted several times about the arrangement since their drink together, and he was looking forward to meeting Ben.

David pushed his marriage out of his mind and turned to cooking supper. He opted for a simple meal of beef stew with mashed potatoes, easy to do because all the vegetables cooked at the same time as the meat. He'd used what he could remember of his mum's recipe and had checked with her earlier in the week about a couple of details.

As the time for their guests' arrival approached, Alan had still not arrived home. That was not surprising after the week he'd had, but it made David nervous. He was not used to entertaining; he and Mona had rarely invited people for a meal except for close family, and then Mona had done most of the work.

He had managed to stay calm all afternoon. He had put the stew in the oven in good time to cook on a low heat, tidied the flat and laid the table. He put snacks and crisps in the sitting room, then nipped into the shower. Finally, Alan texted to say he was on his way. David breathed a sigh of relief and put the potatoes on to boil.

Gavin and Ben arrived exactly on time. When Alan came home a few minutes later, David made the introductions and prepared drinks for everybody. It was when he returned to the kitchen for some ice that he realised his mistake: the room was full of smoke and the smell was foul. The potatoes had boiled dry and the pan was sure to be ruined.

"Oh, fuck."

He quickly turned off the gas and opened the window to get rid of the smoke, swearing quietly to himself. Why didn't anything ever go right? His eyes filled with tears and he sat down at the table, overwhelmed by this latest setback.

Alan came into the room at that moment. "Crikey, Davy, what's that smell? What's happened?"

"It's the fucking potatoes. The pan boiled dry while I was upstairs. I'm sorry, Al. The meal's ruined, and it's all my bloody fault."

Alan grabbed an oven cloth and looked into the pan. "Don't be daft, lad. It's only two or three near the bottom. The others are fine. Leave it to me. Finish the drinks and go and talk to your guests, love. I'll sort it out."

"Are you sure? Thanks, Al."

"Off you go. And don't worry."

"But the smell…"

"Go!"

David allowed himself to be shooed out of the kitchen and went back upstairs to their guests. "Sorry about that. Slight disaster in the kitchen," he announced with a rueful grin. "All sorted now though. Supper'll be ready in a few minutes, guys."

Ben grinned at him. "Don't worry about it. I'm not even allowed in our kitchen in case I set fire to it."

Gavin grumbled, "A bit of an exaggeration – even if he has been known to burn a hard-boiled egg."

Their laughter eased David's tension and he warmed once again to Gavin's easy-going manner. He had already taken an instant liking to his partner.

They talked about Ben's job as a special needs teacher, and their plans for a few days away during the half-term holiday. Having never been outside the UK, David felt vaguely jealous as they chatted about winter sunshine and the bars and restaurants they visited regularly every year. It was another reminder of the different circles in which he was now moving. Would he ever be able to talk about favourite bars in exotic places? He doubted it.

When Ben asked him if he'd been to the islands, David shook his head. "Never even made it to Calais, much less the Canaries," he replied, unable to hide a slightly bitter tone from his voice. "My wife and I used to dream of taking the boys somewhere like that, but of course that won't ever happen now.

"Now, Davy, don't let's get started on that," said Alan, coming back into the room. "I came into say that supper's ready. Bring your drinks and we'll go and eat this sumptuous stew that my boy here has cooked up." As David passed him to lead their guests down the short flight of stairs to the kitchen, Alan winked at him and whispered, "Panic over."

The rest of the evening went swimmingly. Gavin, Ben and Alan swapped stories of their earlier lives on London's gay scene, then Gavin regaled them with tales from his fund of horror stories about weddings he'd photographed. David's beef dish was praised to the heights and he basked in the warmth of their plaudits – but the potato incident still rankled, dragging his mood down.

Christ, can't I do anything right?

Chapter 12

Alan

Towards the end of September, an unseasonable heatwave settled over the UK and dominated the weather for the next three weeks, bringing unusually high levels of humidity in its wake. This left everybody hot, sweaty and tired. Commuting was hell on earth, especially during the rush hour, and Alan arrived home every night almost completely drained.

The agency was in the midst of getting final client sign-off for the Christmas campaigns that would start to roll out within a few weeks. Amongst the recent new clients they had won was a train operating company in the process of mobilising for a new contract that would start at the beginning of December. Launching a completely new franchise meant putting together different elements of previous businesses, so the transition was particularly complex. It didn't help that one or two of the client's senior team didn't seem to believe in the value of marketing, one suggesting that distributing typewritten sheets for timetables ought to be sufficient.

The three weeks after the supper with Gavin and Ben seemed to pass like the wind. Alan worked long hours and was rarely home before nine. He had to work on three Saturdays in a row; he hated it but knew that life would calm down soon, so was not too worried.

Besides, David seemed to be coping. He was relentlessly cheerful when Alan got home, feeding him either home-cooked meals or his favourite take-aways, and keeping the flat spick and span. He told Alan that he was quite happy pottering about all day and asserted that he was steadily recovering from his recent traumas. He'd been in touch with his prospective solicitor, Tom Parkes, and had an appointment to go to see him in a couple of weeks' time.

Alan was not convinced. He noticed that his boyfriend seemed to be getting thinner and his face was increasingly drawn. The smile that had always seemed to be ready on his lips was not there so much, and in the third week he realised that when his lover did smile it was forced and rarely reached his eyes. Caught unawares, there was no smile on David's face, only a look of pain and sometimes utter misery.

Alan asked on several occasions whether everything was all right, only to be told firmly that it was. He knew that was a lie but accepted it for the time being. The combination of the weather and the pressures of work were leaving him so exhausted that he did not have the energy to address the issue. The other effect of his exhaustion was that they had not had sex for a couple of weeks. He assumed that David was not making any moves out of respect for his obvious tiredness, but he also began to wonder whether the apparent lack of interest was symptomatic of David's own state of mind.

Finally, on the third Thursday after the supper, the end was in sight. The last of the Christmas campaigns would be signed off the following day, and they had client approval for the train company campaign. Alan got home earlier than usual in ebullient form, ready to announce that he had a treat in store for the coming weekend. He'd conceived his idea during the week – more joy, he'd thought, to make up for his prolonged absences.

He'd gone for the hottest ticket in town and managed use some connections and call in some favours to snag a couple of tickets for the Royal Ballet's latest triple bill of classic works by Frederick Ashton, Kenneth MacMillan and Nijinksa. He thought a mixed bill would be a perfect introduction to the ballet for David, opening his mind to another art form.

However, that night even the forced smile had disappeared. In response to Alan's enquiry after David's day, he got a grunted "Okay".

"Davy, what's wrong, love? Something's bothering you, isn't it?"

"Nowt. I'm fine," came the snapped reply. David gave a grin reminiscent of a skeleton's grimace.

"Oh, okay. You sure? Because you don't seem very cheerful at the moment and I wondered, that's all."

There was a deep sigh. "I really am fine, Al. Promise." It was clearly a lie, but at least it was accompanied by a more genuine smile.

"Good, only I've got a treat for us tomorrow. I managed to get some tickets for Covent Garden."

"Where?"

"You know, Covent Garden. The Royal Opera House, Davy."

"Oh? What for?"

"The Royal Ballet – they're doing an incredible triple bill and tickets are like gold dust. I thought you'd like it."

"Me? Like ballet?" David snorted. "Whatever makes you think that? All those pretty boys prancing round in tights? I don't think so, Al."

"Actually, all those 'pretty boys', as you call them, work incredibly hard and are amazingly athletic. And frankly, I'm a bit surprised to hear that sort of language from you."

"I'm sorry, Al. It's just not me. I don't want to go. Now can we please leave it?"

"No, we bloody can't. These tickets cost a fortune and I called in all sorts of favours to get hold of them."

"Well, happen you should have asked me first. I'm not going, and there's an end of it."

"I thought you wanted to widen your outlook. Why are you saying no purely on the basis of prejudice?"

"That was before. I know my limits now. It's all out of my league, like most of your posh friends. I'm just an ordinary bloke, a bus driver. I don't belong at t'Royal Opera House."

"So what are you going to do? Sit round here in a tracksuit watching rubbish TV for the rest of your life?"

"Fuck you, Alan Foreshaw. Mebbe I will."

"Fine by me, but don't expect me to keep you."

"If that's the way you feel, maybe I'd better bugger off back to Sedgethwaite where I belong."

At that point, Alan felt a spasm pass through his body. His shoulders slumped and he closed his eyes for a moment.

What was it? Fear? Anger? He didn't know. An icy calm was overtaking him. He knew in that moment that David would be like all the others: in the end he would go, leaving Alan on his own again.

He'd coped before and he would again. He was disappointed but not surprised. He opened his eyes again, put his shoulders back and raised himself to his full height. When he spoke, he realised that his voice had changed as abruptly as his mood, becoming calm and chilly. "Entirely up to you, David. Entirely up to you."

David's face registered the change and he recoiled from the icy tone. He started to apologise, but Alan cut him off. "Let me know what you decide. Now I'm going for a shower and straight to bed."

"But what about supper?"

"Not hungry. I'll see if Tris wants the tickets."

"No, Alan, wait. Don't leave it like this. I'm sorry."

"I am too, Davy. But I can't help who I am, or who my friends are. I promised you that I'd help you open your mind like Tris did for me. If you don't want that, that's fine. I'll know in future."

Alan left the room. He collected pillows and a duvet from a cupboard on the landing, went into the spare room and shut the door firmly.

He awoke the next morning starving hungry and deeply saddened, but still calm and resolute. He showered quickly, grabbed some clean clothes from the wardrobe in his bedroom without waking David and left the flat.

Setting a New Course

Chapter 13

David

It was the first time since David had got back from Yorkshire six weeks earlier that he'd been alone in bed. He lay there for most of the night, castigating himself for his show of temper and his ingratitude. He was been tempted on several occasions to go into the spare room, apologise to Alan and beg him to come back to their bed, but he remembered how tired Alan had seemed, and how much he needed to rest. David eventually fell asleep as daylight began to creep under the blinds in the room. He awoke to an empty flat; Alan had obviously gone off to work.

He groaned again at the memory of their stupid row, the horrid things he'd said and how cruel he'd been. True, Alan had given as good as he'd got, but the row was David's fault. And what had it meant when Alan turned so cold? Was that the end of them?

It seemed as if he'd pressed a button – a self-destruct button, which had turned Alan off. Stupid, stupid, stupid. What had come over him? He knew, of course; it had been the missive from his dear wife. When it had arrived the previous morning, it had blown apart the fragile peace David had been building for himself.

The letter contained all the foul homophobia that had been the hallmark of the previous two, but it also contained another passage. She explained that she and a friend had been doing some research on the internet and had found out all about Alan's firm. She'd discovered that Alan had been tagged in some pictures of Tris and Ian's party on their photographer's web site – and, of course, there'd been one of him and Davy, smiling into the camera, lifting champagne glasses in a toast.

After a whole new rant about rich queers having orgies, she calmed down again and asked what he had been doing there. What on earth made him think that he could hold his own with Alan and his rich friends in London? David would never fit in, she said; after all, he was as thick as five short planks. Why else was he only a bus driver? Much too thick, she said, with no education and, as she put it, "not the right manners for my mother, never mind proper posh folk".

Reading her words had felt like getting an electric shock. By some mischance, she'd hit on the very fears that had been dogging him since the night of Simon's dinner party. He'd been mystified by virtually the whole conversation. Then there'd been the jibe from two of the guests at Tris's party. That had stayed with him, whilst his giant fuck-up after the theatre the other week simply added to the weight of evidence. The letter made him realise that he was cast adrift between two worlds – the old home life that he'd rejected and a new one into which he did not fit, and which left him feeling stupid and ignorant.

The letter had been fresh in his mind when Alan had arrived home brandishing tickets for the ballet; everything Mona had said crystallised in an instant. He could hear her voice when Alan had given him the news; it had been as if she were speaking when David reacted and refused to go. And in the process, he had pushed away the one person whose help could get him out of this mess.

He looked at his phone in case there was a text or a message from Alan, but there was nothing, only a reminder that today was his appointment with Tom Parkes, the solicitor that Tris had recommended. He groaned. It had to be today, didn't it? He toyed briefly with the idea of cancelling but quickly rejected it. Whatever happened, he was going to need some legal advice; it would be sensible to start the process, even if he had to call a halt later.

He roused himself and went to get ready.

David had not been into the area around Lincoln's Inn before, so he was both fascinated and terrified when he arrived there. The buildings exuded a sense of permanence and confidence, as if saying "trust us, we've been here for centuries – we and the people inside know what we're doing". The mellow brickwork and Georgian, multi-paned windows were appealing in their symmetry, somehow restful to the eye. Despite his anxiety, the sight brought a smile to his lips.

His destination was outside the Inn itself but facing the open space of the Fields. The building looked as if it dated from the eighteenth century, but in fact it had been constructed in the 1950s behind a restored façade. The original interior had been destroyed in the Blitz.

David found himself in a cool, grey reception area. All the doors leading off it were polished light oak, as was the furniture. He was greeted by a friendly young receptionist who took his name and asked him to sit down. It was much less imposing than he had expected, but he was still incredibly nervous and wished fervently that Alan was with him. However, everybody had agreed that he should see his new adviser on his own, to put across the facts of the case in his own way in a one-to-one meeting. Tris had reassured him that Tom Parkes had been a close friend since schooldays. He was gay and would be very sympathetic.

Never having had any involvement with lawyers, David didn't know what to expect, but the people flitting about and chatting to one another whilst he sat in reception looked reassuringly normal, even if their accents were decidedly unfamiliar.

After a few minutes, a youngish man came into reception and paused briefly to speak to the receptionist. He was tall and good looking, with a square jaw, hazel eyes and untidy chestnut hair that looked as if he ran his hand through it often. He wore dark-framed glasses and was dressed in a well-cut, mid-grey suit that fitted him like a glove, the jacket slightly flared at the waist and fastened with a single button. He looked as if he belonged in front of a camera in a photographer's studio rather than in a lawyers' office.

He frowned for a moment as he looked round the room, then his face cleared and he broke into a smile that almost took David's breath away. "David Edgeley?" he asked.

"Aye, that's me."

"Tom Parkes," he replied, offering his hand to shake. "Good to meet you, David. Do come through."

David shook the proffered hand, which was warm and soft; it felt comfortable somehow, even if the grip was firm. He followed Tom through the door and into a corridor, then into a small meeting room.

"Do take a seat," Tom said. "Can I get you anything to drink? Tea? Coffee? Water?"

David coughed, his throat suddenly dry. "Water would be fine, thanks."

"Coming right up. Still or sparkling?"

"Still's fine, thanks."

Water poured, Tim sat down opposite him and smiled reassuringly. "So, Tris has outlined the situation to me but I want to get your take on it all, to hear what's happened so far in your own words."

"Okay."

"But first I want to reassure you that everything you say in here is totally confidential and won't be repeated outside this office, despite our mutual friends and acquaintances."

"I understand, Mr Parkes. Thanks."

"Please call me Tom."

David nodded. "Okay, Tom. Where should I start?"

Another reassuring smile. "Tris said that you first met Alan at school. Why don't you start there?"

Hesitantly at first, David started with Alan losing his parents and ended with his departure for London six years earlier. "That was it, really. On the morning after we'd … been together, he asked me to go with him. I was too scared, so I said no. It was a stupid mistake."

"Like you're only the nineteen year old who's ever made a decision they regret," Tom replied with a smile. "I sure as hell know I made some."

"Well, I made another biggie within weeks," David replied with a sigh. "I asked Mona to marry me."

"Why?"

David gave a laugh. "That's a very good question." He paused, wondering what the answer actually was. He'd talked with his sister Jen and Alan about his decision to marry, but even then he'd never actually confronted the question of why he'd done it. "It seemed a good idea at the time."

"Obviously. But why?"

David frowned, momentarily irritated and wondering why Tom was pursuing this.

"I'm pushing you a little because I think it's important," Tom continued. "From what I can gather, your wife is claiming that you only married her as a disguise. God knows, David, you wouldn't have been the first to do that and you won't be the last. But if you want to keep denying that, you need to know why you did marry her."

"I'd known her all my life and I was fond of her. I thought I could be happy with her, and she seemed safe, I suppose. The alternative – Alan, going to London, being with him – seemed risky, dangerous. I didn't do dangerous, at least not without Alan. I wanted to drive my bus and that was all I'd ever wanted. It was only when I was married and actually doing it that I realised it was as boring as hell and not what I wanted at all."

Tom smiled. "There've been lots of worse reasons for getting married. And the kids? Did you want them?"

David nodded emphatically. "Yeah, we both did. But it was a bit of an effort, to be honest, specially for the second one."

"I see. So you wouldn't say your marriage was a success sexually?"

"No. I used to avoid having – you know, making love – as much as I could. And even when we did try, I couldn't always manage it."

Tom smiled. "You were braver than me, David. I never even tried. Just not for me."

"Me neither, as it turned out. When I met up with Alan again, I realised what I'd been missing for all those years."

"So, the two kids came along – Tommy and Kevin, isn't it?"

David nodded and couldn't help smiling at the mention of their names.

"How did you feel about that?"

"I loved them to bits. I think that in some ways the first one saved our marriage. Mona was so focused on Tommy that she didn't have much time for me. That suited me down to the ground."

"But you experienced no sexual attraction towards men during that time?"

David shook his head. "No. I can honestly say it never crossed my mind. I was focused on the family and my job. I was discontented sometimes, but I could never put my finger on the reason. The weeks just seemed to slip by. We were saving for a house, and I had hopes of promotion to inspector, but that was it." He paused, momentarily puzzled by how alien his previous life felt now. How could he have thought it would be enough?

He cleared his throat and took a sip of water before continuing. "That's why bumping into Alan last February was such a shock. Everything suddenly came alive again. It was..." David's eyes filled and he felt a lump in his throat as he remembered sitting in the bus station café and talking to his friend for the first time in six years. "It was incredible."

Tom smile reassuringly. "I can see that. It's quite a story, you know."

"I was terrified, Tom. I didn't know what was happening to me, or why. I realised that there'd been a huge hole in my life since Alan had gone, and now it was filled again."

"What happened after that? I've had the outline from Tris but it would be helpful to get your take."

David quickly ran through the last few months – helping Alan with his aunt's house, making love there, getting the express coach job and staying at the flat. When he got to the bit about the party for Tris and Ian, Tom smiled.

"I remember that – my partner Hugo and I were away and couldn't make it, otherwise I'm sure we'd have met that night."

"Aye, probably. It was a good do." David smiled. He resumed the story and got to the Friday night theatre trip and its aftermath. He recalled his horror in St Martin's Lane when he'd seen Douggie Thorpe looking at him and sneering, remembering the stomach-dropping sensation when he'd realised what would happen next.

"To finish the story," Tom intervened, recognising his distress, "you got back to Yorkshire on the Saturday night, and your wife threw you out?"

"Aye, that's right. She asked me if what Douggie said

was true, and I told her I'd been seeing Alan. She called me a pervert and threw me out."

"Was there any physical violence? On either side?"

"No, though I think we both came fairly close to it at one point. In many ways, it was like a dialogue of the deaf."

"I understand. It must have been pretty terrible."

David shuddered at the memory. "It was. It got worse later when my dad threw me out as well."

"Christ Almighty!"

"It was a bit much, to be honest. So I hitched down to London and got to Alan's. I didn't know what else to do."

"And since? I gather you've had one phone call with Mona, after which you wrote her a letter. Is that right?"

David paused, wondering if he should come clean or not about his wife's letters. But he realised he had no choice; keeping quiet about them was stupid and dangerous. Alan would be pissed about him telling Tom first, but it couldn't be helped.

"Er, she's written back. Several times. None of them particularly pleasant." He proffered the folder he'd been carrying and Tom emptied the contents onto the table. A small pile of lavender envelopes lay there, secured by a rubber band. "I put them in order."

They were silent as Tom read the letters. There was the usual distant roar of the traffic that was a constant in central London, plus the distant sounds of telephones ringing and the receptionist's voice, but complete quiet inside the room.

David did not know how to feel as Tom read. One part of him felt embarrassed that this catalogue of his alleged failings as a husband and a human being should be laid before this comparative stranger; another part of him was ashamed that the letters had caused him to be so dreadful to Alan and possibly threaten their relationship. A third part of him was overwhelmingly relieved that now he had somebody else on his side, somebody with the power and authority to make this better.

Eventually, Tom looked up, his eyes full of sympathy and concern. "David, I don't know what to say." He paused and glanced out of the small window into the gardens beyond. He sighed deeply and turned back. "These are quite some of the most vicious and unpleasant communications I've ever seen – and believe me, as a family lawyer I've seen quite a few. I'm sorry that you've had to endure this."

"Thanks. I ... er ... didn't know what to think, really. Part of me pleads guilty to a lot of what she says, but it's a bit hard coming from somebody you've been close to for six years. I get that she's angry and hurt, and I can understand why. I know it's my fault. But..."

"That's not the point, David. Whether or not she was justified, your wife ended the relationship and ejected you from the marital home. You complied with her demands and have offered to reach a settlement to end the marriage, as she wishes to do. Her interests – and those of your two sons – would best be served by reaching that settlement as soon as possible. It would include an access agreement and making the best financial provision you can for the children. These letters do nothing towards achieving that, so ultimately they are self-defeating. They're also cruel and unnecessary."

"I agree. Can we stop her, though?"

"We certainly can. I'll get a cease and desist letter in the post tonight and copy it to her solicitors. She gave their details in the rational bit of her first letter, didn't she?"

"That's right. Stopping the letters would be fantastic, Tom, and I'd be very grateful. The other thing that's seriously doing my head in is not being allowed to see the boys. Can we do anything about that?"

"As part of a deal? Yes. But I've got to be honest, David – without an agreement, it's going to be extremely difficult to force the issue."

David slumped in his chair. He'd known that for weeks – hell, Jen and her husband had warned him when he'd first told them about Alan in the spring, as had Tris in August – but he'd hoped against hope that an expert like Tom would find a way.

"Don't get me wrong, we're in a stronger position than we were before last year. Under the new law, because your name is on the boys' birth certificates you are designated as having parental responsibility. Even so, if your wife has custody and makes a case about the boys' safety and welfare, it could be difficult to persuade a court to overturn that – especially in your circumstances."

"You mean the gay thing?"

Tom visibly winced at David's question but nodded. "Yeah. Officially the fact that you're gay shouldn't be relevant, especially as you're apparently in a stable relationship even if it is fairly recent. But in practice, there are still some traditionally minded people around. Our best hope is to try for a meeting, to see if we can thrash out an agreement. If not, we can try mediation. Only if all that fails do we go to court. Let's hope it doesn't come to that."

"Fuck."

His meeting over, David left Tom's offices and entered the grounds of Lincoln's Inn Fields; it was a pleasant day, and a few minutes' walk in the fresh air would do him good before returning to the flat. He saw a free bench near the bandstand and sat down, enjoying the autumn sunshine.

He felt much better after his meeting. He hoped that matters would now take on a momentum of their own and all he'd have to do would be to sign things, turn up every now and again and generally do what he was told. He'd liked Tom a lot; charming and sympathetic, he'd immediately won David's trust. The stuff about the boys was disappointing but had not been much of a surprise. Owning up about the letters and finding out that Mona could be stopped from writing them was a real bonus. David felt as if a tonne weight had been lifted from his shoulders.

He now had to fess up to Alan about them and the reason for him being so miserable lately, but he was confident that Alan would understand and forgive him. He spent a few happy minutes making a plan to win him round and to demonstrate his gratitude and love. Then he remembered that Alan was going to be late home tonight because there was a staff leaving party in the office. A pity: David's plans would have to be put on hold for twenty-four hours.

Suddenly he was seized with the need to hear Alan's voice, to say sorry as soon as he could for the previous night's debacle. He reached for his phone but, before he could dial Alan's number, the device lit up with an incoming call.

When he answered it, he heard his mother's voice sounding unusually agitated. Eventually, he calmed her down enough to learn that his father had been taken ill and was on his way to hospital. All plans forgotten, David set off towards Holborn Tube station. Half an hour later, he was on a train north.

When he did get a chance to dial Alan's number, shortly before the train pulled out of King's Cross, it went straight to voicemail. He left a brief message to say that he was heading to Sedgethwaite and that his dad had been taken ill. He noticed that the train had started to move while he was speaking and had entered the tunnel immediately outside the station. When he looked at his phone, he'd lost the connection. He didn't think it would matter because he was sure he'd finished the message.

Setting a New Course

Chapter 14

Alan

It was gone midnight when Alan got home and he was drunk. He'd had a terrible day worrying about David, snapping everybody's head off and, to cap it all, he had lost his mobile phone. He'd no idea where he'd left it but suspected it was on his bedside table, forgotten in the heat of last night's argument and his rapid departure this morning.

Busy in meetings all morning, he hadn't missed it until lunchtime. Once he realised, he'd used the office phone to ring both the landline at the flat and David's mobile but without success. He'd left a message on David's mobile but there had been no response by the time the switchboard closed in preparation for the evening's party.

His firm was not usually known for having spectacular parties but tonight had been different. It was in honour of Maudie, a much-loved senior clerk in the accounts office, who was retiring after more than twenty-five years – in the advertising industry, that was pretty much the equivalent of a whole epoch.

They'd given her a terrific send-off, and the booze had certainly flowed both in the office and in the pub round the corner to which most of the staff had gravitated. Alan had chatted to colleagues in his team, and had a long talk with Ian and with his immediate boss as he sipped his favourite red wine. He'd still not been in the best of moods but he had played his part.

About nine-thirty, his evening's steady drinking on a virtually empty stomach suddenly caught up with him. He sat quietly in a corner of the bar, his head spinning violently and feeling vaguely sick. One of his team passed him a bottle of mineral water and he drank it down. He was about to leave when somebody mentioned going for a Chinese meal, reminding him again of how hungry he was.

Deep down, Alan knew that he ought to go home and face the music from last night's shitstorm, but he realised that his current state was not ideal for settling arguments. Also, if he were totally honest, there was a tiny part of him deep down that was still cross with David for his attitude and wanted to punish him. And there was also a rather larger part of him that dreaded what he might find at home and feared another row. At that moment, going for a Chinese seemed an excellent way of putting off the evil moment.

The food helped to sober him up a little but you couldn't eat without having a drink to wash it down with, could you? No, of course not. The result was that a taxi dropped Alan outside his building at eleven-thirty, and he made his way unsteadily up the stairs to the top flat.

"Hi, I'm home," he called out as he closed the front

door behind him. There was no response. "Silence was the stern reply," he muttered as he climbed the stairs up from the kitchen. He looked into the front room, saw it was empty and went into the bedroom they shared. Also empty. Where the hell was his Davy? Alan shook his head in an attempt to clear it, but that only made him dizzier.

He sat down on the edge of the bed, trying to come to terms with the fact that David was not there. In his befuddled state he couldn't work out what that meant and what might have happened. Should he be worried? Call somebody? Probably.

But he was so tired. With so little sleep the previous night, a long day and a skinful of booze, he'd about had it. He so needed a rest. He could lay back here, have a little doze and then find out about what happened to the boy. He lay back on the pillow, smiling at the thought of his Davy, and fell fast asleep.

When Alan awoke on Saturday morning, three things quickly became clear: one, that he'd slept all night in his clothes; two, that he had a mouth like the bottom of a parrot's cage, and three, that he had the most God-awful headache. Just to complete the picture, the weather had broken, and rain was lashing against the window.

He turned his head gingerly to look at David's side of the bed but it was cold and clearly had not been slept in. He frowned. What the hell was going on? He started to get out of bed and moved too quickly, almost leaving half his brain behind, but he had to move because he needed the bathroom. Once he'd emptied his bladder, he swallowed a couple of paracetamol tablets and returned to bed to decide on a course of action.

He lay down again and stared miserably at the wall. In the absence of evidence to the contrary, he had to conclude that David had gone – exactly as he'd expected him to and exactly like everybody else in his life.

Christ! What now? What have you done? You idiot!

He closed his eyes, unwilling to look the world in the face, and promptly fell asleep again. Waking up two hours later, he felt much better physically even though his mood was still black. He saw his phone on the floor beside his bedside table and picked it up to check the time, only to realise that the battery was completely flat. He grimaced. His to-do list for the next few minutes was growing – shower, coffee, breakfast, charge phone, find out what had happened to his stray boyfriend, make a grovelling apology. He felt completely unequal to any of the tasks.

He plugged his phone into the charger but couldn't face switching it on, not before his shower. He walked slowly and deliberately to the bathroom so as not to upset his balance or equilibrium. As he stood in the shower, his brain gradually started to function again. He relaxed as the hot water cascaded over him and the tension in his body dissipated.

Alan wasn't surprised that David had gone. He had become convinced on Thursday night that their argument would be fatal to their relationship, hence his abrupt change of mood. Once he realised that departure was inevitable, his defensive screens came up and his emotions shut down. Rather than continue the argument, or try to persuade David to another point of view, he'd switched off and retreated to the spare room.

He didn't know what had made him be so nasty to the man he loved, but he couldn't stand to see David gradually deteriorating and refusing to explain what the problem was. His own outburst had been as a result of his frustration and disapproval at the way David was spending his time. As a tactic, that had hardly proved inspired.

The cooling of the water brought him back to reality. He towelled himself dry and went into the kitchen to make some coffee. Back in the bedroom, he stared at his phone once again, still frightened to press the button to switch it on, terrified that his fears would be justified. If he didn't listen to his messages, they wouldn't be real.

After a few more moments, he realised that this was nonsense; he had to do it and face the consequences. With a trembling finger, he found the on/off switch and pressed it. After a few seconds, the small screen lit up and showed that he had voicemail messages and several texts waiting for him.

He sat down on the bed and dialled the message service. The first message dated from yesterday lunchtime. "Hi, it's David," said the familiar voice, the sound of it acting like a balm to Alan's soul. "Just to say that I'm on my way home to Sedgethwaite, because..." There was a faint click and the message ended.

Alan hit the button to end the call. He didn't want to hear any more. So he'd been right. David had gone, pushed away by Alan's tongue-lashing on Thursday night, presumably in an attempt to put his life in Yorkshire back together, poor lad.

He sank back on to the bed, rolled onto David's side and buried his head in the pillow to try and catch even a whiff of his scent. He felt numb, unable to come to terms with what seemed to be happening. He clutched David's pillow and stared unseeingly out of the window, oblivious to the stormy day outside. He shivered despite the central heating and pulled the duvet over himself.

He faced the horror of being parted from his best friend again after only a few months of their re-acquaintance. As soon as he'd clapped eyes on David sitting in the cab of that bus in Leeds the previous February, he'd known what had been missing from his life for the previous six years. But he'd never expected to have the opportunity to keep his friend in his life. David's arrival to stay for good had been a huge bonus. For a few weeks Alan had felt complete – but now it had all gone wrong. His own irascibility and impatience had forced David to run away.

He squeezed his eyes shut against the tears that were trying to flow but they flowed anyway, soaking into the pillow. His gaze shifted to the blank wall next to the window and he stared at it, picking out faint brush marks and tracing the joins in the lining paper. At that moment, his future seemed to be as blank as the wall. There didn't seem to be any way back.

He was awoken from his reverie by a knock at the door. He groaned and was inclined to ignore it, but the polite knock increased in volume and he heard the letter box open. "Alan Foreshaw! I know you're in there!" It was Simon. "Shift yourself, open this bloody door and tell me what the fuck is going on."

Alan levered himself off the bed and grabbed a tissue to

wipe his face and blow his nose. Despite everything, he couldn't resist a smile at Simon's sense of the dramatic as he headed for the stairs. "Okay, Simon, On my way."

Chapter 15

David

Saturday morning found David in bed at the Edward Street house. Given how matters had been left with Alan, he wasn't entirely sure whether he should be there or not, but he'd needed somewhere to sleep and had the key with him, so here he was.

As on his last visit, he'd spent the night in Alan's old room. It had seemed the natural thing to do and he'd slept surprisingly well in the circumstances. Mental exhaustion, probably, after the past week.

He lay in bed and closed his eyes, trying to piece together the events of the previous day to make sense of them. It had been shortly after noon when he'd left Tom's office and got the phone call from his mum. He'd managed to get a train north to Leeds within the hour, and taken a cab straight to the hospital. He'd arrived around four and found his mother and sister in the waiting room, looking anxious and tearful.

The diagnosis had not been good: a severe ischaemic stroke caused by the narrowing of the carotid artery, which, his mother explained, was in his dad's neck and carried blood to his brain. The doctors had decided he needed surgery to unblock the artery and his father was in the operating theatre.

"They said it would take up to two hours," Jen told him. "After that he'll be monitored in a recovery ward for another three."

"Will he make a complete recovery?" David asked anxiously.

His mother shrugged. "It's too soon to tell, love. He'd lost the use of his arm and couldn't talk properly after it happened, but the doctor said that might be temporary. At least there's a chance there'll be no lasting effects."

"That's good." David hardly dared asked his next question; he was convinced that he already knew the answer. If it had been caused by stress it was something else he was going to have to feel guilty about, but he had to know for certain. "What brought it on? Do they know?"

Marion Edgeley looked at him sharply. "It wasn't through worry about you, David Edgeley, so you can forget that for a start."

David gave a small rueful grin. "How do you know?"

"Because he was quite calm about it all. He was only being obstinate, really. In any case, he said he'd just had one of the best rounds of golf he'd played for years."

"Oh, okay." He paused and frowned. "If you're sure. I'd hate to think..."

"Stop it, David," said his sister sharply. "You've got enough on your plate without taking the blame for this on yourself."

"Tell me about it," he replied with a groan. Jen reached

out and drew him into a hug. It was all he could do not to burst into tears but he managed to keep himself together. The last thing his mother and sister needed right now was for him to break down. He needed to be strong for once in his life, for them.

They settled down to wait. Eventually David offered to fetch them a hot drink from the cafeteria, glad of the opportunity to stretch his legs and to check his phone. There was one message from a number he did not recognise.

As he queued to be served, he listened and heard Alan's voice. It sounded clipped and distant. "I'm ringing from the office because I've left my mobile at home, I think. Wanted to remind you that it's Maudie's leaving do tonight, so I'll be out late. Can't stop. Talk later. Bye."

David leant against the cafeteria counter and sighed deeply. What the hell was he supposed to make of that? There was no mention of their argument or his meeting with Tom, simply a bald statement uttered in a matter-of-fact tone – no more than a diary update. Did Alan assume that the row was already in the past? Or was the call only a matter of politeness?

He was brought out of his speculations by someone nudging him from behind. "Hutch up, lovey, they're moving," a voice said.

"Yeah, sorry. A bit distracted." There was no more time for reflection since he was now at the head of the queue. He bought the hot drinks and traipsed back along the endless corridors to where his mum and sister were waiting. He gave himself another stern lecture on the way. He was here for his family. He had to stop fretting about Alan, at least until his father's surgery was complete and his condition better understood.

When he got back to the waiting room, his mother and sister were talking to a young guy in a white coat – a doctor, David assumed, even if he hardly seemed old enough for the job. They shook hands before the doctor excused himself to return to his duties.

"Dr Wahid has been telling us that the operation is done and was a complete success, love," his mother told him.

David breathed a sigh of relief and hugged her. "That's great news, Mum. I'm so pleased."

She smiled at him. "He's in recovery now and should be on the ward by eight tonight. Apparently we can see him then for a few minutes."

The three hours they'd waited to see his father passed relatively quickly. Eventually, a nurse came to fetch them. Only two people at a time were allowed into the room, so David was left on his own for a few minutes while his mother and sister went in. He took the opportunity to send Alan a text, updating him on the situation. It wouldn't be read immediately but at least would offer some reassurance when Alan was eventually reunited with his phone.

Eventually, Jen appeared, looking angry and upset.

"Hey, Sis, you look glum. What's the matter? Is he not doing well?"

"He's fine, David. Remarkably so, in fact."

"Brilliant! Can I go in then?" he asked, rising from his seat.

His sister's eyes filled with tears. "I'm sorry, David,

love. He doesn't want to see you."

Lying in bed now, more than twelve hours later, he could still feel the shiver down his spine he'd experienced at Jen's words. "Mum and I tried to persuade him, David. But he's adamant, love. I'm so sorry."

He'd suddenly felt an overwhelming need to get out into the open air. He managed to speak despite the huge lump in his throat. "In that case there's no point in me staying. Tell Mum I'm sorry. I'll see her tomorrow."

He set off, ignoring Jen's call for him to stop, brushing her away as she tried to restrain him. "Leave me be, Jen. I'll be fine. I'm going to Edward Street to try and talk to Al. I can't stay and argue this out. I'm just so tired. Night, love."

"If you're sure."

"I am, Jen. Now get back to Mum and Dad. I'll phone you tomorrow."

And so he'd come here. If he couldn't be with Alan, at least he was in a place closely associated with him, in a bed where they'd made love. Fortunately he'd had the presence of mind to call at the chippy on the main road, so at least he'd eaten. He'd dialled Alan's number, but it had gone straight to voicemail again.

He'd left another long message, apologising again for Thursday night and saying how much he needed his Al right now. He could only hope that he hadn't ruined everything by his pride and obstinacy. He'd felt better for having expressed some of his feelings in the voicemail and fallen asleep quite quickly.

That was still his mood on Saturday morning, after his long sleep. He checked his phone for any message or missed calls but there were none. He got up and went into the bathroom to relieve himself. While he was in there, he heard a ping on his phone. Unable to supress a feeling of elation, he raced out to grab it but crumpled as quickly as a burst balloon when he realised that it was only a chatty text from Gavin inviting them both for supper the following weekend.

David looked at the time – it was gone ten. Surely Alan was home by now and reunited with his phone? He shrugged. Maybe he'd met somebody and was still out. No – surely he wouldn't do that, would he? There could be something wrong. Maybe he was ill or there'd been an accident. David began to picture Alan lying in a hospital bed somewhere or, even worse...

Shit, that was it – an accident was the likeliest explanation. He began to pace up and down the bedroom, wracking his brains for a way to find out what was happening. Then it struck him; he grabbed his phone and found Simon's number in his contacts.

David felt much better as he ended the call with Simon. He'd been reassured that Alan was at home in the flat and not lying in a hospital bed somewhere; he'd also benefitted from a good deal of quiet reassurance from the man who was now his neighbour and, increasingly, a close friend.

Ever since David had met him on the night of the rail strike in June, Simon had been kindness itself; somehow David had felt an almost instant bond with him and they had grown closer. Being of a similar build had helped, even if in other ways – background, upbringing and education – they were so different. But none of that mattered; David and Simon knew instinctively that they had each other's backs and would be friends for life.

David felt slightly better, but all the problems and uncertainties that he faced were still there. He didn't know where he stood with Alan after Thursday night, he'd been rejected again by his father and, underlying everything, there was the throbbing pain of missing his sons.

He'd promised to have brunch with Jen and Mark, so shifted himself to get ready. He was about to set off for his sister's house, a ten-minute walk away, when he noticed that it was bucketing down with rain. He called a cab.

Although he'd seen Jen the previous evening, this was the first time he'd seen Mark for a few weeks. It was clear from the look on his brother-in-law's face that he was shocked at David's appearance. The look was masked quickly after a glare from his wife, and Mark assumed a neutral expression.

They chatted amiably enough while Jen dished up their food. The kids were out with their friends on various weekend activities, which included ten-pin bowling, swimming and music lessons. David smiled; in the past, he'd often felt sympathy for Jen and Mark having to ferry their kids around all the time and realising that he would have to do the same for Tommy and Kevin in a few years' time. Realising that this was another aspect of their lives from which he would probably be excluded prompted yet another sharp stab of regret.

Food eaten, Jen turned to David with her characteristic bluntness. "Well, brother dear, judging by the look of you

I can't say that London life seems to be suiting you."

David closed his eyes. He'd been dreading this inquisition ever since she'd invited him round. His immediate instinct was to brush her off with a bland "I'm fine", but he knew she wouldn't let him get away with that; she was her mother's daughter, after all.

"It's been a pretty shitty few weeks, to be honest. I can't make any headway with Mona, I'm missing the kids so much, and Alan has been frantically busy at work. I've been on my own a good deal and it's all getting me down a bit, to be honest."

"Any news on the job front?" Mark asked.

David shook his head. "Plenty of opportunities but I haven't had the energy to follow them up. Besides, my head's so full at the moment that I doubt I'd be able to concentrate properly."

"I can see that, love," Jen said. "There are days when I'm in the car and my mind's whirring away that I don't even remember driving home."

"We all do that sometimes," Mark added.

"Aye, but it's a different prospect hurtling down the M1 at night at seventy miles an hour with fifty passengers behind you."

"I see that," Jen said. "But that's not all, is it, love?"

"No, I suppose not. I miss the boys so much. Not being allowed to see them is hell."

"Mona's still adamant, is she?"

David nodded. "Totally. Though how she's managing on her own, I don't know."

"Lots of help from Mummy, I suspect," Jen replied with the same acid tone in her voice that always crept in when she referred to Mona's mother. She had never taken to Cheryl Spensley and the antipathy was mutual. "Mind you, from what I heard the other day, not everything is sweetness and light in the Spensley family. I think Cheryl and Brian are a bit fed up with being taken for granted."

David scoffed, "That wouldn't surprise me." He straightened up at the prospect of more news. "Have you seen them? The kids, I mean? Were they all right?"

Jen smiled. "Relax, love. They're fine. Mum and I have our spies. Mum's cousin Ivy is four doors down, and don't forget my friend Rosemary lives round the corner. We're keeping a close eye on what's happening."

David sat back, relieved. "She's been writing to me. Mona, I mean. Seriously nasty things about me, our marriage, Al – you name it. The letters have been getting under my skin. I saw a lawyer yesterday morning and he's going to try to stop them."

"That's horrible, David!" exclaimed his sister. "What did Alan say?"

"He doesn't know."

"What?"

David looked Jen in the eye. "He doesn't know because I didn't tell him. He's been so busy at work and so tired, and I've been such a bloody nuisance sitting about all day and sponging off him that I didn't want to make it worse."

"David Edgeley, you're an even bigger fool than I thought," Jen's voice grew louder with indignation.

"Jen, careful," her husband warned. "Shouting doesn't get you anywhere."

She shook her head and made as if to start again, but then paused and sighed. "No, you're right. I'm sorry, David."

"It's okay. Anyway, you're right. I should have told Al. But I'm sure he didn't realise what he was letting himself in for when he signed me up."

"I'm pretty sure he did." Jen smiled gently. "But that's not the real reason you're so upset, is it?"

David was tempted to steer the conversation away, but he knew his sister too well to try it. He sighed. "It's what Mona says in those letters. I get cross and hate her for some of the foul things she writes, but deep down I know she's right. The marriage breakdown *is* my fault, and I don't deserve any happiness out of it. I was so selfish, only thinking of myself. It's wrong being with Alan, loving him, having a nice life with his rich friends. I should be here, taking responsibility for my wife and kids. It is *wrong*, Jen – and I shouldn't have done it."

Jen turned to Mark. "Love, will you just pop outside and put the cross up in the garden? I think we'll set the crucifixion for about three this afternoon. Is that okay?"

Mark gaped for a moment then grinned at his wife.

David was genuinely shocked. "Jen! What on earth do you mean?"

She shrugged. "Merely that if you're determined to turn yourself into a martyr, David Edgeley, I'm happy to oblige."

"But..."

"But nothing. I know you made a mistake in marrying her, but that doesn't mean you had to face a life sentence of being miserable for her sake. You're lucky, David – you've got a second chance at your happiness with somebody you love. Not everybody gets that. So for Christ's sake don't throw that away simply to assuage your guilty conscience."

"I'm not throwing it away! I'm trying to keep it!"

She shook her head. "Relationships need nurturing with honesty and trust. Keeping secrets is the last thing you should be doing. Besides, I'd lay a pound to a penny that Alan knows there's something wrong and is worried to death because you won't tell him what it is."

David sighed as he realised the truth of what his sister was saying. "You're right, of course."

"When am I not?" she replied smugly, prompting a snort from her husband. "And you'll tell him?"

David nodded. "I will. Thanks, Jen. I do love him and I know I'm lucky. I'm just so frightened of buggering it all up."

"Good," said Jen with a firm nod. "And you won't. Bugger it up, I mean. Not if you keep being open and honest. Now, I'd better get myself up to the hospital and give Mum a break. Are you coming?"

David nodded. "I'll come for Mum's sake. I'll sit with her while you're with Dad. I don't suppose he'll have changed his mind about seeing me."

Chapter 16

Alan

When Alan opened his front door, Simon was standing looking rather red in the face and obviously agitated. "Alan Foreshaw, would you mind telling me what the fuck is going on?"

Taken aback by his friend's anger, Alan stammered slightly. "Wha…? Who…? Wait … where's the fire?"

Simon pushed past him and started to climb the stairs towards the kitchen. "There's no fire,' he said over his shoulder. 'Only your fucking boyfriend is going frantic because you can't – or won't – speak to him, you idiot. I hope you've got some bloody coffee on the go."

"Oh." Alan had known for a long time that Simon was formidable when roused; he had a sharp tongue and the ability to seem much larger than his five-foot-six frame. But this was the first time he'd ever been on the receiving end of his friend's genuine anger.

"You might well say 'oh', Alan Foreshaw. There David is, worried to death because his father's had a bloody stroke, and you won't talk to him so now he's also frantic about you."

"Whoa. Wait. Did you say stroke?"

"Yes. Don't you listen to your messages?'

Alan spoke slowly as he absorbed Simon's news. "We had a bit of a row on Thursday night and I thought he'd gone home to Yorkshire for good. By the time I'd heard the first voicemail, which cut off after he said he was on the train north, I decided not to listen to the others. I couldn't face them. I was so frightened that I'd fucked up, Si."

Simon's face softened a little but he still harrumphed at this explanation. "As if he'd leave you, you silly bugger."

"Why not? Everybody else has."

Simon drew Alan into a hug. "You're so going to have to get over this fear, sweetheart. The only way David will ever leave you is if you push him away. You forget, I've watched you two grow into this relationship for the last eight months – I've seen the way he looks at you, as if you're the emperor of his world. He can't take his eyes off you if you're in the room. He literally hangs on your every word."

"Then why hasn't he confided in me for the last three weeks? I know there's been something wrong and I've asked him and asked him, but he brushes me off. I can't help him, can't protect him, if he won't talk to me, Simon."

"I know it's difficult, and I don't know what the matter is because he hasn't told me either. You'll have to persuade him to talk. But I do know that you've been working all the hours God sends for the last few weeks and every time I've seen you, you've looked like death warmed up. At a guess, he didn't want to bother you."

There was a pause while Alan found a clean mug and

poured Simon some coffee. They sat down at the kitchen table. "I suppose you might be right, but…"

"You've got to try and see things from David's point of view, love." All trace of anger had now gone from Simon's voice. "He's completely outside his comfort zone and the last few weeks have probably robbed him of every last bit of self-confidence he ever had – which I suspect wasn't much in the first place. He's in a strange, terrifying city, socialising with new people who have a completely different way of life. Of course he's scared and out of his depth. Who wouldn't be?"

"Yeah, I know. But he's got me. He knows I've got his back."

"Yes, but I suspect he doesn't trust that yet. My guess is that he's frightened that he won't be good enough for you and you'll get bored with him. I could see that with the Victor Hugo business at Joe's the other week. And I could have kicked myself after our dinner party earlier in the summer. He looked so lost that night and it was partly my fault."

"Right. I can see that, I suppose…"

"Not to mention his position here. After six years of being the breadwinner in his own household, he's suddenly lost that too. This isn't his home yet, it's yours, and he must be feeling like an interloper. You know what it's like when you're staying with somebody – you feel you have to be on your best behaviour and it's difficult to relax. Of course he doesn't want to upset you or make too many demands, especially when he's seeing how bloody hard you work."

Alan felt as if Simon's words were drawing back a curtain, letting light flood into his mind. Everything he said made sense and explained so much of the awkwardness that had crept into his relationship with David. But he was sure there was something else, and he had to get to the bottom of it. "And what's this about his dad?" he asked.

"From what I can gather, he had a stroke yesterday morning. David got the call around twelve and that's why he hared off to Yorkshire. Apparently it's quite serious, and they operated straight away to clear an artery."

"Christ. Poor lad. I'd better ring him."

"You can do that on the way to the station, Alan. He needs you, love. I don't think all's well with his dad, but he wouldn't say much about it. The sooner you get there, the better. He's staying at your house."

Alan sprang into action, glad to have something to do to distract himself from reflecting on what a giant fuck-up he'd made. Packing, grabbing a snack, thanking Simon profusely and getting himself to King's Cross in record time, he flung himself on the next Leeds train with moments to spare and breathed a huge sigh of relief.

He might be facing a lot when he got there but at least David was still in his life. They could sort out the rest together. They always did.

The train made good time as far as Doncaster, but came to a grinding halt between there and Wakefield. The guard explained that the way ahead was blocked by a faulty train and he couldn't say how long they'd have to wait. Alan groaned with frustration; he was so worried about David and couldn't wait to see him to make sure he was all right.

He stared out of the window to try to work out where they were but could only see his own reflection and the raindrops sliding down the glass.

Sunset was still a couple of hours away but it barely seemed to be daylight, and the rain was bouncing down as they reached their last stop. Alan stared at his phone – at least there was a signal here. He'd already tried to ring David's mobile a couple of times, but it had gone to voicemail; the last time he'd left a message, but couldn't say much of what was on his mind in front of fellow passengers on a crowded train. He tapped out a text message instead to say that he was on his way north but there was a delay. There was no immediate reply. He sent Simon a quick text to say that they'd been delayed, and another to Tris to say he'd be in Yorkshire for a few days.

He'd barely sent the latter when his phone rang. It was Tris, wanting an immediate update. Alan explained about David's father and said there were other issues that they needed to sort out.

"Yes," Tris said. "Ian mentioned that you'd been like a bear with a sore head at the office this week. What's up?"

"It's a long story, Tris – and I'm not sure I know all of it yet. Something's been bothering David for a while now and he wouldn't tell me what it was. To be honest, it started to get me down on top of everything at work. We had a bit of a row on Thursday night, then David's dad had this stroke yesterday. I don't know where we stand."

"Bloody hell, Alan. You two seem to be like magnets attracting all the drama, don't you?"

Alan laughed. "I suppose you could put it that way."

"Anyway, you need to sort it out, old love. I'm sure

everything'll be all right."

"So am I, deep down. It all still feels right. Got to work at it a bit, though."

"That's the spirit."

They chatted for a while longer. Tris thanked Alan profusely for the ballet tickets he'd passed on after David's refusal to go and ended the call. Alan felt a good deal steadier after the chat with his best friend and went back to staring out of the window. At long last the train began to move. They'd be ninety minutes late into Leeds, the guard told them.

Chapter 17

David

David spent a couple of hours in the waiting room at the hospital, chatting with his mum and his sister as they alternated at his father's side. His dad hadn't changed his mind about not wanting to see David, but that came as a disappointment rather than a surprise.

He couldn't get away immediately because they'd been promised an update from the doctor after further scans. David's relief at the news they received was profound; the operation to unblock the artery had been entirely successful, and the scan suggested that the brain had sustained little or no damage from the temporary loss of blood supply. His dad was expected to make a full recovery and would leave hospital on Monday or Tuesday.

David took his cue to make a move at the end of the conference. He tried, but failed, to wave off Jen's offer of a lift. "I'm glad of the break, to be honest," she said when they reached the car. "The smell of the disinfectant gets to me after a while, and sitting in that ward looking at the other old men is so bloody depressing."

David smiled. "At least you had somebody to look at. All I had in the waiting room was a load of old posters about VD."

"Oh, charming. I thought it was called STI these days."

"Yeah, that's how old the posters were."

His sister laughed. "Anyway, the news about Dad is good, isn't it?"

"Yes, it is. I'm so relieved. I'd hate for anything to have happened while we're like this, you know?"

"I understand, love. I could see on Friday that you were all set to blame yourself for his stroke."

David nodded. "I was. I thought the stress might have done it. When they explained about the artery, I felt like a tonne weight had been lifted off me."

They reached the house in Edward Street moments later. David smiled when he saw the lights on. "Thanks for the lift, Sis. You going back to the hospital?"

"No, I've got tea to get for the kids and Mum said she'd be all right. I don't think she'll stay much longer."

"Great. I'll talk to you tomorrow, Jen. Thanks so much for the ride." He kissed her on the cheek, got out of the car and looked up at the house. It seemed to loom above him against the dark, cloud-heavy sky. He dashed across the road and up the steps, trying to dodge the rain that was still pouring down.

Once inside, he shut the front door and leant against it, closing his eyes and breathing a sigh of relief. He was grateful to be alone again, to try to process everything and hopefully recover some equilibrium.

Despite his conversation with Jen, the situation with his father still weighed heavily – not only the illness, but also the continued refusal to see him. Dad was putting up stolid resistance to pressure from his wife and daughter, simply refusing to budge. This, on top of everything else that was going on in his life, was almost intolerable. David's head was spinning with all his thoughts and fears and the thoughts that continued to reverberate around his head. It was as if his brain was existing inside an echo chamber; it was a horrible feeling and he hated it.

He glanced down at the floor, and there it was: a familiar, lavender-coloured envelope, addressed simply to David Edgeley in his wife's handwriting. There was no stamp, so it had been delivered by hand. He picked it up and went into the front room, collapsing onto the sofa. He flung the letter on the coffee table and stared at it.

As with all the others, he knew that it would be stupid to open it and read the contents but – as on the other occasions – he clung to the hope that this one would be different. There was always the chance, however remote, that this would be the one in which her attitude would change, in which she'd grant him access to the boys and agree to a settlement.

Judging by the fact that she'd delivered it by hand, she had to know that he was in Sedgethwaite so she probably knew about his dad. Surely this might be the time for a change of mind? He hesitated for a moment then seized it, tore it open and began to read.

A few moments later, he flung the letter back on to the coffee table and put his hands over his face. Not only had she not changed her mind, this letter was somehow worse: she was now accusing him of being responsible for his father's illness. In the process, she had highlighted all the fears he had been trying to suppress since his mother's panic-stricken phone call on Friday.

Despite all the reassurances from his family, David's nagging feeling of responsibility had not gone away; to see it reinforced in writing, even if the suggestions were inspired by malice, made it seem real. His misery was doubled by being alone. He was convinced that he'd blown it with Alan and he had no friends of his own, only Alan's, who were two hundred miles away. He had no job, probably no home, nobody to turn to and no wife or kids. God, what a fool he'd been!

He started to sweat and his breathing got shallower as his heartbeat increased. Then the pains in his chest started, quickly growing sharper, like knives. He started to pant for breath and felt dizzy. He toppled sideways onto the sofa and lay there, wondering if this was a heart attack and he was going to die.

Part of his brain realised that he was having a panic attack. He closed his eyes and forced himself to breathe more slowly and deeply, counting his breaths. Gradually the pain in his chest subsided and he started to feel better. He stopped sweating and felt cold, despite the central heating.

Suddenly he was overwhelmed with exhaustion. He didn't think he'd ever felt so tired in his life. He lifted his legs onto the sofa, reached over, grabbed an old travelling rug that lay folded on the back of the sofa and threw it over his legs. That was better. He closed his eyes and went out like a light.

Chapter 18

Alan

As he left the station to join the taxi queue, the lights from surrounding buildings were reflected off the streaming wet streets. The air was full of the sound of tyres on wet tarmac accompanied by the beat of windscreen wipers. Alan remembered days like this from his youth, and he'd always hated them. It was not stormy; there was little wind, simply a steady downpour as if somebody up in the sky had turned on a huge tap. It put Alan in mind of Noah and his ark. This must have been what it was like when the deluge began.

It was too wet to walk across Leeds City Centre to get to the Sedgethwaite bus, so he decided to get a cab all the way even though it seemed a bit extravagant. Fortunately, the driver was not a chatty soul, and Alan was left to his own thoughts as they fought their way through the traffic jams towards his aunt's old house. He peered through the rain to try and get his bearings until, eventually, he started to recognise familiar landscapes.

The Edward Street house seemed distinctly forlorn on

this wet Saturday afternoon. It was dark apart from a faint light visible through the stained-glass panels in the front door. The curtains were drawn in the front room. In the little daylight that was left, it was clear that the exterior paintwork was looking dowdy and decidedly flaky in places. Rain overflowed from a blocked gutter and ran down the wall. He made a mental note to get that fixed, otherwise they'd be having damp problems.

Alan paid off the taxi, dashed to the front gate and climbed the three steps to the porch. He found his key and let himself in. The heating was on, which made the place feel less desolate, and light spilled from a lamp on a small side table inside the front room.

If he shut his eyes, he could have been coming home from school on a winter's afternoon. He listened for his aunt's voice calling out, telling him to "get those wet things off" and get himself into the kitchen. In those days, it would have been filled with the scent of baking and a fresh scone or butterfly cake would be waiting for him. He smiled at the memory – especially since David would probably have been with him, come to share homework and hoping for a quick game on the Nintendo before he had to leave for home.

The house looked spick and span, which came as a surprise until Alan remembered that David had spent a good deal of time sprucing up the house when he'd stayed a few weeks earlier. He'd evidently done a good job.

He assumed that David was still at the hospital with his phone turned off, which would explain the lack of response to Alan's texts and voicemails. He was about to go through to the kitchen to make himself some tea but the lamp being on in the front room seemed odd. He pushed open the door a little wider and saw a body lying fast asleep on the sofa, wrapped in his aunt's old travelling rug.

He looked down and saw a sheet of paper lying on the coffee table next to a lavender-coloured envelope. He'd seen a similar one on the doormat at the flat the other Saturday morning.

It was a letter. Alan didn't mean to pry but he couldn't help catching a few words, those written in capitals and underlined. He saw "queer", "pervert", "cocksucker" and "not their father", and realised instantly who it was from. Something told him that was not the first letter Mona had written. Suddenly, he understood; it was like the final pieces of a jigsaw fitting into place. At last, David's brooding, his loss of self-confidence and his growing unhappiness all made sense.

Alan experienced a whirlpool of conflicting emotions: anger about the contents of Mona's letter, sympathy for how David must be feeling, frustration that he had not shared what had been going on. However, these feelings were dwarfed by Alan's remorse at having been oblivious to David's deteriorating mental state. He must have been going through hell and Alan simply hadn't noticed.

Involuntarily he made a noise, an odd combination of a sob and a gasp of horror. It was sufficient to alert David to his presence. He woke up, blinked and pushed himself up into a sitting position. "Al? Is it really you? Oh, my God. What are you doing here?"

"Didn't you get my messages?"

"What messages?" David reached into his pocket for his phone then realised it was off. "Sorry," he said. "I must have forgotten to switch it on again when I left the hospital."

Now he was upright, Alan could see David's face clearly in the lamplight, the tracks of tears and the redness of his eyes. There were deep, dark bags under them too, whilst his skin was pale, almost ghostly. "You've been crying, Davy. Whatever's the matter? Is it your dad?"

David gave a small smile. "No, he's doing fine. No, it's another of Mona's lovely little notes. Rather got to me, I'm afraid."

"Another? Have there been more, like ... like this?"

David nodded. "Several. I've got photocopies – I left the originals with Tom on Friday morning."

Alan couldn't help his wave of irritation. "You mean you could tell your lawyer about them but not me?"

"I know. I'm sorry."

Alan picked up the paper and had a closer look. It was foul, two pages of scrawled invective, a vicious combination of all the homophobic words Mona could muster and invective about David's fitness to be a father or even his right to exist. This was followed by accusations that his father's illness was obviously David's fault.

"The bitch." Alan flung down the paper back. "How long, Davy? And how many?"

"A couple in that first week but after that she warmed up. She's been averaging one every two days for a couple of weeks."

"Christ Almighty. Why didn't you tell me?"

David shrugged. "You were busy. Any road, there wasn't much you could do and I didn't want to worry you. Anyway, I probably deserve it all."

v "And you don't think I'm worried now, seeing you like this?" Alan struggled to keep the rising note of irritation out of his voice. "And *nobody* deserves abuse like this, you silly ass."

"Please, Al." David's face crumpled again as more tears threatened. "Don't shout at me – not you as well."

Alan felt something break inside him and his own tears welled up. He didn't reply but sat next to David on the sofa and took him into his arms. He tucked his lover's head under his chin and held on for dear life. "I'm so sorry, Davy. Oh, my love."

They stayed quiet for a while, Alan rocking David gently. Every sob, shake or shudder from David's body pierced his heart. He kissed David's temple repeatedly whilst continuing to hold him tightly and murmur words of apology and reassurance.

Eventually David calmed, but they stayed where they were for a few minutes longer. "Thank you, Al," he whispered eventually. "Been feeling so shitty."

"We'll talk in a while, Davy. You're shivering, baby. Let's get you warmed up with a bath. I'll sort out some food out and then we can talk. How does that sound?"

David nodded but seemed unwilling to move. "Great. I feel better now you're here. And why are you here, by the way? What happened?"

"Er, Simon happened. I had an almighty hangover after a boozy session at work last night, and woke up with him banging on the door."

"That would have been after I phoned him, I suppose."

Alan grinned. "He did mention getting a call from you – in between giving me a good telling off, the bugger.

Anyway, we can talk about that later. Bath first."

After helping David to climb the stairs, Alan left him in the bedroom while he went into the bathroom and turned on the taps. Glancing round, he realised that refurbishing this room would be a top priority; it needed a shower that was big enough for the two of them.

After a few minutes, the water was ready. "Come on, let's get you into the bath." Alan went into the bedroom to find his boyfriend with his shirt off but clearly struggling with the rest because he was shivering uncontrollably. As Alan helped him, he noticed how thin David was; his jeans hung loosely from his hips and his ribs were much more prominent. Alan asked himself how on earth he could have missed all the signs. He could not come up with a satisfactory answer.

David followed into the bathroom. Alan helped him off with his jeans and briefs and David sank back into the water with a sigh.

Chapter 19

David

As he lay in the bath, David realised what a fool he had been to allow himself to get into such a state. In his own defence, he'd known how busy Alan was at the office and hadn't wanted to bother him but he should have been able to cope with nasty letters from his soon-to-be ex-wife.

But each letter had acted like water on a chalk cliff, soaking through the porous surface, steadily undercutting the structure until the whole thing collapsed in a heap. Each letter had further damaged his already fragile morale, spreading poison through his mind, whilst in the background was his constant worry about Tommy and Kevin and what this separation was doing to them. The constant pain he felt at missing them was like a bad toothache, adding to the burden he felt. The combination had almost completely undermined him. At the same time, events had conspired against him: the theatre evening, the burnt potatoes when Gavin and Ben had visited, and lastly the row over the ballet tickets.

His big concern was that the argument with Alan would

leave its mark. Largely through force of circumstance they'd barely spoken since Thursday, but he couldn't forget Alan's icy stare and the tone of his voice as he'd left the room that night. He feared that there was more than that. It didn't help that a combination of Alan's tiredness and David's disinclination meant that they hadn't made love for over three weeks.

David had been determined not to make things worse during Alan's busy period at work. He'd wanted to keep the mood light during the little time they'd had together, but his energy levels had steadily diminished and his ability to do even the most mundane of domestic tasks had drained away. It had been a huge effort just to get to Tom's office on Friday morning. Maybe Alan's jibe had been right on Thursday night: David was only fit for sitting about all day in his tracksuit watching rubbish telly.

David felt that he was trapped in no man's land with no way out. Alan's feelings would fade – probably already had, given the change in his behaviour – and he would stop loving him. Mona and his dad already had, so why not Alan as well? It was this realisation that had precipitated the crisis this afternoon.

Now, as he lay soaking in the bath, he could feel the tension draining away. He didn't know why: his situation had not altered much during the last couple of hours. But, even as the thought crossed his mind, he knew that was untrue. Admitting the existence of the letters and his true state of mind changed everything, and Alan's reaction, his gentleness and kindness, had reminded David of why he loved him so much.

He washed himself then started to get out of the bath as

Alan came back in to help him. It was time to talk, to face up to it all.

"That was grand, Al. Thanks."

They were sitting at the kitchen table over the remains of a Chinese meal. The food had been fantastic, and the fact that Alan got all his favourite dishes had made it even more special. Mind you, Alan had seemed to like them as well judging by the huge amount of food they'd consumed.

"So, Davy. Talk to me. What's been going on?"

David took a deep breath, wondering where to start. He avoided Alan's eyes and did not reply for several moments. After a while, he looked directly at his lover. "It started with my letter to her the other week. The one I wrote on the Saturday before I left Sedgethwaite."

"I remember."

"I made the mistake of putting our address on it. It seemed polite at the time, and I thought she needed to know where I was, in case ... you know, if anything happened over the boys."

"Seems sensible. Go on."

"That's when the letters started. She replied to mine and started off quite reasonable, but halfway through it was as if somebody'd thrown a switch. It got nastier and nastier until she obviously ran out of steam." He paused and gave a weak smile. "I was okay with most of that – it wasn't any worse than what she said on the phone. But a few days later the next one arrived."

He gave a deep sigh and Alan took his hand. "Was it bad,

Davy?"

He nodded. "All about what a useless husband I'd been, especially in bed. She said she was surprised I'd managed to father two children. And she said I'd been a rotten father, never helping her and taking no notice of the boys." He broke off as his emotions threatened to spill over again. "It's not true, Al. I loved her, I really did, and the boys. I'd have done anything for them, for her. I tried my best when they were babies but I had to work, to do overtime, to keep paying for everything."

He took a shaky breath. "The next letter had all sorts of stuff about the size of my prick and not satisfying her. It was horrible – not only because of what she said and the language she used, but the way she wrote off everything we'd had together as if none of it had been any good.

"Next she was on about you and me – how we'd conspired against her all through school and this was the culmination of your hatred of her that went back ten years and more. Some of the things she said about you were ... just awful." He paused and shook his head. "She talked about what we did ... you know, together. She bet I was your bitch and you'd use me and then discard me, 'cos you'd also realise I was no good. I can't get the words out of my brain. Now, every time we're together in bed, all I can think of is that sodding letter."

Alan covered his face with his hands then slowly lowered them. "Jesus, Davy. I'm so sorry." David could see the tears sparkling in his eyes as his lover squeezed his hand, encouraging him to carry on.

"The next letter went back to the sex thing. And on that, of course, she was right. I was a lousy lover and I dreaded having sex with her. Nobody was more surprised than I was when she announced she was pregnant." He gave a short laugh. "When I managed it for a second time, I was over the moon." His expression quickly lost any trace of amusement. "She's right about me being a rotten father and betraying my family. So when she questions whether I deserve to have a nice life with you, she's right about that too. I don't deserve a nice life. And I certainly don't deserve you."

Chapter 20

Alan

"And I certainly don't deserve you."

Alan bridled when he heard those words. "That's not true, Davy, and you know it." He stopped himself and closed his eyes, suddenly feeling out of his depth. What could he say? He knew that David was a gentle soul, lovable and unfailingly kind. For Mona to twist that and make him think of himself as inadequate or hateful was intolerable. But there was no point in arguing about the details of David's marital life or the conception of his children; Alan couldn't offer any contrary arguments because he hadn't been there. David needed reassurance and comfort, not an argument.

"Whether you deserve me or not, David Edgeley, you've got me," he said. "And whether you're 'worthy' or not, I fucking love you. And my God, if I've done anything over the past three weeks to make you doubt that, I'm so fucking sorry, Davy."

David blinked at him, unable to speak.

Alan carried on. "Whatever's happened and whatever

she thinks of you now, she's got no right to persecute you and make your life a misery. I hope Tom can make that stop straight away. I wish you'd told me, that's all."

"As I said, I didn't want to worry you, especially when you were so busy at work."

"I'm sorry you thought that. I've been a pretty shitty boyfriend to you recently. "

"No, Al, you haven't. It's my own stupid fault. I should have been stronger."

Alan moved from his seat and took David into his arms. "Oh, my sweet. This isn't about strength or weakness. You're rightly upset and seeking help to deal with it isn't weak, it's common sense. You must stop talking yourself down, Davy. I should have been taking care of you and I wasn't. If I had been, I'd have seen there was something wrong and made you talk about it."

As he uttered those words, Alan realised the underlying truth. He hadn't been there for David during the last three or four weeks and, in a sense, he still wasn't. He'd enjoyed the romance of their time together over the summer and had been content to revel in the physical side of their relationship; these, coupled with David's presence in his life, had been enough to satisfy his own emotional needs. He realised with a shock that, in the six weeks or so since David's arrival in London, he hadn't actually been fully engaged in them, in their relationship. He'd not made any changes to his routines or attitudes, much less helped David integrate fully into his life. Come to think of it, he hadn't even gone out of his way to make him feel particularly welcome. That all had to change, and quickly. And it would.

Later in bed, Alan snuggled up to David and took him in his arms. "I hope you know how much you're loved, Davy."

"What, even when I get myself into such a state?"

"Especially then. I was thinking about it earlier. Even when we were kids, you'd get a bee in your bonnet and your anxiety levels would go up and up until you almost burst. Then I'd have to calm you down."

David laughed. "I suppose you're right. I've never thought about it. Now you mention it, though..."

Recognising that they were about to go down another rabbit hole of criticism of David, Alan shifted the direction. "I always knew how to calm you down and I liked it that I could. Being able to help you meant a lot."

David squeezed his hand. "Thanks, love. Specially for tonight. I had a panic attack before you arrived, I'm afraid."

"Ah, that explains a lot. What brought that on?"

"It was that last letter when she said my dad's illness was my fault. I'd already been half-thinking that all weekend and seeing it in writing made it worse."

"She really is a cow, Davy. I don't know how you put up with her for six years."

"She wasn't like that when I was married to her, Al. I suppose you could argue that this change in her is my fault too. It seems to have made her incredibly bitter."

"Maybe – but she could be a bit of a harridan at school."

"Happen. She's getting more like her mother. She's certainly wreaking havoc now. It was her that caused the argument over the ballet tickets."

"How so?"

"She sent me a note on Wednesday last week about my life in London and how I couldn't fit in with yours. I don't know where she got that from, but by God she hit the target with that one. It hit me straight between the eyes, playing into all the fears I've had from the start."

"Really?"

"Yeah, Si's dinner party, Tris's party, the theatre the other week, burning the potatoes – everything seemed to conspire to make me feel out of place."

"Oh, Davy. You mustn't think like that."

"Why not? It's true, isn't it? Here am I, a working-class lad, a bus driver from Yorkshire. What have I got in common with barristers, solicitors and antique dealers who live in the posh parts of London?"

"For a start you're gay, like them. Number two, they're my friends – and number three, and most important of all, they all like you for who you are, Davy, as they do me. I'm not so different from you, you know. You're young, good-looking, sweet-natured and you have a terrific sense of humour. None of them care a fuck if you eat peas with your knife or can't tell your Bach from your Bieber. They're interested in you as a person and they like what they see."

"But..."

"But nothing, Davy. Are you telling me that Marion Edgeley's son can't hold his head high and talk intelligently to anybody he meets? Because if so, I'd better let her know – and I can just imagine her reaction."

"Not fair! You can't deploy my mum in an argument like that."

Alan joined in the laughter. "Why not? You know it's true – she'd have a fit if she ever heard you say that you weren't good enough."

"Yeah, you're right. She'd give me a proper telling off. She told me the other week how disappointed she was when I married Mona. Said she'd wanted me to better myself."

"Right. Trouble is that I'm not sure that a future with ... what did she once call me? Oh, that's it – 'that Foreshaw hooligan' is quite what she had in mind."

David laughed and Alan loved the unrestrained sound, revelling in the sparkle that had returned to David's eyes. "Actually, she says she always knew that we were soul mates."

"Hmm. Very sharp, your mum." Alan moved so that he was hovering over David then dipped his head for a kiss, which quickly moved from gentle to passionate. Their bodies entwined and their hips began to move. "God, I love you, David Edgeley."

David grinned up at him. "Prove it."

So he did.

Chapter 21

David

David lay in Alan's arms in a state of blissful contentment. Judging by the deep breathing in his ear, Alan was already asleep. Despite his tiredness, David needed a few minutes to get his brain into some sort of order.

Their lovemaking, which had ended in spectacular orgasms for them both a few minutes earlier, had been deeply moving. They had not felt that level of intensity since their nights together in the summer. Work pressures and all the tensions they'd been working through had undoubtedly taken the edge off, but it was back now.

After exchanging kisses for what had seemed like hours, David had felt a deep need for Alan to be inside him. He'd wanted to express the depth of his love by experiencing once more the intensity of a physical connection between them.

Alan had prepared him carefully, punctuated by kisses and gentle caresses, and eventually David had laid on his back and lifted his legs to allow Alan access. He'd pushed in carefully and gently until he was fully seated. Their eyes had locked as Alan begun to thrust into him, and it had all felt even more intimate as Alan leant forward to kiss him. David had wrapped his legs around Alan's waist to draw him in.

Their physical closeness was exactly what David had craved. He'd needed no hand to bring him to climax; instead he was brought there by the friction of their two bodies grinding together. Alan had followed soon afterwards, crying out David's name as his body shuddered uncontrollably.

Afterwards they'd cleaned themselves up and cuddled together under the blankets in the same way as they had all those years earlier on Alan's last night in Sedgethwaite.

David had never been so glad to see anybody in his life as he had been when he'd opened his eyes at teatime to see Alan looking down at him on the sofa. If David had had any lingering doubts about the strength of their relationship after the last three weeks, the concern and tenderness on Alan's face had dispelled them.

He was convinced that they would learn the lessons of the last few weeks; they would learn to express their feelings, problems and fears to each other and sort them out together. Without any scintilla of doubt his future lay with Alan in London, and he had to dispel thoughts of not being good enough to be his partner. It was ironic, he supposed, that his wife's letter had expressed all his own doubts and fears. Seeing them laid out before him in writing, he realised how groundless they were. He needed to stop being ruled by them and to take control of his life for once, instead of only reacting to events and other people's wants. In any case, he now had the incentive to prove Mona wrong.

That was liberating enough, but now he also realised that the doubts that had made him so hesitant about committing himself to a life in the capital had to stop too. His first task this week was to stop faffing about and get a job.

And with that resolution, he succumbed to his tiredness and drifted off to sleep.

The weather improved a little the next day and they were able to get out for a walk. Alan had arranged to take Monday off, but needed to be back in London to work on Tuesday. After consulting Jen and Marion, they'd agreed that David could go back too. There was no point in hanging around in Sedgethwaite when his father was so much better and wouldn't see him.

After their walk, they spent some time working out what they were going to do with the house if they were going to keep it as they'd planned as a base for David's visits with the boys. Walking through it provoked all sorts of childhood memories, and they had a high old time laughing about their various escapades. They finished by mid-afternoon and curled up on the sofa to watch an old movie on TV.

There was still some coal left in the bunker outside, so they lit the fire and then made love on the rug in front of the hearth. This time, David topped – he loved the way Alan fell apart as he moved gently inside him. They climaxed together and afterwards dozed in front of the fire. Later in bed, they fell asleep in each other's arms, all signs of tension between them long gone.

As he drifted into a dreamless sleep, David reflected on what a perfect day it had been. It was confirmation – if any were needed – of the strength of what he and Alan had together.

They'd decided to aim for a lunchtime train back to London, so they could spend a leisurely morning getting breakfast and packing up. Alan made notes about what they'd decided to do with the house while David chatted over the phone with both his mum and his sister.

At around ten-thirty, his phone rang again from a landline number he vaguely recognised. As he pushed the button to answer, he remembered: it was his father-in-law.

"David? Is that you? Brian Spensley here."

"Yes, Brian. How are you?"

"I'm fine, thanks. Sorry to hear about your dad. How is he?"

"Thanks. He's on the mend – may even go home today. What can I do for you?"

"Mona's been on the phone in a bit of a state and I wondered whether you could help."

"I can try. What's the matter?"

"She says she's had a letter from a firm of London lawyers threatening her with prison or something. Do you know what the hell's going on?"

"That'll be from my solicitor. It's called a cease and desist letter, Brian. They've sent it because of the letters she's been writing to me."

"Surely a wife's allowed to write to her husband?"

"Yes, but not foul, abusive letters every other day."

"What?"

"You heard me, Brian. Since I last saw you, she's been writing the most horrible things, and I need it to stop."

"She didn't mention that."

"I bet she didn't."

"But why the threat of prison?"

"That's a last resort, and it would only happen if we had to get a court order which she defied. That'd be contempt of court. At least, that's what my lawyer said."

"The letters. Are they really that bad?"

"Yup. I'm at Alan's house in Sedgethwaite for another couple of hours if you want to come and see for yourself."

"I think I might, if that's okay. I need to get this sorted in my own mind."

"That's no problem. To be honest, I'd be glad if you saw them." David gave Brian the address and ended the call. He found Alan downstairs in the kitchen and quickly explained that they were expecting a visitor. "It's a good opportunity, Al. Brian's about the only one who might be able to talk some sense into Mona. She usually listens to her father – eventually. If we can get him on our side, maybe we can settle this."

"Sounds a good plan. Should I make myself scarce?"

David smiled and shook his head. "I'd like you to be here, if you don't mind."

"Of course. Happy to, if you think it'll help."

"I'm sure it will."

Brian arrived about ten minutes later. David showed him

into the front room and introduced Alan. The atmosphere was more than a little tense for a while – after all, it's not often your wife's father is introduced to your boyfriend. However, being the gentle soul that he was, Brian shook Alan's hand and remarked that he remembered him from his school days.

"I asked Alan to be present," David explained, "because he saw what effect Mona's letter had on me."

Brian sat down in the chair by the fireplace, whilst Alan and David sat next to each other on the sofa. Alan maintained contact by sliding his hand discreetly under David's thigh.

David passed a folder across. "These are photocopies. The originals are with the lawyer, except the one she delivered here on Saturday afternoon."

Brian took the sheets out of the folder and started to read. David could not help a brief feeling of satisfaction as he saw the colour drain from his father-in-law's face, but it was quickly replaced by sympathy. It couldn't be pleasant to be confronted with what your own daughter was capable of.

Brian got through the first two letters in silence but couldn't help muttering, "Good God alive," at the start of the third. He was silent again after that, right through to the end. Putting the papers aside, his face was a picture of unhappiness. "I'm sorry, David. You didn't deserve any of that. No wonder you got the lawyers involved."

"I suppose the question is," said Alan, speaking for the first time, "whether you can persuade her to stop."

"Oh, she'll stop all right. You leave that to me."

David was shocked at the tone in his father-in-law's

voice. He'd never heard him strike such an authoritative note in all the years he'd known him.

"And, what's more, we're going to settle this. I've had enough of being taken for granted as an unpaid child minder while she sits at home and writes this rubbish. Where does she get all the words from, anyway? How does a daughter of mine know the sort of things she writes about in those letters?"

"I wondered that, too," remarked Alan. "I mean we weren't exactly the best of friends at school, but I don't remember her having such a vicious streak."

"Me neither," added David. "She never behaved like this while we were together."

"I blame that bloody vicar that Cheryl's been going to lately."

"You mean the Rev Archie?"

"That's the one. All the stuff he spews out, anti-gay, anti-this, anti-that. It doesn't seem very Christian to me. Cheryl goes to his church and she's been taking Mona with her the last few weeks."

"And the boys?"

"No, she leaves them with me every Sunday."

David didn't know how to respond, so he remained silent. After a few moments' thought, Brian spoke again. "If I can persuade her, would you be willing to try some form of mediation?"

"Of course," David replied. "I think that might be the best way forward. I'm prepared to try anything."

"Leave it with me. Maybe as a starting point we could all meet with the lawyers present."

"Sounds okay to me."

With that, Brian left, muttering another apology for his daughter's behaviour.

Chapter 22

Alan

The three weeks after their return to London were comparatively calm. Alan had plenty to do at work, but not at the frenetic pace that had dominated the previous month. In Sedgethwaite, David's father had gone home and continued to improve. Meanwhile, David was in a much better frame of mind and making progress on the job front. He applied for a driving job with a coach company nearby and was hoping for an interview.

Brian Spensley had been true to his word and the letters from Mona had stopped. He'd also let David know that he was still working on the idea of a meeting, though it was unlikely to take place before the New Year.

Alan felt calm and happy, relieved that he and David had worked through their differences. Their relationship seemed to have been strengthened by their experience – and that was as it should be. He had never been in a committed partnership like this before and was conscious that he still had a lot to learn. He still felt guilty for the way he had allowed David's mental state to deteriorate and done nothing about it.

Alan realised that David might have had more practice at relationships because of his marriage, but to some extent that was a disadvantage,. Having spent six years cloaking his real feelings, there was little wonder that he had tried to do the same again.

Their friends continued to be concerned for them and were extremely supportive. Simon especially had grown close to David, much to the latter's benefit. Under Simon's tutelage, David was developing very good dress sense. He'd changed his hairstyle too, cutting it shorter and using product to make it stand up on top. It was all in line with the latest trends, Simon assured him. Alan loved the look and, more importantly, he loved the way the changes were doing wonders for David's self-confidence. This, coupled with his own determination, had changed David's approach to life in London. He now listened intently to what was being said and was confident enough to admit to not knowing stuff, interrupting and asking questions.

The thing that Alan appreciated most was the return of laughter to their life. Verbal sparring had been a feature of their friendship for many years, and Alan had missed it earlier that autumn. Now that David seemed more settled, his sense of humour had returned. Despite the fact that there were still many unknown factors in their situation, especially over the boys and David's father, the uncertainties no longer seemed to weigh as heavily on him.

Alan was determined to keep following Simon's advice about making sure there was joy in their lives. He arranged meals out, two more West End shows and David's first classical concert. Judging by the looks on his face, David was certainly finding his new life joyful.

Most importantly, they also found time to simply be themselves, to cuddle up under a blanket and watch their favourite films, and to make love several times on lazy Saturday mornings before meeting friends for brunch.

The approach of the holidays meant the last class before a four-week break. Alan's studies had been going well and he was on schedule to complete his marketing degree within twelve months. In the ever-competitive world of advertising, his relative lack of formal qualifications had always been a concern, especially if he ever wanted – or was forced – to leave the firm he'd been with since he'd arrived in London six years earlier. He'd already got his Institute of Marketing qualification and, with his degree, he could afford to relax a little – especially if he got a first or a two-one. A combination of academic qualifications and an employment track record that showed he'd started at the bottom and worked his way up should stand him in good stead for the future.

In addition to his natural talent, Alan found the whole subject of marketing absolutely fascinating so the course had been a pleasure. He left the class in an upbeat mood, with a tonne of assignments for the Christmas break.

When he got home, it was to the news that David had secured an interview with the coach company. It was scheduled for the following Monday. The look on David's face when he gave Alan the news was a pleasure to behold, and their celebratory hug lasted a long time.

The approach of Christmas made this period of contentment even more special. Alan remembered how excited David used to get during the build-up to the festive season when he was a kid. Accordingly, on the third Saturday after their return from Yorkshire, Alan suggested a trip into the West End for a look round the Christmas shop in Selfridges and a tour of the lights.

He never forgot the wonder in David's eyes as they strolled round the West End, looking at the lights in Bond Street, Carnaby Street and the Seven Dials area as well as Regent Street and Oxford Street. David's enthusiasm was totally infectious.

After leaving Seven Dials, they headed for Soho and ended up in Wardour Street, revelling in the relaxed atmosphere, in being amongst so many of their own kind and the thousands of people simply having fun on a Saturday night. In the middle of the crowds, Alan felt David's hand slide into his own, so he turned and kissed him on the cheek. It was the first time that either of them had made a public display of affection, and it was exhilarating.

They managed to get a table in Balans, the famous all-night gay restaurant and a decades-old Soho institution. David lapped up the relaxed vibe and the friendly service; his eyes were barely still throughout their meal as he soaked up the atmosphere.

As they sat over the remains of their wine and waited for coffee, he became quiet and thoughtful.

"A penny for them?" Alan asked.

"Oh, you'd be wasting your money," David replied, his smile returning. "No, I was wondering what the nineteen-year-old me would have thought if he'd known that this was what life in London was like."

Alan laughed. "If you'd been like me, you'd have thought it was like having all your childhood treats rolled into one. It was so bloody exciting, Davy."

David nodded. "I'm sure it was. Weren't you scared, being on your own in the big city?"

"Bloody terrified, at least for the first few weeks. I'd booked into a cheap hotel but I couldn't afford to stay there for too long and it was pretty grotty. I found a flat share through an ad in one of the gay papers. I got on well enough with the other guys – there were four of us altogether, and two were seriously hot. But then I met Tris, so I didn't stay long."

David laughed. "Yes, the Gods were certainly smiling on you that night."

"You're not kidding, Davy! I owe him so fucking much. I sometimes wonder what would have happened if he'd tripped over somebody else's feet in the Salisbury that night."

"You'd have been all right, Al. You'll always land on your feet."

"I dare say. But what about you? Were you saying earlier that you regret not coming with me when I asked you to?"

"Part of me does, I suppose. Maybe if I'd known then what I know now, I might not have been so terrified at the idea of being gay."

"I get that," Alan replied. "Liking boys when you're isolated in a Yorkshire town is a very different prospect from living amongst thousands of other gay people in London."

"Though it's equally possible to be lonely here, I expect."

"Absolutely. I've experienced that sometimes, despite having my friends round me."

"Looking back, I was lonely at times even when I was living with Mona and the boys. We seemed to exist in different worlds."

"I certainly missed you during those first few weeks, Davy. So much. Not seeing you every day felt as if somebody had cut my arm off."

"I know what you mean. If you'd got in touch again after a couple of weeks, I think I might have changed my mind and come down. But who knows how it would have turned out? In any case, if I hadn't got married I wouldn't have the boys and I can't regret them." Mention of Kevin and Tommy inevitably meant that sadness flickered across David's face, but even that didn't spoil his good mood. "Anyway, I'm here now and that's what matters. No sense in brooding over the past. It's the future – our future – that matters now."

It was gone midnight by the time they'd finished their wine and drunk their coffee, so they wandered hand in hand through to Shaftesbury Avenue and waved down a passing taxi to take them home. They sat close in the back and held hands. Alan had never felt more strongly for David than he did during that journey and he wouldn't have changed a thing about their evening.

Once in bed, they moved naturally into each other's arms. Their kisses were gentle and affectionate. At one stage, they pulled back and Alan stared into his lover's eyes, still sparkling so much that it was as if the Christmas lights had taken over.

"Thank you for tonight, Al. I had a lovely time."

"Me too. Love you so much, Davy."

"Love you too."

Their lips met in another round of kisses, which grew steadily more passionate. After a while, David broke away and moved to straddle Alan, their erections brushing and causing them both to moan. "I need to feel you inside me, Al. Can I ride you?"

"Of course, sweetheart. Whatever you want tonight, my love." Alan lay back with his eyes closed, delighting in the feeling of closeness with David's body. He felt David shift as he reached across to grab the lube from the bedside cabinet.

Alan felt David's thighs flex and shift as he quickly prepared himself. There was another click as the bottle opened, and Alan hitched his breath slightly as he felt the cool of the lube on his cock, quickly warmed by David's hand.

Alan felt David shift again as he lifted himself again and guided Alan's cock to his entrance. Then there was heat and tightness as David impaled himself, slowly and steadily, until he was fully seated. David wriggled his hips slightly and gave a small sigh of contentment.

He opened his eyes to the sight of his lover leaning over him, face scrunched up in concentration as he waited for his body to adjust to Alan's cock. He reached up to draw David down for a passionate kiss. David began to move, rotating his hips slightly as well as moving up and down. Alan thrust upwards in sync and they quickly found a rhythm. The pace picked up. Alan gripped David's erection, tightly and pumping in time with their thrusts.

David began to babble between his groans as Alan closed his eyes once more and gave himself over to the sensations he was feeling. He started to whisper "yes, yes" every few seconds, his whispers growing in volume until they became shouts of joy and triumph as his climax stole up on him. David, too, reached the point of no return and they finished together, shouting with joy.

Alan felt completely boneless as David carefully lifted himself and flopped down on his side next to him. Neither of them spoke for a moment as they struggled to recover their breath, then Alan turned his head to look into David's eyes. They touched noses and each gave a small giggle.

"Wow," Alan remarked.

David's giggle turned into a laugh. "Wow, indeed. That was ... as good as all the Christmas lights put together."

"Given how much you loved the lights, I'll take that as a huge compliment. And I agree – definitely better than all the Christmas decorations in the world."

David excused himself and went to the bathroom, quickly returning with a cloth that he used to clean Alan gently, almost reverently. Then he hopped back into bed and lay his head on Alan's chest in the crook of his arm.

"It was a perfect day, Al. Thanks so much for showing me the lights." With a small sigh, David's breathing changed and Alan was aware that his lover had fallen asleep.

He lay there for a few minutes more, relaxed, absorbing the feel of David's body resting next to his. It was one more magical moment amongst so many of late, and the prospect of many more brought a small smile to his face as he too fell asleep.

Chapter 23

David

David's interview took place at the beginning of the following week. The company to which he'd applied was based a couple of miles away and had a depot next to a busy railway line. The facilities were modern, and they had a fleet of some sixty coaches operating a mix of sightseeing, touring and private hire. They'd recently won a contract to run a couple of express services for one of the big national players, and needed to recruit more drivers as a result.

He was nervous but also excited to be back in a depot, to inhale the smell of the place which, to him at least, was a magical combination of oil, exhaust fumes and raw diesel; to hear the sounds of fitters' voices and the clang of their tools from the workshop, and to stand next to the vehicles themselves. David couldn't put a date on his fascination with buses and coaches, nor could he rationalise it because it had always been a part of him. His mother joked that it dated back to when he could sit in his pram and point at them, and he wondered sometimes whether that was very far from the truth.

He found his way to the offices, housed in a modern block in one corner of the yard, where he reported to the receptionist. The ground floor housed reception, a large traffic office – the hub of the operation – and the drivers' room, with other offices on two floors above. He was to be interviewed by the traffic manager, Alex Winter.

He was asked to take a seat in reception and told that Mr Winter would be with him in a couple of minutes. Five went by before David heard footsteps bounding down the stairs. He looked up to see a youngish guy of about his own age. He was tall – about six feet, David reckoned – with light-brown hair and a short, well-trimmed beard. His outstanding feature was a broad smile that made dimples either side of his mouth and caused his bright hazel eyes to sparkle.

They shook hands and Alex took him up the stairs into a small meeting room. As David followed, he made a determined effort to avoid checking out the sight of his prospective boss's snugly fitting trousers. David was not used to finding men other than Alan attractive, and usually did not notice them, but he was drawn to this man, feeling a buzz of some kind in his presence. He was unsure whether it was charm, charisma or pure sex appeal, but it was definitely there.

He took the seat he was offered and Alex sat down opposite him, shuffling papers on the table before looking up with a welcoming smile. "So, welcome to Leigham Coaches, David. Why don't you tell me about yourself?"

David launched into his much-rehearsed words about his long-term fascination with buses and coaches and the fact that he'd never wanted to work in any other industry.

He outlined his experience and how he'd ended up being part of the launch team for the new Yorkshire-London service earlier in the year.

Alex asked one or two questions about how that had worked, and about customer relationships. He also wanted to know how David felt about prolonged motorway driving, explaining that the firm was a newcomer to express operations, having only won the contract a couple of weeks earlier.

The more they talked, the more David relaxed and felt comfortable in Alex's company. It was clear that his references had been taken up and that Alex had spoken to Jack Davis and Len Hedges, his mentors at Sedgethwaite & District.

"One last question, David. What brings you to London? You seem to have been settled in your last company with a good track record and prospects for promotion. What happened?"

That was the one question that David had hoped would not be asked, not because he felt he had anything to hide but because he didn't know how he should answer it. He was sure that he shouldn't lie because he knew from experience that it almost never worked. It was more a question of how much of the truth he should tell. Would coming out as gay at this stage jeopardise his prospects? Or was it better to be entirely honest from the start?

He and Alan had discussed the question over the weekend, but hadn't come to a conclusion. He could duck the issue and talk about domestic problems, but David's gut instinct was to be open and honest. After the experience of being forcibly outed at work in Sedgethwaite, he never wanted to be in that position again.

Aware that he had to speak, he looked into Alex's eyes and saw that they were full of sympathy and concern. That decided him. "I recently realised that I'm gay," he said. "My wife chucked me out and my father rejected me. My oldest friend, who's here in London, took me in and he's now my boyfriend." The words came out in a rush, almost tripping over one another. David held his breath while he waited for a reaction.

Alex smiled. "Wow. You seem to have had quite a time. Coming out is difficult, isn't it? Thanks for trusting me enough to be honest with me. It always helps, I think."

"I agree. I was outed by my union chairman, so I didn't want a repeat performance with a new job."

"Jesus, David! You won't have a problem like that here, I can promise you. We recognise the union, though they're not particularly strong – with seasonal work and the transient nature of the London labour market, people tend not to stick around for too long. Anyway, our union chairman occasionally moonlights as a drag queen, so I don't think you'll have any difficulties there."

David laughed. "You're probably right." He hesitated again, wondering whether to let Alex's remarks lie. But he wanted to know, so the best thing to do was ask. "So, did you mean earlier when you said about coming out...?"

Alex nodded. "Yes, me too. My partner Tony is the FD here – we've been together for seven years. We met when my dad recruited him around the same time I joined the business."

David smiled. "What a lovely story. Thanks for sharing."

"You'll meet him soon if you join us."

"Well, here's hoping."

"So the thing is, David, that we're coming up to our quiet time. There probably isn't much we can do for you until February. If that's okay, we could start you then, give you a couple of weeks' route learning and training ready for when our new contract starts. How does that sound? Or do you need something sooner?"

"Actually, February would be perfect. There are still some issues to resolve in Yorkshire. If I can get those sorted next month, that would leave me clear too."

"Sounds ideal. I'll confirm in writing in the next day or two," Alex replied, standing up and offering his hand. David quickly stood and grasped it. "See you in February."

"That's grand, Alex. I'll look forward to it."

David more or less skipped down the road from the depot. He couldn't believe his luck not only in picking such an apparently good firm, but also getting a boss who seemed kind, sympathetic and, to be honest, stunningly sexy. The fact that he was gay was the icing on the cake.

When he got to the bus stop for his journey home, he shot a quick text to Alan.

DAVID >>Interview gr8. Offered job to start Feb

There was a pause. David was about to get on his bus when his phone pinged with a reply.

ALAN >> Fantastic news. Get yr gladrags on – we're going to celebrate tonight. Be in touch later. Luv U.

As he sat on the bus back to Clapham, David couldn't keep the smile off his face. The job should suit him down to the ground; he could hardly wait to get behind the wheel again, and the nature of the work was perfect. He'd loved the few months he'd spent on the express coach service and returning to that sort of work was a real bonus.

Getting this job represented another milestone in his quest to build a new life in London. Being back in work would enable him to pay his way and make him feel less like a sponger. Okay, so he knew Alan didn't see it that way, but David did and he couldn't wait for it to end. It would also mean that he could support the boys if and when the row with Mona was resolved.

He reached the flat half an hour later and picked up the post from the mat before going upstairs. Most of the stuff was for Simon and Peter, but there was one letter addressed to David in a thick, expensive envelope. It was from Tom Parkes; Mona had agreed to a meeting that was to take place at the offices of her solicitors in Leeds. She'd insisted on being accompanied by her parents and had agreed that David could also be accompanied by up to two people. Tom suggested that David might want to ask Alan, or one or both of his parents. He added that the date for the meeting had provisionally been set for Tuesday the ninth of January and asked David to confirm his availability and who he would be bringing.

David clutched the letter to his chest and sighed. What could be more perfect on this already spectacular day? A meeting was not the same as reaching an agreement, but it represented a huge step forward. He had no doubt that this was his father-in-law's doing; he would be for ever grateful to Brian Spensley if they could only get everything resolved.

Chapter 24

Alan

Alan was wrapping up a meeting when David's first text about the result of his interview came through, but he got back to him as soon as he'd said goodbye to his clients. The two of them were not in the habit of texting backwards and forwards during the day, so he was a little surprised when he got a second message from David within an hour.

When he opened it and read the contents, he immediately dialled David's number. "Hey, Davy. Thanks for your text. That's great news!"

"Thanks, Al. I still can't believe it – specially not today of all days."

"What exactly does Tom say?"

David explained the terms of the proposed meeting. Alan drew in a sharp breath at the mention of the mother-in-law. When David got to the bit about his own supporters, Alan immediately responded, "Davy, of course I'll be there if that's what you want. But if you think I might make matters worse, I'd understand that, too. It's your call – I'll come with you to Yorkshire whatever happens. I can book the leave today."

"I do want you in the room, Al, no question. If Cheryl Spensley doesn't like it, she can do the other thing."

"Right. Let me go and sort out my leave and I'll see you in a couple of hours. Don't forget your gladrags – we've certainly got something to celebrate now!"

Alan had been mulling over the idea of a treat for the evening – either as a celebration or, if necessary, a commiseration – but he hadn't decided what form it should take. Should he invite their friends or keep it to the two of them? Should they go out and, if so, where? The other Saturday at Balans had been perfect – fun, relaxed with superb food – but it was too soon to go back there. He wondered how he could replicate that buzz but take the romance up a notch.

He suspected that Tris would have the answer and was about to dial his number when Ian wandered into his office. "Ah, Ian, you'll do."

"Oh, thanks so much. So kind, so condescending. Er … what for?"

"Sorry, that rather came out backwards. I was about to ring Tris for some advice but you know as much about eating out as he does – so can I ask you?"

Ian laughed. "Of course. What's the occasion?"

"A celebration. David's got the job he was after and his wife has agreed to a meeting."

"Wow! That's fantastic news, Alan. I'm so glad." He grinned. "I like celebrations. Can we come too?"

"I'd thought of that, but maybe later in the week?

Besides, haven't you got dinner with your favourite client tonight?"

"Oh, shit. I'd almost managed to forget about that. Did you have to bring it up? Maybe I should send you instead."

"Not bloody likely. Anyway, it's you he fancies."

Ian groaned. "Don't remind me – he gets awfully handsy during the second bottle. He was like an octopus in the taxi when I escorted him back to the hotel last year."

Alan grinned at him. "I remember. Tris said it took you a week to get over it."

"Yes, I had nightmares for ages afterwards. God, the things I do for this firm."

"Yes, but Sir Digby is one of our oldest clients and they do place three million pounds worth of business through us every year. Isn't that worth a quick grope in a taxi every now and again?"

Ian sighed. "I suppose so, but it does make me sound a bit of a whore. The awful thing is that I quite like the old boy – when he's sober. It's just that he gets all soppy and affectionate after he's had a few. He doesn't mean any harm, though. Anyway that's my evening mapped out. What are you after?"

"A cosy, intimate dinner. Good food, but not fantastically posh."

"There's a great Italian place tucked away at the bottom of Marylebone Lane that might suit. I can't remember what it's called. It's a few yards up from Wigmore Street on the left-hand side."

"Oh, I know the place – Massimo's. Jimmy Anselm took me there for lunch a couple of months ago. That's a fabulous idea, Ian. Thanks. I'll see if I can get us in."

"My pleasure. You should be all right on a Monday if they're open. May I go now, please, oh mighty one?"

"Of course. Didn't you come in for a reason?"

"Probably, but I can't remember now. Your news was much too exciting."

Alan laughed. "I can't disagree with that. So how about Thursday for the four of us to go out?"

"Sounds good. I'll consult the oracle and let you know."

"Great. And have fun with Sir Digby."

"Gee thanks, pal."

Alan looked up the number of the restaurant, dialled and booked a table for eight-thirty. Perfect.

Alan finished his main course before David, so he had a chance to sit back for a moment and study his partner. There was almost no comparison between the shivering, exhausted man that Alan had found on his arrival at the Edward Street house four weeks earlier.

David had put back some of the weight he had shed and lost the deep bags that had seemed to dominate his face. His eyes had lost their dull look and regained their sparkle. There was still a way to go: the business over the kids was still bothering him, and there were still times when his attention would wander and he was obviously somewhere else.

Even so, Alan felt optimistic tonight. He was sure that the new job and the meeting were two more building blocks in their new lives. The meeting with Mona would help enormously with the next stage of David's recovery from the traumatic events of that night in August.

David finished his main course and put down his knife and fork. He looked up and grinned. "Were you staring at me, Alan Foreshaw?"

"Curses, Edgeley. Caught in the act."

"What's up, Al? Was I doing something wrong?"

"No, no. Not at all. No, I was just thinking how much better you were looking, since we got back from Yorkshire."

"Oh, God, yes. Si said I looked like a character out of *Ghostbusters* when I got back. Mind you, you look better too. There were times in October when I was convinced you were about to keel over."

"Tell me about it. Talk about crazy. It's been the same every bloody year since I started at the firm. Every time we say we're going to be better organised and get through the Christmas campaigns more calmly."

"What goes wrong?"

"I can sum it up in one word, Davy. Clients."

David frowned. "How do you mean?"

"We can be as organised as you like at our end, ideas aplenty, sending draft copy – you name it. But if the clients won't make a decision until the last possible moment, we're stuffed."

"Ah, I see. And because they are Christmas campaigns, everybody has much the same deadline?"

"Exactly. Still, they do pay us lots of lovely lolly, so I shouldn't complain too much. But tell me more about your interview. We haven't talked about that yet."

David's face took on a mischievous look. "What if I told you that my new boss is a rather handsome, youngish gay man?"

Alan laughed. "I'd tell you to go and get a job somewhere else. Can't be doing with rivals for your affection."

"All I can say is 'tough luck', sweetheart."

"Are you serious?"

"Certainly am. He's called Alex Winter and he's six foot of gorgeousness, as Simon would have it. And yes, he's gay, because he told me when I told him. But he's also in a relationship with the company's FD."

"Well, well. Who'd have thought it, eh? And you liked him, Davy?"

"Oh, absolutely. We got on like a house on fire, even before the gay thing cropped up."

"So what happened?"

"He asked me why I'd left Sedgethwaite and the old firm, so I told him."

"All of it?"

David nodded. "Yep. It was a split-second decision, but I didn't want to start a new job without telling the truth. Life's too complicated for that – trying to remember what you've told to whom. I couldn't be doing with it."

"No, I think you're right, Davy. Anyway, it must have gone okay, because he still offered you the job."

David smiled again. "And came out to me."

"Pretty impressive stuff. You must have ramped up the charm."

David buffed his nails on his jacket lapel. "Just one of my many talents."

"But seriously, Davy. You think you'll be all right there?"

"Yeah. I really liked Alex, and the place seemed to have a friendly atmosphere."

"That's good. I hate to think of you being unhappy anywhere."

"I know. Thanks, Al. No doubt it'll have its moments, same as any job. But it's what I've always loved doing, so I'm sure it'll be fine. Also, not too many late nights – and no overnight duties, at least on the run I'll be doing."

"That's good too. Where will you be going?"

"They've won two contracts, one for a service to Bournemouth and the other to Stansted Airport. Alex wants me to focus on Bournemouth, at least initially."

"Wow. So lots of trips to the seaside. Can I come with you?"

David laughed. "I don't think I'll be seeing much of the sea. Only the bus station, a quick break then straight back, I expect."

"That's a shame. I imagined bringing my bucket and spade."

"Silly bugger."

"I'm very pleased for you, Davy – even if I'm worried about you having a hot boss."

"Who's totally spoken for, don't forget."

"Oh, okay. But I know from experience the effect you have on people. You can certainly rev my engine at any time."

"Al, stop it, you're making me blush."

Alan grinned mischievously at him and moved his leg under the table to rub against David's. "I like making you all red in the face."

Much to Alan's disappointment, his Davy-baiting session was interrupted by their waiter, asking if they'd like to order dessert. Having debated the merits of tiramisu and profiteroles, they decided to order one of each and share. When the order had been sorted, David used the opportunity to change the subject. "One thing I wanted to ask you, Al. What about Christmas?"

Alan smiled, glad that David had brought the subject up because he'd been hesitating to raise it for the last few days, uncertain how his lover would react. "I'd been wondering about that too. What do you want to do?"

"I don't see any point in going up to Yorkshire, at least not this year. Mona wouldn't let me see the boys and I'm not welcome at home, so... I dunno. But I don't want to interfere with your plans."

Alan couldn't help but smile. David was so cute when he was being diffident. Alan had imagined them spending Christmas together as most couples would, and he couldn't understand why David was being so tentative. It was if he were still uncertain about his place in Alan's life. He supposed he could be offended by that, but he wasn't; he understood.

Alan took David's hand and looked him directly in the eye. "I rather assumed that I'd be with you somewhere. It doesn't matter where, as long as we're together."

David visibly relaxed. "Oh good. I'd thought so too, but I didn't want to take anything for granted."

"Silly sod," Alan replied. "Where did you think I'd want to be?"

David shrugged. "I don't know. I hoped, you know..."

"Davy, Davy, Davy. We're together now, and it's a 'for ever' job as far as I'm concerned. Who else would I want to spend Christmas with?"

"I suppose I knew that, but I didn't want to assume. I

know it's daft, but I'm still not used to … you know … us."

"I know, love. I do understand, believe me. It's not been easy for you. But we're on the right path now, don't you think?"

"Aye, lad. Definitely," David replied exaggerating his accent slightly. "And it's a 'for ever' job for me too, by the way."

Alan smiled back and nodded. "Right, so that's sorted. Now, what would you like to do for Christmas?"

They were interrupted as the waiter brought their desserts and took their coffee orders. When they were alone again David asked, "What have you done for the last few years?"

"I've been to Tris's parents for Christmas lunch several times. Since Tris and Ian got together, I've tended to spend the rest of the day on my own, catching up on sleep."

"Sounds very restful. You can imagine what ours have been like."

"Did you stay at home?"

David laughed. "Absolutely not. Mona was horrified by the idea of having to cook Christmas dinner, especially for a houseful of people. No, we alternated between the two sets of parents, then we went to the other set on Boxing Day. It should have been my mum and dad's turn this year." He paused and swallowed hard. "It's going to be bloody hard, I'm afraid. I don't suppose I'll be full of the Christmas spirit."

"Bound to be, love. Do you want to go to Yorkshire just in case? To be on hand?"

David shook his head. "I thought about it, but I think it'd only make matters worse to be so near and yet so far. I reckon it'd be easier to stay down here, if you don't mind."

"Davy, I don't mind at all. I'm in your hands. I'm sure we'll need to be up there in future years when you've got access to the boys, but for now it's your choice. Whatever we do, I shall be happy so long as I'm with you."

"Thanks, Al. That goes for me too."

The matter unresolved, they left the restaurant and strolled back into Oxford Street for a spot of window shopping and another look at the Christmas lights. After that, Alan hailed a cab to take them home. He sat quietly in the back of the taxi, holding David's hand and pressing against him, shoulder to shoulder. He smiled to himself; it had been a good day, and the dinner – undemanding, intimate and relaxed – had been a terrific way to celebrate. He hoped it was the first of many such outings.

Chapter 25

David

"What do you think of it so far?" Alan asked.

David took a sip of champagne and beamed at him. "Fabulous. Totally magical." They were standing in one of the bars at the Royal Opera House during the interval of *The Nutcracker*. Alan had snagged a couple of tickets from a client who was one of the Royal Ballet's corporate sponsors so here they were, enjoying the quintessential Christmas ballet three nights before the big day, sipping complementary fizz.

David had spent the evening trying to keep his eyebrows at their usual height, having decided that wandering around all evening with eyes as big as saucers would be decidedly uncool. He was nervous, of course – who wouldn't be on such an occasion, with all the posh accents and elegant clothes? But he'd noted during the pre-theatre reception and again now that the accents were not universally posh and the clothes, whilst fashionable, were certainly not all stiff and formal. The overall impression was of people thoroughly enjoying themselves. He could certainly relate to that. He couldn't help reflecting on how jealous his mum would be if she could see him now. She had loved the ballet ever since she was a young girl and had seen Margot Fonteyn dance in Leeds, and she had always dreamt of visiting this theatre to see a live performance.

When Alan first mentioned the invitation, David had been enthusiastic and pushed aside memories of his truculent refusal to attend a few weeks earlier. He still blushed when he remembered how horrible he'd been that night, both in spurning Alan's attempt to cheer him up and in dismissing the whole idea of ballet as an entertainment in which he could ever be interested.

It had only taken a few minutes of tonight's performance to change his view completely. He was blown away by the sweep of Tchaikovsky's music, the power of the live orchestra and the spectacular scenery – and that was before he'd had the opportunity to appreciate the skill and athleticism of the dancers. As with his previous experiences in the theatre, goose bumps rose on his skin and he found his eyes filling. He grabbed Alan's hand the moment the curtain went up and clung to it tightly until it went down again.

He was aware of Alan speaking again, so ripped his mind away from his memories of the first act.

"Most of the most famous dances are in the second act," Alan remarked. "So you've got lots of treats to come."

"Oh?"

"Yeah. 'Dance of the Sugar Plum Fairy', 'Waltz of the Flowers' and the 'Pas de Deux'. They all come after the interval."

"It's funny that the music seems so familiar. I suppose

Mum must have played it a lot when we were younger."

"And it's always on the telly at Christmas. I bet she watched it every year if she was that keen."

"Oh, absolutely. We three kids used to moan about it because it always clashed with a big film on the other side."

Alan laughed. "I remember. I think one year you stomped out and came round to me to watch a movie."

"So I did! It was a repeat of *Superman*, wasn't it?"

"You're right. We must have been about fourteen. I can remember that I used to fancy Christopher Reeve something rotten."

Their reminiscences were cut short as they were approached by one of the executives from their host company. He recognised Alan and shook hands with him, welcoming him to the event. At first David was horrified at the idea of having to talk to him, but quickly remembered his mantra that everybody was here to enjoy themselves. He squared his shoulders and responded to the man's smile. He was in his mid-fifties with elegantly styled hair and an immaculate suit. His faced was tanned and his smile was warm.

"David Edgeley," he said, offering his hand for a shake.

"My boyfriend," added Alan.

"Ah, right. Welcome, David. I'm Guy Baxter. Are you in marketing too?"

Hit with a sudden inspiration, David replied, "Sort of – frontline customer service. Travel."

"Fascinating – and so important."

David nodded enthusiastically. "Yes, I'm a great believer in looking after customers. After all, travelling can be quite stressful and I find that reassuring people helps a lot."

"Yes, people are outside their comfort zones, I suppose," Guy mused.

"Exactly, and they often behave rather oddly as a result."

"Quite so, quite so. And are you enjoying the show?"

"Oh, very much, sir. Thank you so much for your hospitality."

Their exchange of social niceties was interrupted by the bell to signal the start of the second act. Guy shook their hands once more, and left them. David looked up and caught Alan looking at him with a broad smile on his face. "What's that for?" he asked.

"Oh, nothing," Alan replied, his eyes sparkling now with amusement. "Just admiring the new David's social skills."

David immediately felt crestfallen. "Did I do anything wrong? Did I put my foot in it?"

Alan laughed. "Certainly not, Davy. It was perfect – you were perfect. I'm trying to get used to this show of confidence. It's – you are – fantastic."

"I might have looked confident, but I certainly didn't feel it. Was I right to duck the driving bit?"

"Davy, it was fine. You are in customer service, after all – in many ways, that's the most important aspect of your job. And I thought your remarks were shrewd and observant."

"Thanks."

They were separated briefly in the crowds returning to the auditorium, something which a few weeks earlier would have made David a little panicky. It didn't worry him nearly as much tonight and Alan's praise for his encounter with Guy Baxter had left him with a warm feeling inside. It had been a small thing, a brief chat of little consequence, but such an event would have left him tongue-tied and miserable a few weeks earlier. It was a small victory but it felt like a triumph.

"God, it's chilly out there," Alan said as they opened their menus. "What are you going to eat, Davy? Any ideas?"

"I was thinking black bean soup and the burger. I could do with warming up."

After the end of the ballet, they had walked briskly down to Exeter Street and supper at Joe Allen's. As Alan had promised, the second half of the show was full of highlights. The magic of the costumes and scenery, the exuberance and drama of Tchaikovsky's score and the technique and artistry of the dancers had taken David's breath away on a couple of occasions, and he'd spent most of the time with tears of joy in his eyes. This might have been his first visit to the ballet but without doubt he was totally hooked and couldn't wait to see more.

Now he sat back and looked round him. Even though it was almost eleven, the place was packed with a mixture of evening diners coming to the end of their meals and the post-theatre crowd. The combination of loud laughter, animated chatter and the noises from the kitchen and the bar, with Jimmy's piano playing in the background, created the ambience for which the place was famous.

The atmosphere alone was enough to warm David after their chilly walk down Wellington Street. His body, which had been tense from trying to keep out the cold, gradually relaxed.

"All right?" Alan asked.

"Couldn't be better, Al, thanks. That was a great night."

"Glad you enjoyed it, love. The look of wonder on your face – I could barely keep my eyes off you."

David laughed. "Silly bugger. Why would you want to gaze at me all night?"

"'Cos I think you're awesome."

"Shut up, Al. You're making me blush. There's nothing special about me, I can assure you."

Alan grinned at him. "Well, I think there is. And, as you almost said to Guy Baxter tonight, customer perception is everything."

David huffed a laugh. "Okay, okay. I suppose I'll have to accept that, in your eyes at least, I'm awesome." He blushed again. "But I'm still a rotten father, a cheating husband and a lazy bugger who's spent the last twelve weeks doing absolutely sod all."

The smile left Alan's face as David recited his shortcomings. "You'll not be surprised to know that I disagree. I'm not going to argue about it tonight, but you have *not* done sod all for twelve weeks. You've cooked and cleaned and washed and ironed for me, and done it all beautifully. In fact, you've been quite the domestic goddess."

David couldn't help laughing at this description, despite the sudden darkening of his mood. His amusement dispersed the sudden descent into gloom that had been about to overtake him. For all that he was having a good time and enjoying his new life, sometimes he remembered that this was all an escape from the realities of his existence.

He didn't feel entitled to be happy and it did no harm to remind himself of that every now and again.

Aware of Alan's appraising look, he was pleased that the waiter chose that moment to arrive and take their orders. The pause enabled him to recover his equilibrium. "Cute," he remarked as the waiter walked away.

"New, I think," Alan replied, also grateful for the change of subject. "Don't remember seeing him before. So, do I take it that you'd like to come to the ballet again?"

"Try and keep me away. It was fantastic. I loved everything about it."

"I'm so glad. I don't know why, but I was sure that it would be right up your street."

David shook his head. "I don't understand it either. It never interested me as a boy – mind you, I suppose that was the Billy Elliot syndrome at work. It wasn't something Yorkshire lads did, all that 'poncing about', as Dad used to call it."

"He didn't approve?"

"Certainly not. If there was one thing guaranteed to send him off to the pub, it was when Mum wanted to watch the ballet. I suppose I absorbed his attitude and that's what made me react badly the other week."

"I did wonder where that had come from. It sounded so unlike you."

"Looking back, I can see now that it was all part of my cunning plan to deceive myself."

Alan smiled at the *Blackadder* reference but then looked puzzled. "Care to explain?"

"I can see now that there were several things at home and at school that I deliberately avoided because they weren't 'manly' enough. Watching cultural stuff with Mum on the telly was one of them. I always enjoyed that sort of thing with her until I hit my teens, then I started to push it all away. Neither Dad nor Robert was interested – they really hated some programmes, like dance – and I thought I had to be like them. If I did that, I was in no danger."

"Christ, Davy. Why didn't you tell me?"

"It didn't matter, Al. That's what I'm saying. It seemed the right thing to do back then, and it didn't cause me any anxiety. I wanted to fit in, be loved, feel safe. Following Dad's rules seemed the best way to do it. It wasn't a conscious thing at the time but, looking back, I understand that's what I was doing. It was that version of me that sent you off to London and refused to come with you."

"And the version that got married?"

"Spot on."

Their starters arrived. David took a couple of spoons of his soup before resuming. "Realising that over the past few weeks has helped so much."

"The new you?"

David nodded. "Those letters Mona sent seemed to unlock everything. The person she was criticising wasn't the real David Edgeley, it was another version that I'd constructed, the person I needed to be in order to survive. As that version, I was bound to fail – as a lover, as Mona's husband and as my father's son – because I was putting on an act."

He paused, taken aback by his own words. The thoughts he was expressing were genuinely new; he instinctively recognised the truth of them but couldn't help but be surprised by his self-revelation. "Six years ago, you were the only person ever to see the real me. When you left, I put that version away and locked him up. He stayed there until you came back." He paused again and smiled. "Thanks for not losing the key, Al."

Veering off Course

Chapter 26

Alan

Alan awoke to the sight of credits rolling on the television screen. It was Christmas night, and he and David had got home from lunch with Tris's parents around five. They'd made some tea, put on the television and parked themselves on the sofa, snuggling together under a throw. David Lean's black-and-white version of Great Expectations had been playing on BBC2 and they'd watched the rest of that before switching over to the Harry Potter film on BBC1.

At some point Alan had dozed off, still full of turkey, stuffing and Christmas pudding, not to mention several glasses of some extremely fine claret that had been followed by some equally impressive vintage port. When he'd fallen asleep David was glued to the film, clearly loving every minute of it. Not that Alan hadn't liked it too, but his eyes had grown too heavy...

David noticed him stirring and snorted. "Ah, it's awake."

"Did I doze off? Sorry. Was it good?"

"Brilliant. Loved every minute of it – terrific cast and the special effects were fantastic."

Alan smiled. "Good. A proper Christmas treat." He yawned and moved to snuggle against David's side but his boyfriend moved away.

"Sorry, got to pee," David said. "Do you want a drink or something?"

"No, thanks, love. I'm fine."

"Okay, back in a trice."

Alan levered himself upright and glanced at the TV screen. He noticed the opening credits for *EastEnders* and reached for the remote to switch off. He wasn't in the mood for a soap opera and the angst that usually went with it. They'd had enough of their own this autumn. Alan was determined to keep all trauma at bay over the holidays if he could.

He'd succeeded so far, mainly by keeping David so busy and distracted that he hadn't had time to think much about his kids. In addition to the visit to the ballet, they'd been to the cinema, gone out for dinner with Simon and Peter and watched several films on DVD. Alan had amassed a large collection, including many of their favourite films from their teenage years, and it had helped to keep their focus on those times, rather than their time apart.

Today had been magical. They'd woken early and spent most of the morning making love more slowly than they'd ever done before, each savouring every moment. Even now, Alan could remember how David had felt inside him and how hard he'd come while their eyes had been locked together. He wriggled with pleasure at the memory.

Lunch with Tris's parents had been a delight. David had been nervous at meeting new, 'posh' people and had been stressed on the way there but, once he'd arrived and been introduced, he'd relaxed in the warmth of the reception he'd received. The lunch had been delicious as always and afterwards they'd sat around the table chatting over the port with Ian, Tris and his parents, who'd taken quite a shine to David. Finally, sitting cuddling together watching Harry Potter had been ... well, magical.

David had been gone for a while and Alan wondered where he was. The toilet had flushed several minutes ago, but there was no sign of him. Alan frowned and stood to go and find him. After checking the kitchen and bathroom, he found David in their bedroom, standing in the dark by the window. "Hey," he said gently.

"Oh, hi."

"I wondered where you'd got to. Are you okay?"

"Yeah, I think so. Sorry, I was standing in the bathroom and a memory of last Christmas flashed into my mind. It brought it all back, you know? Not getting to play Santa with the boys, wondering what they're doing and what they think about me."

Alan could tell from his slightly hoarse tone that David had a lump in his throat. There was nothing he could say, though. It was not a problem that could be fixed; they would just have to get through it.

He rubbed David's arm and felt him relax. David turned slightly to face him and Alan wrapped his arms round him. David put his chin on Alan's shoulder and tucked his face into his neck. They stayed still and quiet for a few moments; the only motion was Alan gently rubbing circles in the small of his boyfriend's back.

Finally David pulled back and glanced up with tear-filled eyes. "Sorry, Al. Way to ruin the day, eh?"

"Don't be daft, lad. I'd have been surprised if you hadn't thought of the boys at some point – it's Christmas Day, after all. The only consolation I can offer is that we've got the meeting date, so there is some progress."

"Aye, you're right. It's just me being daft."

"This time next year, Davy, we'll make it up to them. I promise."

David smiled at him a little wanly. "I'd like to think we'd get the chance."

"I'm sure we will. Now, how about we go and watch another movie? Your pick this time."

Later, as they lay in bed together after another round of sex, this time rather more boisterous than their early morning love making, Alan returned to thoughts of how the future might pan out.

This would probably be the last Christmas holiday they would spend in London for the foreseeable future; given any sort of access agreement, David would want to see the boys at this time of year, so they would have to be in Yorkshire. Not that he minded; he was fond of his old home in Edward Street, and looked forward to modernising the house in the new year. By the time they had finished, it would be a good place to visit for weekends and holidays. He was sure that spending time with the boys, and possibly even David's family, would be fun. Even so, he would miss Tris and Ian and Tris's family. They'd been so welcoming to him over the last few years.

Still, nothing was for nothing. He couldn't help

comparing his mood tonight in David's company with how he'd felt on the previous three Christmas nights once Tris and Ian had moved in together. Each time, he'd come home alone to an empty flat, feeling a strong sense of anti-climax after such a sociable day full of joy and laughter. On those occasions more than any other during the year, he'd felt the lack of somebody in his life with whom he could share memories and compare notes.

This year had been so different. He had David, and it was everything he could have wished for – comfortable, domestic, reassuring – just plain *right*.

He smiled to himself as he drifted off to sleep. Best. Christmas. Ever.

Setting a New Course

Chapter 27

David

The week between Christmas and New Year was dominated by the news of the Asian tsunami and its aftermath. Like millions of others, David and Alan sat in front of their television appalled by the destruction and human misery that played out before them.

It was brought a little closer to home when Simon popped upstairs to see them with the news that Peter's elder brother Charles and his family were missing. They were on holiday in Phuket, Thailand when the tsunami struck on Boxing Day morning.

"Gawd knows what happens if he doesn't turn up," Simon lamented. "It'll make Peter the heir to the estate and the title and everything. Mother will try to whisk him off and marry him to some suitable gal so that he can produce an heir. There'll be hell to pay when Peter refuses. His mother will blame me – my 'malign influence', as she calls it – so there'll be yet another row about that."

"Have you met Charles?" asked David, not fully familiar with the full details of this family drama.

"Oh, yes, sweetheart. He's lovely, as is Rachel, his wife. She and I are great friends, and they have two of the most adorable kids, Guy and Will. It's only Mother who kicks up such a fuss about Peter being gay. Even then, I think she'd have been all right if he'd dated Prince Harry – 'right class, don't you know'. She's such a bloody snob. God, I hope they're all right."

"I can't imagine what it must have been like," Alan reflected. "I was on that beach a couple of years ago and it seemed so tranquil."

"Will you not be coming to Tris's party, Si?" asked David.

"We'll see. If they turn up safe and sound in the next two or three days, I'm sure we'll be fine. If not, who knows? I honestly doubt it, luvvie."

"I'm sure Tris and Ian will understand," Alan said. "It'd be a shame, though."

"I agree – I'd hate to miss it. We had such a wonderful time at their betrothal do."

"Yeah, that was an awesome party," said David wistfully. "Once I could actually pluck up the courage to walk in."

"Which reminds me – they've set a date for their civil partnership now the law's gone through," Alan said. "They're aiming to be one of the early adopters, so hopefully it will be the thirtieth of December next year."

"Wow, that's quick work, only ten days after it takes effect," Simon remarked wistfully. "I wish I could get Peter to move that quickly."

In the event, the news was good. Peter's brother and family were found safe and well and would be amongst the first group of Britons to be repatriated. They were the lucky ones; almost two hundred others wouldn't be coming home.

David and Alan spent the rest of the week quietly. They spent several lazy mornings in bed making love, getting up in time to make brunch. They went for a walk across the common a couple of times, wrapped up against the cold. David thought Alan looked adorable in the bobble hat with matching scarf that he'd bought him for Christmas. Its main colour was tiger lily, which seemed to be one of the colours of the year, and it certainly suited him.

They chatted and laughed as they strolled, exchanging memories of boyhood walks across Town Moor in Sedgethwaite. "I always remember your Auntie Mary used to give us crumpets for tea," David said.

"God, yes. I haven't had crumpets for years," Alan responded. "You always used to get butter down your chin."

"Did not."

"Did too."

"That's 'cos it used to melt and run straight through the crumpet."

Alan laughed. "That's because you couldn't wait for them to cool down before putting the butter on." He suddenly went quiet and his eyes got a faraway look.

"What are you thinking about now?" David asked, recognising the signs of Alan getting nostalgic again.

Alan laughed gently. "Nothing really. I had a sudden memory of one time when I was sixteen and we had crumpets. How much I wanted to lick the butter off your chin."

David laughed. "Oh, you naughty boy. If only I'd

known." He paused and thought for a moment. "I wouldn't have stopped you if you had."

"Seriously?"

"Seriously," David echoed, nodding. "I knew it was special between us. I suppose I'd known ever since that first day in the playground when you were so sad. But I didn't know what it meant, so I ignored it. I wish you had, Al."

Alan abruptly turned off the path, taking hold of David's hand and pulling him. He stopped by a tree and drew David into an embrace. "I wish I had, too, Davy. You've no idea how much."

David found his lips locked in a passionate kiss, but it was over too quickly. Instead, Alan led him back onto the path in the opposite direction, back towards the flat. "God, I need to get you home, Davy," he said, his voice almost a growl.

"Yes, me too." David grinned. "But I thought we could call in at the baker's and see if they've got any crumpets left."

Much to their disappointment, the shop had sold out but when they got back to the flat Alan insisted on licking David's chin anyway. David dissolve into gales of laughter, which only subsided when Alan's mouth became more sensuous and moved to David's lips. They adjourned to the bedroom and supper was a bit late that night.

On the Wednesday afternoon, they took the bus to Chelsea and wandered along the King's Road window-shopping. It was David's first visit to this part of London and he loved the quirky shops and small boutiques. He saw a couple of shirts that he liked but flatly refused Alan's offer to buy them, instead making a note to return as soon as he started to earn some money.

It was getting dark when they found a small teashop in a side street and managed to grab the only spare table. The only down side was when a large elderly lady at the next table huffed with disapproval when she noticed them holding hands. On the other hand, their afternoon was made when they discovered that "tea and crumpets" was a menu item.

"We simply have to order them, Al."

"Naturally," Alan replied. "But I need to know what my prize is when you prove me right and get butter on your chin."

"Hmm. I'll have to think about that. I might be up for letting you lick somewhere else when we get home. Would that do?"

Unfortunately, their disapproving neighbour heard the comment and made another noise of disapproval, her "well, really" clearly audible.

David rolled his eyes at Alan who smiled back reassuringly. "Seriously?" he asked.

"Still an issue sometimes," Alan muttered. They ignored the woman, who continued to glare at them as they held hands in full view and chatted about their visit to Tris and Ian for New Year's Eve.

The crumpets were served under a small domed dish and were delicious – better, Alan said, than the ones his Auntie Mary used to buy. When David got butter down his chin, Alan had to be dissuaded from carrying out his threat to lick it off there and then. He was eventually deterred by another disapproving stare from their friend at the next table.

As the judgmental glare grew even more severe, David burst out laughing, whispering that if their fellow customer got any redder in the face she'd explode. Alan started to laugh too; each time one stopped, he caught the other's eye which would start him off again.

Eventually, the woman rose from the table, muttering "disgraceful behaviour" and "shouldn't be allowed" before heading for the door. "And a Happy New Year to you too, dear," David called out, which sent them both into yet another burst of laughter.

When they left the café, the temperature had dropped sharply since the last of the daylight had gone. They hurried across the road to get the bus back to Clapham. On the bus, they sat close and held hands again. "Does it bother you?" David asked. "When somebody like that gets huffy?"

Alan shook his head. "Not really – I suppose I've got used to it over the years. And, in fairness, it's comparatively rare. How did you feel?"

"I found it funny while it was happening, like we did years ago when adults disapproved of what we were up to. It seemed cool to be rebelling. But now, thinking about it, I realise that I'm not a little boy any more so I'm not so sure that I do find it funny. She didn't think I was being naughty, Al, she hated me. There was so much malice in that woman's face, especially when she was leaving – the look she gave me was poisonous. And why? Just because of who I love? I don't understand it."

"Neither do I, Davy. But we must be aware that it's going to happen every now and again, even in these so-called enlightened times. I thought you were incredibly brave in the teashop. You were very strong and I was proud of you."

"Thanks. I didn't feel brave – upset, I suppose, and pissed off with her."

"I hope it didn't spoil your crumpets."

"Certainly not. They were grand, weren't they?"

Alan laughed. "They were indeed. And what's more, you got butter on your chin, yet again proving my ninja memory."

That brought back memories of their shared enthusiasm for *Teenage Ninja Turtles*. "God, I haven't thought about them for years," David said. "We had great fun with them, didn't we?"

"Yeah, you definitely wanted to be Michelangelo, didn't you?"

"Oh always. And you were Leonardo."

"Yeah, the level-headed leader. A role made for me."

"Oh, sure. With that other guy as Rafael – what the hell was he called? Ginger?"

"That's him. Ginger McPherson. Left in the fourth form when his parents went back to Scotland. He was good fun, Ginger, if a bit of a hothead – which was why he was Raph."

They paused, grinning at this powerful memory of their early teenage years.

"Who was our Donnie? Can you remember?" Alan asked.

"Oh, yes – our techie. God, what was his name? I can picture him – the perfect nerd. Thin and a bit weedy, with black-framed glasses. Richie... Raymond... Ronnie! That's it. Ronnie Charlesworth."

"God, yes. I remember him now. He got the technology bug big time, didn't he?"

"And how. Last heard of in Silicon Valley."

"You're kidding."

David shook his head. "Nope. He got a first-class degree at Imperial in London and went on to do his masters at Stanford."

"Wow. That's seriously impressive for a Beckett's Hill boy."

They talked about their childhood for the rest of the journey home, and their confrontation in the teashop was quickly forgotten. Back in Clapham, the flat felt warm and comfortable. *Home*, David thought as he took off his coat. He realised that this was the first time he'd had that thought, and it brought a smile to his face.

Chapter 28

Alan

It was New Year's Eve, two days after their excursion to the King's Road, and Alan stood in the bedroom putting the final touches to his appearance for Tris and Ian's New Year's Eve dinner and party, plus an overnight stay. David was still in the shower, but there was no hurry – they didn't need to leave for another half an hour or so.

The dinner was due to start around eight-thirty and was an intimate affair with eight of Tris's closest friends including David's solicitor, Tom, and his partner Hugo. It promised to be interesting. Alan liked them both very much but he was particularly fond of Hugo, whose work as a graphic artist he loved so much that he'd persuaded his boss to commission several designs over the past few months. The dinner would be over by ten-thirty, after which other friends and acquaintances would start to arrive for the party to see in the New Year.

Alan wondered how the evening would go. He was acutely aware of how intimidating David had found previous social events involving his friends, and he very much wanted this one to be much better for his boyfriend. He didn't think he needed to worry too much; David had made huge strides since his low point at the time of his father's stroke. He was much more confident, surer of his place in London and in Alan's life.

Witness the scene in the café on Wednesday. Alan had been so proud of the way David had coped with the waves of hatred coming from that old woman at the next table and the fact that they'd been able to joke their way through it. It had been hilarious when David had delivered the *coup de grâce* with his feigned good wishes for the new year. Alan had been so proud of him.

The quiet week they'd spent together over Christmas had been blissful. In many ways, it represented the culmination of the process of reconnecting that had begun way back in February. The closeness they now enjoyed was at least on the same level, if not stronger, than it had been at the height of their adolescent friendship. All the growing apart that had gone on after Alan had left for London had been reversed; it was as if the six years of separation had never happened.

They seemed to know what the other was thinking and could laugh, joke, take the mickey out of each other as they always had done. Their affection for each other, always there, had deepened into love. That had all sorts of consequences: it meant that Alan couldn't keep his eyes off David when they were in the same room, that they instinctively needed to touch as often as possible, whether brushing shoulders, holding hands or stealing quick kisses. If they sat at the table to eat, their legs would become entwined as if drawn by a magnet. Watching TV or listening to music always meant snuggling together on the sofa, and bedtime meant making love and falling asleep in each other's arms.

Alan recognised that this closeness might not last when the novelty wore off or they were back facing the pressures of everyday life, but in the meantime he revelled in it. He'd not enjoyed this level of physical closeness with another human being since the death of his parents when he was nine. He felt as if every touch or hug was feeding his soul with warmth and comfort.

He smiled at his own reflection in the mirror. If this was what life was going to be like in future, then bring it on. He gave his hair one more pat, picked up his jacket and went towards the sitting room, leaving the bedroom space for David to get ready. He glanced at his watch. "Davy! It's nearly ten to. The cab'll be here in twenty minutes, love."

"Just finished." David emerged from the bathroom with a towel round his waist.

As always, the sight of his boyfriend like this took Alan's breath away and – also as usual – David spotted the fact and played on it. He gave a big grin, dropped the towel and sauntered sexily up the stairs to where Alan was on the landing with a huge grin plastered all over his face.

"Like what you see, big boy?"

Alan laughed. "You know fine well I do, sweetheart. But we'll be late if you don't get a move on and that'll get Tris all in a tizzy before the night's even begun."

David paused in the bedroom doorway. "I know. He's a great one for his timetables, isn't he? Bless him. I think he missed his vocation – he should have been a scheduler of some sort."

"Now get going or I'll have to smack that beautiful behind for you."

"Oh, promises, promises. You'd have to catch me first." David disappeared into the bedroom still chuckling. Alan was seriously tempted to follow through on his threat, but he knew exactly what would happen if he stepped over the threshold so he went into the sitting room to wait.

With exactly three minutes to go, David emerged from the bedroom and appeared in the door of the sitting room. He looked stunning in a dark-blue velvet jacket paired with black evening trousers, a white evening shirt and black-velvet bow tie. It was a classically elegant look, chosen with Simon's help and bought with the vouchers Alan had given him for Christmas.

"Wow, Davy. You look stunning."

David blushed to the roots of his hair but couldn't keep the smile off his face. "Do you like it? Si thought you would."

"I love it – you're certainly going to turn some heads tonight. I'm so proud of you."

"Thanks. I know I'm saying it and I shouldn't, but I'm proud of me too." He laughed. "I wonder what Mum would think of me tonight."

"She'd be chuffed to bits, Davy. We'll send her a picture later. Now come on, let's go and set about welcoming 2005 in style."

Chapter 29

David

The car they'd booked pulled up as they reached the front door and they sped off towards Kensington. They shuffled close together, and Alan took David's hand and intertwined their fingers. As they crossed the river, David couldn't help but remember that first journey to Tris's house. He snorted quietly to himself at the memory.

"What are you thinking about?" Alan asked.

"I was remembering Tris and Ian's party in July. Travelling like this reminded me of the cab ride that night. I was so bloody terrified."

"Why?"

"For a start, I was late. I'd been delayed by that pile-up on the M1, if you remember. That meant I hadn't got changed, so I was arriving at this incredibly posh house in my coach driver's uniform. It was also my first ride in a black cab."

Alan laughed gently. "You never told me that bit."

"No, it got lost in everything else that night. But yes, I was shitting myself – I missed two cabs because my wave was too tentative. When one did stop, I was so nervous I could hardly get the words of the address out."

"Oh, Davy. I'm sorry."

"It wasn't your fault, love. I was being stupid."

"And then you nearly ran away."

"I did. When I got out of the cab and looked round, the area seemed so incredibly posh. And Tris's house seemed huge. It wasn't for the likes of me."

"Poor love," Alan said.

David felt a squeeze of his hand, which made him smile. He could afford to do so now because he'd grown used to it all and he knew more about Alan's friends. "I'll never forget how kind Tris was that night and when I stayed with him in September. He's a lovely man."

"He is that, Davy. He is that."

"So, what happens tonight? Is there anything I should know?"

"I don't think so. We're having dinner first and there'll be eight of us – you, me, Tris, Ian, Tom, whom you know, and his partner Hugo. You'll love him. Then there's Greg and his partner – I think he's called Dai, so Welsh I assume. I've not met them. Greg works in Tris's chambers."

"Sounds fun."

"It is, usually. About fifty or so turn up after ten-thirty for the big party and it usually goes on until about three, but we can disappear upstairs whenever you've had enough."

"Will it mostly be the same crowd as at the party in the summer?"

"Pretty much, I think. One or two people might be missing – family obligations and so forth. And Ian tells me that the two who were bitchy about you that night got crossed off the list."

"Seriously?" David was touched that Tris had done that; after all, they hadn't been that bad calling him Alan's bit of rough. To be fair, he had looked a bit like rough trade when he'd first arrived in his uniform.

"Definitely. He was so cross about that business. It was so bloody rude. As Ian said, neither of them wanted friends like that."

When they arrived at the Kensington house, Ian greeted them warmly at the door and settled them into their room. "Front right as usual, Alan," he said. "Sorry Tris isn't here to do the honours – bit of a panic in the kitchen."

Alan laughed, knowing of old Tris's huge eye for detail when he hosted important events like this. He'd been the same at the betrothal do in the summer, checking and re-checking to ensure that everything was perfect. "In the kitchen? Nothing major, I hope?" Both Tris and Ian were excellent and enthusiastic cooks, but they'd booked outside caterers for tonight.

Ian smiled. "No, it was about the decorations for the trifle they're serving at supper – whether to use edible glitter or hundreds and thousands on the top. I said life was too short to argue but I was overruled *firmly*. So I was beating a retreat when I heard the doorbell. Now you two have arrived, I'm safe to vacate the kitchen area completely. Anyway, dump your bags and come down when you're ready. I've got some fizz on ice."

"That sounds seriously tempting." David smiled. "We'll be down in a minute."

Ian left them with a small wave.

"Poor Tris does get so stressed on these occasions," Alan

remarked fondly. "He likes everything to be perfect."

"Judging by the party in July, he's pretty good at it."

"Oh, he is. But I do worry that he gets so worn out running round that he doesn't actually enjoy the event when it happens."

An hour later, the eight dinner guests were enjoying their main course of *fillet mignon*, beautifully cooked and immaculately served. It was clear to everybody round the table that their host had started to relax now that everything was under way.

David had never tasted food like this before. The steak melted in his mouth and the vegetables were simple but delicious: mashed potatoes of exquisite lightness, mushrooms and green beans. He sipped his wine; he hadn't caught its name but he'd ask Tris later, because it was also fantastic.

Growing up, his mother had tried to interest the family in nicer ingredients and more adventurous cooking. She'd never met with much success, especially with his father whose ultimate condemnation was contained in the phrase "makes a change, Marion", which translated as "it was okay but please don't serve it again". Watching and occasionally helping his mother to cook some of her "posh nosh" recipes, they had always seemed complicated and elaborate and the result never quite worth all the effort. He'd learned to cook simple dishes like the beef casserole he'd made for Gavin and Ben, but always shied away from more complicated recipes.

After his marriage, he and Mona had always stuck to plain cooking like sausages or chops. Their meals tended to feature lots of chips, and fast food – pizza, burgers and fried chicken. The kids loved it, so it was easy.

He was brought back from his food-induced reverie when he realised that the guy sitting on his right, Tom's partner Hugo, had asked him a question. David asked him to repeat it, excusing himself by saying that he'd been carried away by the food.

"Exquisite, isn't it?" his companion asked. "I was saying that Tom mentioned that you'd recently moved down from Yorkshire. I wondered how you found London."

David laughed. "Big and scary, especially at first. But I'm starting to get used to it. Have you lived here long?"

Hugo nodded. "About five years. I spent a lot of time travelling abroad for my job but I settled here when Tom and I got together. I found it big and scary at first, too. What helped me was realising that there's no such thing as London. People say it's actually a collection of villages, and in many ways that's true. You'll probably never get to know Crouch End or Cockfosters ... but why should you? There's no need to worry about what happens in Palmers Green or Pinner. What matters is your bit of Clapham and wherever you work."

"That's fascinating. I never thought of it like that. I only ever thought of it as one huge place that I'd never truly get to know. What did you do when you were abroad?"

"I was a TV news cameraman."

"Wow, that sounds exciting," David replied. He felt over-awed again but pushed the thought away. This man was charming and good-looking too, with his blond hair and penetrating blue eyes. *No deceiving this one*, he thought.

"A little too exciting at times, I'm afraid, especially in the Middle East. When they started shooting the messengers, I decided it was time to give up. Besides, I started to lose faith in TV journalism. It became too much about the images and not enough about the story."

David wasn't sure that he understood but he dived in anyway. "You mean that the pictures keep getting more graphic? Because I've certainly noticed that."

"Yes, there is that, but it's also that the broadcaster gives prominence to items based on the quality of the pictures they've got, rather than the news value of the story."

"Right, I get you. So what do you do now?"

"What I always truly wanted to. I'm a graphic artist."

"Oh, of course! I remember Alan mentioned that when I first met Tom. You've done some work for Alan's firm, haven't you? He was singing your praises."

Hugo blushed slightly. "Yes, Alan's been very helpful, recommending me and so forth."

"He loves your work."

The blush grew stronger but Hugo smiled too, gratified by the praise. "Thanks. And you? A bus driver, I believe?"

"Yes, a bit mundane, I'm afraid. But it was my passion growing up and I still love the job."

"My grandad was a bus driver. He worked for a company called Midland Red in Banbury."

"Good Lord, really?"

"Yes. He was passionate about it, a bit like you, David. He used to love driving round the villages, chatting to his regulars."

"That sounds idyllic. I had some regulars in Yorkshire,

but people were too grumpy there to chat much."

Hugo laughed. "Most people around Banbury were always very cheerful, except possibly my father. He was – is – so sniffy about it. He always hated that grandad was 'on the buses', as he put it. He's such a bloody snob."

"Driving professionally isn't always easy."

"You're telling me. I did a spell as a part-time delivery driver a few years ago. I've never been so exhausted at the end of a day. You make thousands of split-second decisions during every shift – and if you're driving a bus, you're responsible for the passengers as well. Not to mention all the customer relations stuff."

David laughed. "You're not kidding. That can be the toughest bit."

"I'm sure. You need so many skills to make a good job of it. Good luck!"

"Thanks, I'm sure I'll need it, being a stranger round here and all."

"Well, remember what I said. Remember all the villages and you'll find it easier to get your bearings. How long have you and Alan been together?"

"As in living together, since September. But we've been friends since we were nine. What about you and Tom?"

"We met at prep school, so we must have been about seven, I suppose. We became lovers at the age of sixteen, but then I got this job as a news cameraman so I was away for long periods. Poor old Tom, it drove him bonkers. We broke up for a while." Hugo grimaced. "That was hell."

"Alan and I were apart for six years when he came to London. That's when I got married and had a couple of kids."

"Ah, the mist begins to clear. Are you Tom's client in an access-cum-divorce case?"

David nodded.

"I get it now. Tom is careful only to talk generalities to me – no names, no pack drill. I knew of your case but not the names. How's it going?"

"It's difficult. We have a meeting in a few days. I'll know more after that."

"Tom said he'd be away for a couple of nights next week."

"He's been very kind, Hugo. I'm so grateful to him."

"Yes, he is – kind, I mean. But don't be deceived, David. There's a good deal of steel under that cuddly exterior. He'll look after you, I'm sure. Once he gets the bit between his teeth, he's away – as I'm reminded every time I forget to pick up my wet towels in the bathroom."

David laughed. "That bad, eh? I shall have to remember to mind my Ps and Qs. But thanks for telling me. I've got every confidence in him, given what I've seen so far."

The arrival of pudding punctuated their conversation naturally, after which Hugo got involved in an intense discussion with Tris and Tom. David sat back and watched the proceedings for a while, reflecting on how lucky he was to have met all these lovely guys and how different it was from everything he'd been used to. He might not be the sharpest knife in the drawer, but that didn't seem to matter; they'd made him feel welcome and so much a part of their small family.

The next thing he noticed was a pair of hands caressing his shoulders and Alan's voice in his ears. "You okay?"

"More than, Al. That was a fabulous dinner, wasn't it?"

"Certainly was. That steak. Amazing. You seemed to be having a good chinwag with Hugo."

"Yes, he's lovely. His grandad was a bus driver. He was telling me how good Tom is."

Alan laughed. "Yeah, well I think our Hugo might be a tiny bit biased on that subject."

"I can see why he might be," David replied. "But on the other hand, he probably knows him better than anyone."

"The party's getting underway downstairs. We should say hi to Simon and Peter. Dance with me later?"

"I'll see if I have a place on my card, Mr Foreshaw."

"Why, thank you kindly, Mr Edgeley," Alan replied in a faux-posh accent. Reverting to his own voice, he added, "I knew letting you watch a rerun of *Pride and Prejudice* over Christmas was a bad idea."

"Cheeky sod! It's you that's got the crush on Colin Firth."

"Point, I suppose. But I did hear all your little whimpers every time Mr Bingley came on screen."

David's face assumed a dreamy expression and he sighed gently. "Ah, yes. Dear Crispin – God, he was so good-looking in that show."

"I'll give you that. Very pretty, but you must admit that his character's a bit of a wimp."

"I'll admit no such thing. Besides, Mr D'Arcy's far too stroppy – all those black moods and faces like thunder. If being surly and looking bored all the time is your thing, I shall have to see what I can do to oblige." He drew his forehead into a frown, half-closed his eyes and pouted his lips. "There. How's that?"

Alan started to laugh. "You look about as butch as

gerbil."

David huffed, "Well, if you think I'm jumping into a lake for you after that remark, you've got another think coming."

"What's this about jumping into lakes?" David recognised Simon's voice and went over to give him a hug.

"Nobody's jumping anywhere," David assured him. "We were talking about the men in *Pride and Prejudice*. We've been watching it the last couple of nights. Alan was just comparing me to Colin Firth, weren't you, *dear*?"

Alan also hugged Simon, before answering. "Yes. Unfavourably."

Simon assumed a shocked expression. "What's this? Dissent between the Edgeley-Foreshaws? I sense juicy gossip. Spill."

"No dissent, Si. Put your scandal notebook away. We were only comparing notes on our favourite guys in the series."

Simon grinned. "No contest, darlings. Has to be the guy who played Mr Wickham. Adrian somebody..."

"Lukis," David supplied.

"That's the one. Dark and a bit menacing but could really turn on the charm when he wanted to. I love a good villain."

Alan laughed. "Is that how you see Peter? As a good baddie?"

"No, silly. He's a big black Labrador – all soft and cuddly. And loyal. And friendly. Oh, and well endow—"

"Simon." They turned to welcome Peter who was returning with two glasses of champagne. "TMI, sweetie."

Simon giggled. "Oh? Okay."

Peter bent and kissed him on the top of the head. "Yes, you promised. Nothing too risqué, remember? Especially about the size of people's equipment."

Simon beamed up at his partner. "What's my reward, then?"

Peter looked at Alan and rolled his eyes. "You'll find out in heaven."

"Is that Heaven the disco or heaven the religious construct?"

Peter laughed. "Actually, I was thinking of heaven in my arms. You said this morning..."

Alan and David interrupted him, exclaiming "TMI" in chorus. Simon started to laugh, despite having a mouthful of champagne, prompting much coughing and spluttering. Eventually order was restored.

Tris, ever the concerned host, came over, looking worried. "Everything okay?" he asked.

"Fine, Tris," Alan replied. "No problem. It turns out that inhaling champagne, even the finest, is not a good idea. Simon laughed at the wrong moment."

"Not an unusual occurrence, I might add," Peter added.

Simon gave him another pretend glare. "I'll have you know that I work hard on my sense of humour. It's what has kept me sane all these years."

"Even if it drives the rest of us mad," Alan replied with a grin.

"He's right, though," Tris said. "They do say that if you can laugh at yourself, it'll make you happier and healthier."

"That's me," Simon responded brightly. "I find myself hilarious."

"And with good reason," replied Peter, putting his arm

round his boyfriend's waist and giving him a squeeze. "You certainly brighten my life, sweetheart." He kissed Simon on the temple, prompting a chorus of "Aahs" from his three companions. "Especially this week."

"Oh, God, yes," Alan intervened, suddenly remembering the trauma he and Simon had endured over Peter's brother and the tsunami. "How are they?"

Peter sighed. "Okay, I think. They got back home yesterday evening. I spoke to my brother on the phone last night and he said he was fine, though he certainly didn't sound it."

"I'm not surprised," Tris said. "It must have been hell. The sheer speed of events and the shock of it all..."

"I know," Peter replied. "But at least they survived and are home. They can recover in peace, hopefully."

Everybody was quiet for a moment until Alan broke the silence. "So, Tris, we were just discussing our favourite men in *Pride and Prejudice*. Who's yours?"

"Oh, Larry Olivier, undoubtedly," he replied, laughing. "That 1940 film isn't half bad, and he was so handsome."

That took the four of them off into a discussion about 1940s' film stars. David tuned out but stood there watching and smiling. The four of them were probably his favourite people in the world, together with Ian who was on the other side of the room chatting to Tom and Hugo.

They'd been so unfailingly good to him over the last few months. Tris had been kindness itself that first Sunday night in London and ever since, his actions closely mirrored by Ian. Simon and Peter had been so supportive too. He glanced across at Simon, who was giggling again at a remark of Peter's. His sense of humour made him terrific fun but also disguised a fiercely loyal man who had taken David to his heart and been his rock on more than one occasion. He'd been so lucky, finding them.

Lastly, there was the man standing next to him, shoulder pressing into his. David felt the warmth of Alan's hand holding his and his thumb moving backwards and forwards, gently caressing and calming his nerves. Talk about falling on your feet.

He was woken from his reverie by Alan who whispered in his ear, "Come on, it's nearly half-eleven. Let's dance."

David allowed himself to be led downstairs to the spacious front room they'd cleared for dancing. The room was busy enough without being too crowded, and they quickly found a space on the floor and slipped into each other's arms.

"Having a good time?" Alan asked as they swayed together.

"It's been great, Al. I was just thinking, upstairs, how lucky I've been – not only meeting you again but having such an awesome bunch of friends. They've been grand."

"That's at least partly down to you, Davy. They love you because you're you. I was so proud of you tonight, chatting away – especially Hugo, whom you've never met before. Tris says he doesn't always relate well to strangers."

"Pfft. Nowt special about me, lad," David replied with a grin on his face. "I like people, that's all. I thought he was a lovely guy. I really liked talking to him – and Tom's great too."

"Whatever. I happen to think there is something special about you, Davy. And I bless the day I got on your bus last February."

"So do I, Al. So do I."

They were interrupted by their host, clapping his hands. "Nearly time, guys – grab yourselves a glass and we can offer a bit of a view of the firework display from the balcony or you can watch them on the TV. Anyway, five minutes to go."

"Balcony?" asked Alan.

"Definitely." They grabbed glasses of champagne and moved outside into the fresh air. The sharp cold of the winter night caught them by surprise but they stood together and drew warmth from each other. After a few moments the countdown began, followed by the chimes of Big Ben sounding on the thin night air across from Westminster and echoing from the TV inside the house. As midnight struck, David found himself in Alan's arms again. "Happy New Year, Davy."

"Happy New Year, Al. And thanks for everything."

Across the square to the south east, the first of the fireworks lit the sky from the Thames on and around the London Eye. David smiled to himself but wasn't much bothered about the pyrotechnics. He was much more interested in kissing the man in his arms and making sure they started 2005 as they meant to go on: loving one another.

After a few moments, David felt a tap on his shoulder. He broke the kiss with Alan to be greeted by a smiling Tris. "Don't I get a New Year kiss as well?"

"Not as spectacular as that, I hope," remarked Ian, who was standing slightly to one side. "I might get jealous."

Chapter 30

Alan

Alan shivered as he and David stood in the taxi queue at Leeds station. It was the Saturday after New Year and they'd travelled north to be ready for Tuesday's meeting.

It wasn't raining, but the sky was gloomy and there was a keen easterly wind blowing. One that "went right through you and buttoned up on t'other side", as his Auntie Mary would have said.

"Jesus, it's cold," David remarked, standing close and trying to use Alan's body as a shield against the breeze that penetrated their shelter as if it wasn't there. "I'd almost forgotten how cold it can get up here."

"London wasn't exactly balmy this morning."

"True, but it feels much worse here."

"Never mind, we'll soon be home. Hopefully Hilda's put the heating on for us. We can light the fire too and warm up with a nice cuppa."

"Sounds great."

At that point two cabs drew up together and took the people in front of them, moving them to the head of the queue. Another long gap followed with no sign of a vehicle.

"There's a match at Elland Road today, so I expect they're all stuck in traffic," David remarked, remembering Saturday afternoon chaos during the football season from his days on the Leeds run from Sedgethwaite.

"Does it still get busy, despite the relegation?"

"Oh, I think so. The supporters have been very loyal even though the team's in a lower division. It's not the results that'll sink them, but the debts."

"Yeah, I read that. They're in bad way, aren't they?"

"Certainly are – they had to sell the ground last autumn."

Their conversation about the woes of Leeds United FC following their relegation from the Premier League was cut short by the arrival of a cab. "Thank God for that," Alan muttered as they piled into the warmth of the vehicle and gave their address to the driver.

It was starting to get dark by the time they arrived in Edward Street. There was a lamp on in the hall, which was a sign that their neighbour had been in. The heating was up to temperature and there was a note in the kitchen, next to a small package.

"Crumpets! Fantastic," David said, picking up the note. "She says that she remembered these were our favourites. There's bread, butter, milk and eggs in the fridge, she says, plus some bacon. Oh, bless her!"

"That's so kind. We must call in before we go and thank her," Alan replied. "We can take her some chocolates. Now, do you want to unpack or light the fire?"

"Neither," David replied firmly. "At least not until we've had that cup of tea."

"Good point. I'll go and put the kettle on."

A couple of hours later, they were in the front room, toasting their toes and replete after eating their crumpets. There'd been more laughter over butter leaking out, and David had insisted on cleaning Alan's chin with his tongue rather than a napkin, This had inevitably led to a fairly heavy make-out session on the sofa, which was heading into something more when they were interrupted by David's phone. He was tempted to ignore it, but then took a quick look at the screen. "Sorry, got to take this," he muttered. "It's Mum."

"Okay," Alan replied with a grin. "Talk about cock blocker."

David grinned at him as he pressed the button to accept the call. "Hi, Mum. How are you doing?"

Alan knew he ought to move and give David some space but he was too comfortable. Besides, when he did try to shift to give his boyfriend a little more room on the sofa, David held him in place. Alan was not close enough to hear the other end of the conversation. It started off conventionally enough, with David saying that they'd arrived a couple of hours ago, and yes, Hilda had put the heating on for them. No, they had no plans for tomorrow and yes, they would be free to go round for a meal.

David's eyebrows shot up and he looked at Alan wide-eyed and anxious. Alan heard him ask what his dad would say and saw David's face change in front of his eyes as his mother spoke at length. David chipped in with an occasional "yes", "well, obviously" or "no, quite".

Eventually the conversation ended with "Al too?" and, "Okay, then, see you tomorrow about one." David ended the call. He put his phone down carefully and looked up at Alan, his eyes full of uncertainty. "As you might have gathered, we're going to Mum and Dad's for Sunday lunch."

Alan felt his stomach drop with nerves. "Er ... wow. Um great, I think."

"It'll be okay, Al. Dad's changed his mind at last. Apparently, Brian Spensley went round to see him this morning and they had a long talk."

"Well I'll go the foot of our stairs, as Auntie Mary would have said. What prompted that, do you think?"

David shrugged. "I've no idea. I mean, Brian's pushing hard for a settlement – hence this meeting on Tuesday – so maybe he sees my parents as part of that."

Alan moved across and hugged David. "Doesn't matter really. The point is, your dad's changed his mind. That's really great, Davy. I'm so pleased for you."

"It's certainly a turn up for the book. I'm staggered, quite honestly. It's completely out of the blue. Last time I spoke to Mum on New Year's Day, Dad still wasn't having any."

Alan gulped. He was pleased – chuffed to bits, in fact – but he was also nervous. He didn't want to butt in where he wasn't wanted, and he didn't think he could cope with being no more than tolerated for David's sake. "There's no need to take me. I heard you ask, but I can easily stay here and work on the house."

David looked at him with wide eyes, clearly surprised by the idea that Alan might not be welcome. He shook his head. "No way, Al. Mum was most insistent that you should come as well. Besides, I wouldn't go if you weren't welcome. You're family now, more than ever."

"Oh," Alan shrugged. "Okay." He couldn't help his reaction to this sudden change in their lives. He'd known David's family almost the whole of his time in Sedgethwaite and had been showered with affection by them until he went to London. Being with the Edgeleys had helped him enormously during his teenage years when life with his rather austere aunt had threatened to get on top of him.

He was suddenly hit by the realisation of how much he owed them. And how had he repaid them? By buggering off to London and not getting in touch for six years. And when he had come back, what had he done? Disrupted everything, destroyed their son's marriage and driven a massive wedge between David's parents and their two grandsons.

And now they planned to welcome him back into the house as a member of the family and feed him? Mentally, he snorted to himself. If he were them, the only thing they'd be feeding him was hemlock laced with cyanide with an arsenic topping.

He became aware that David was watching him, his eyes full of concern. "I can almost hear your brain working. You're thinking that they blame you for what's happened, aren't you?"

Alan nodded. "When you think about it, how can they not?"

"Easily, Al. Mum and Jen certainly knew I wasn't very happy at the beginning of last year, and neither of them wanted me to marry Mona in the first place. There's no way they'd blame you for my marriage falling apart."

"But what about the kids? Surely..."

"Surely nothing, Alan Foreshaw. The problem with us

seeing the kids is down to Mona. Nobody else – with the possible exception of her bloody mother. So don't you go thinking that you'll be any less welcome in the Edgeley household tomorrow than you were six and more years ago."

David's vehemence made Alan smile. "You're a proper spitfire when you get going, Davy."

"Well, you're a silly bugger sometimes, always expecting people to think the worst of you."

Alan couldn't help laughing. "All right. I surrender. I'm coming with you tomorrow. And I promise not to expect the worst."

Sunday lunchtime arrived and Alan found himself sitting in a cab on the way across town to David's parents, regretting his agreement to come. He realised how empty his promise about not fearing the worst had been, because that was exactly what he was doing.

He accepted the logic of David's arguments but that did not stop him from feeling guilty about crashing back into these people's lives after a gap of nearly seven years. As they pulled up outside, he felt David's hand slip into his.

"You'll be fine, Al. Trust me."

Alan paid the driver and joined David on the pavement before heading up the short flight of steps to the front door of the Edgeley family home. He swallowed hard as the door opened to reveal David's mother Marion smiling broadly. As they approached, she flung her arms open wide, gathering them both into hugs and kissing them on the cheek. "My two favourite boys. Welcome home, darlings."

David grinned. "Thanks, Mum. Good to see you."

"Yes, it *is* good to see you," echoed Alan, feeling better as the warmth of the welcome drained the tension away.

Marion ushered them both inside through to the large kitchen at the back of the house. Once there, she turned to Alan and looked him up and down. He began to feel nervous again under her appraisal, but then she gave him a broad smile. "So, Alan Foreshaw, eh? It's long time, love. More handsome than ever, I see."

Alan smiled back. "Aye, Marion. It's good to see you – it's been too long. And you're looking as beautiful than ever."

Marion scoffed. "I doubt that. What with this one worrying me to death and an obstinate husband, it's a miracle I've any hair left."

"There's no need to worry about me, I'm a good boy," David interrupted with a grin.

His mother scoffed again. "You might have been a good boy, David lad, but that never stopped me worrying about you. Specially now, when you're all those miles away amongst millions of southerners."

"Oh, that's all right. He's got me to look after him," Alan said reassuringly.

"Yes, exactly," Marion replied tartly. "And I well remember the mischief you two got up to when you were younger. You always egged each other on and I bet you still do."

"No, no, Mum," David replied. "We're the men on the Clapham Omnibus nowadays. Models of respectability."

"And I'm the Duchess of Cornwall."

"Oh, excuse me, Your Royal Highness," David responded using his poshest voice. "I had no idea. Pardon me for being so rude."

Marion reached out and cuffed the back of his head. "Get on with you," she said. "Now go and fetch your father. He's in that shed of his, pottering as usual. Tell him lunch is in half an hour."

"Right you are, Ma'am. I'm on my way." David's tone stayed flippant but Alan noticed the tension in his body. David had confessed in the cab how nervous he was about this reunion with his father and now the moment had come. As he reached the back door, he turned back and caught Alan's eye. Alan winked at him and gave him a look of reassurance.

"And don't stay there nattering all afternoon," Marion called after him.

As soon as David was out of the back door, Marion turned to Alan. "How is he, Alan? Is he really all right? I was so worried about him when he was here after George's stroke."

Alan smiled. "So was I, love. The poor lad got himself into such a state. But he's much better now – he's settling down in London, I think, and he's got the job starting next month. If we can sort Mona and the boys out this week, so much the better."

"And you? Are you okay with all of this – the boys and all?"

"I'm fine. More than fine." He suddenly remembered how easy David's mum was to talk to; she always had been. It wasn't just that she was sympathetic, she also made you trust her; you could be safe in the knowledge that nothing you said would shock her or prompt her to be judgemental. "Honestly, meeting up again with David last year was the best thing that could have happened. It made me realise what I'd been missing since I went down to London."

She nodded. "I understand. I can't say that I was exactly pleased about the marriage breaking up, but I think David will be the happier for it despite worrying about the boys. I don't know whether he told you, but I expected him to come to London with you six years ago. I was a bit disappointed when he didn't."

Alan looked up in surprise. "He didn't mention that. Mind if I ask why?"

Marion smiled. "Because I always thought that there was more to David than he realised himself. I thought he needed to get out of Sedgethwaite and lift his sights beyond driving buses."

Alan nodded. "I can understand that. I always thought he was brighter than me at school, but he would never have it. He always said he was thick. Don't know why."

"Simple, Alan. He's his father's son. Once he gets an idea into his head, it's almost impossible to shift him. George also under-rated himself when he was younger. He wouldn't accept promotion from the shop floor when he was first offered it." She paused, before adding with a twinkle in her eye, "I soon changed his mind."

Alan suddenly recalled part of the conversation he'd overheard between Hugo and David on New Year's Eve. "I understand your concerns, Marion. But equally David doing a skilled and responsible job that he loves, and he does it extremely well. That counts for a lot. There are millions of people who never ever get to do that.”

Her face registered surprise and she did not respond immediately. He worried for a moment that he'd overstepped the mark but then a smile spread over her face. “I'd never thought of it like that, Alan. Thank you.” She glanced up at the clock. “Look at me blathering on. I must get the Yorkshire puddings on – Jen and her brood will be here in a minute.”

“Right you are.”

At that moment, the back door opened and David and his father came into the kitchen. Alan noticed that David looked a little pale, but both he and his father were smiling. Alan raised an interrogatory eyebrow and received a small nod in return. He breathed a sigh of relief, and moved to greet David's father.

Chapter 31

David

David remembered only too well the walk from the kitchen down the garden to his Dad's shed. When he was a boy, and in trouble for some sin or other, it seemed long and nerve-wracking, after he'd been summoned for a "discussion". It certainly felt that way this Sunday morning, although the cold and damp weather ruled out any thought of dawdling to put off the evil moment.

In those days, the shed had smelt of pipe smoke with an undertone of methylated spirits from the small camping stove on which his dad made himself cups of tea. In the last few years, he had given up smoking his pipe and had run a power line out there, so the spirit stove had been replaced by a kettle. The shed had somehow never seemed the same again to David.

It was a place of order, with tools for both DIY and gardening all immaculately clean and beautifully arranged. There was a workbench in one corner and a couple of old desk chairs in another next to the kettle. There was now an electric heater as well; the place felt very cosy when David opened the door and walked in.

He was still unsure how he should open the conversation, but in the end decided to behave as if there'd been no break in their relationship. "Hi, Dad. Mum said you wanted a chat."

"David. Aye, lad. Come in. Good to see you. Take a seat. Do you want a brew?"

"I'll be right, Dad, thanks. Not long till dinner, Mum said."

"Oh, okay. How are you doing?"

"Good, thanks. Enjoying life in London."

"Got a job yet?"

"Aye. Starting next month. Coaches, again. Express, like I was doing here before I left."

"Good. You enjoyed the long runs, didn't you?"

"I did, yes. This'll be mainly to Bournemouth."

"Oh, seaside. Sounds fun. It'll be busy in the season, like."

"Expect so. And you, Dad? How are you doing now?"

"Fine, fine. I get tired a bit more but otherwise the same as ever."

"That's good. I was worried in case you had – you know, problems."

His father shook his head. "Not so far."

"Good. So what did you want to say?"

"Aye, well. I wanted to say that ... um ... about your marriage. That ... er, I've been thinking about it and what you said that night about not living a lie. And I understand a bit more."

"Mum said that Brian had been to see you."

"Brian Spensley? Aye, he did. He said that Mona had

been giving you a hard time, but he'd listened to you and understood. He wanted me to know." His father paused. "And he reasoned if he could do that as her father, I might be able to do it as well."

David couldn't help a wry smile to himself. He bet that went down like a lead balloon, a comparative stranger telling his dad what he should think. "And you thought he had a point?"

"Happen he did. But I wanted to say that I didn't mind about Alan being gay and all. That wasn't the point. I was worried that you were dumping your wife and the kids on a whim. And, like I said that Saturday, breaking promises you'd freely given even though they'd possibly been given as a disguise at the time. I hated the thought of you just walking out."

"I didn't marry Mona as a disguise, Dad. I know people do that but I didn't. I loved her, and really intended to make a go of it. I might have done if Alan hadn't got on my bus that day."

"I knew you two were always close. It never occurred to me that it was that close."

"Nor to me, Dad. But part of me realised it that morning and the feeling got stronger and stronger. Even then, I didn't know what to do, especially about the boys. I was very aware of all the responsibility, believe me. A few days later, the London job came up and it seemed like fate was knocking at the door."

"It must have done. I can see that."

"But I had no plan to leave, Dad. I thought I'd probably have to at some point, but I was still trying to work out what to do, trying to find the words to tell Mona, to be honest with her. Then Douggie Thorpe spotted me that Friday night and that was it." David sighed. "The rest you know. She threw me out the next night. Can't say as I blame her. And I suppose in some ways she did me a favour."

"How so?"

"Forced me into a decision. It's still a mess, I know, but at least there's some sort of plan if we can get Mona to agree on Tuesday."

"Oh?"

"Aye. We're proposing weekend visits once every four weeks, when the boys would stay with us at Edward Street. I'd support them financially, obviously."

"Fine. Well, you know your mother and I will help with the boys if Mona'll let us. Jen too, I'm sure."

"Thanks, Dad. I'm sure she will, once we can settle down. The boys love you both so much."

"Good. They're grand little lads." There was a pause, in which David wondered whether anything else needed to be said, then his father rose from his chair. "Well, nearly dinner time. We'd better get ourselves inside, otherwise there'll be trouble. And I need to say hello to that lad of yours – must be nigh on seven years since I saw him last."

The Edgeley family had never been big huggers but, rather to David's surprise, he found himself in an awkward sideways hug with his father, who patted him on the shoulder. "Good to see you, David, lad. I'm glad you're back."

They got back to the Edward Street house shortly before five after a large, filling and raucous family lunch. David felt tired after all the tension earlier in the day about the prospect of the reunion with his father, but he felt warm and happy inside in a way he hadn't since the events of that August Saturday night.

Being back at the heart of his family took away a dull ache that, alongside missing the boys, had underpinned his life for the last four months. The way they had received Alan had pleased him most; he'd been welcomed as if he'd never been away. From his father's handshake to his mother's farewell as they left, his parents and sister had made it clear that Alan was now very much part of the family. Alan's presence had been one aspect of the day that required no comment or special accommodation. In fact, now he thought about it, Alan had fitted in rather better than Mona ever had, which was probably why she had tried to avoid Edgeley family lunches whenever she could.

As they shut the front door behind them, David moved into his boyfriend's arms. "Thanks, Davy and well done," Alan whispered into his ear.

David laughed, "What are you thanking me for?"

"Being you and looking out for me today."

"I did keep an eye on everything, true, but there was no need. Once I'd had the chat with Dad in his shed, I knew everything would be okay."

"Was it all right?"

David nodded and smiled. "Yes, so like Dad. A bit abrupt and he never knows what to say about personal stuff. He's been like that ever since I can remember. But he's solid for us now, Al. And if we can get the access sorted, he and Mum are on board to help however they can."

"That's fantastic, Davy. I'm so pleased."

"Me too. It's a better outcome than I could have hoped for." He kissed Alan on the end of his nose. "Helped of course by the awesomeness of my boyfriend."

"Of course. Goes without saying."

"Nice to be on our own again, though. I could hardly keep my hands to myself and I kept wanting to touch you all through lunch. It was really tough, you being at the other end of the table."

"Well, you can touch me all you want now," Alan replied, waggling his eyebrows. "I think I might need a lie down after all that socialising this afternoon."

"That sounds like a seriously good idea, Mr Foreshaw."

"So glad you agree, Mr Edgeley. After you."

"No, no, I insist. After you."

Alan started to laugh at David's faux-refined accent. "Just get up the bloody stairs, Edgeley."

David grinned, then raced up to their bedroom, undoing his shirt as he went. By the time Alan reached the doorway, David was bare-chested and reaching for the button on his trousers, quickly unfastening them and letting them pool at his feet. His excitement was clearly visible in the tight white briefs he was wearing. Alan couldn't help but stare and lick his lips at the thought playing with the beautiful body in front of him.

David's voice broke his trance. "Snap to it, Foreshaw. Clothes off, boy."

Alan quickly complied, shivering slightly as the cool air in the bedroom hit his skin. He followed David under the covers and they moved together, holding each other close against the chill of the sheets.

Legs entwined, they started to kiss. David didn't think he could ever get enough of these early stages of their love-making when he could revel in the feeling of being held in Alan's arms. He felt safe and calm and loved in those moments; if they were apart for any reason, it was these sensations he craved, much more than the delights of penetration and climax. He closed his eyes and relaxed into Alan's embrace as they rolled slightly so that Alan was on top. "Love you so much, Al."

"Hmmm," came the reply. "Love you too, Davy."

The undulations morphed into thrusts as the two felt their erections brush against each other and their kisses became more passionate. "God, I love this," David whispered. "The feel of you against me. So wonderful, Al."

Alan smiled down at him. "Me too, sweetheart. Do you want to come like this?"

"Mmm. Love to."

Alan reached across to the bedside table for the lube, rubbing it between his palms to take the chill off. He reached between them and took hold of both their cocks, at the same time renewing the thrusts of his hips.

"Fuck, Al. That's good. So good."

"That's it, baby. Come for me. Love you so much."

Their mouths met in a bruising kiss before David cried out as his climax dominated his senses. Moments later, he felt Alan's release shooting between them, mixing with his own. They lay there for a few moments, enjoying another lazy kiss. After a moment or two, Alan rolled off and they lay side by side, recovering their breath.

"Thanks, Al. That was terrific."

Alan turned his head towards David and grinned. "It was, wasn't it? Not sure it's terribly good for the digestion after all that roast beef and Yorkshire Pudding, but what's a few burps between friends?" He hopped out of bed. "Back in a trice."

He disappeared into the bathroom and came back with a warm, damp facecloth, which he used to clean David up. Afterwards he quickly got back into bed. "It's still chilly. We'd better get this central heating checked over soon."

David laughed. "Another task for the list." He took Alan back into his arms and kissed his nose. "I'll soon warm you up again."

They snuggled together under the blankets, Alan's head resting on David's chest. The sound of Alan's breathing quickly slowed, a sure sign that he'd fallen asleep. David stayed awake for a while longer, replaying the day's events in his mind. His chat with his dad had cheered him immensely. Until he'd come face to face with him in his shed, David hadn't quite realised how much he'd missed his father. It had been slightly awkward but that was nothing new – it was how they were.

And then there was this, now. Simply lying there and holding somebody he loved felt glorious. He smiled, closed his eyes, and fell quickly into a contented doze.

Chapter 32

Alan

Even though the lunch with David's parents had gone well and had been an enjoyable occasion, Alan recognised that the nervous tension before and during the day had taken its toll on both of them. He was grateful that they had twenty-four hours' rest before the session with the lawyers the following morning.

They spent the morning in bed, dozing and making love. Hunger had eventually driven them to get up and Alan nipped down to the corner shop to get the ingredients for an all-day breakfast. Afterwards they sat down and went over the final draft of the opening statement that David would make the following morning, setting out his case for an agreement with Mona. They'd been e-mailing it backwards and forwards with Tom over the previous few days as the lawyers laid the ground for the meeting.

Tom had explained that it was important to be prepared. "Lawyers don't like surprises, so we try to ensure that we know what's going to happen in advance – as much as anyone ever can."

He was travelling north that evening and staying overnight in central Leeds. Alan and David had arranged to meet him at the station and join him for a late dinner to go over the papers one final time. As they drove into Leeds, Alan noticed that David was tensing up again. It was inevitable, he supposed; there was a such a lot riding on the meeting and settling the issue of David's marriage was fundamental to sorting out their own futures.

During the evening, Tom repeated that that he was more than happy with the draft that Alan and David had worked on. David seemed to relax after that; Tom's praise was clearly designed to make him feel confident in what he had to say and the plan seemed to succeed. Nevertheless, Alan was still worried about how the meeting might turn out. He knew that David was as well, whilst Tom also confessed to some nerves. "I can't put my finger on the reason," he explained. "And the work with our opposite numbers has been remarkably smooth. But I've got a gut feeling."

This put Alan on the alert and he watched David's reactions carefully in case he got upset. To his relief, everything seemed okay – at least on the surface. After dinner, they travelled home to Edward Street and fell straight into bed, but neither of them slept well.

David was restless. Every time Alan was about to drop off, he was jerked awake by his boyfriend moving his legs or turning over. Eventually, about three, Alan got up, made them a hot drink and tried to get David to talk about what was worrying him.

It turned out that David was worried about having to step outside his comfort zone once again. He was totally new to the world of lawyers and how they worked. He liked Tom and was reassured by his quiet competence, but one of the things he feared most was being in the presence of Mona's lawyers. He was fearful of what might be said about his sexuality and his and Alan's relationship.

There was also the prospect of being in the same room as his wife for the first time in four months. Alan could well understand that the memory of the shouting match with Mona in the kitchen on that Saturday night still was still raw; it was inevitable that David should now feel panicky about seeing her again.

"All these things are going round and round in my head. Every time I close my eyes, my mind starts to zip from one thing to the other," he explained.

The combination of a hot drink and talking about his fears seemed to settle him; that – plus some reassuring cuddles – eventually enabled them both to get at least a couple of hours' sleep.

Tuesday morning found them sitting in the waiting room of the ultra-modern and rather swish offices of Mona's solicitors in Leeds city centre. They sat close, thighs pressed together. Alan was holding David's hand, and trying to keep them both calm. It was another wet day, though the penetrating cold of Saturday had gone. Nevertheless, Alan felt David shiver a little.

David released Alan's hand as the receptionist came into the room with some coffee for them. "Mrs Enderby and her parents have just arrived," she informed them. "We shouldn't keep you long now."

"Thanks," David said, his voice unsteady with nerves.

Alan took hold of his hand again and squeezed gently. "You okay?"

David nodded. "I will be once we get going. It's the waiting I find difficult."

Alan grinned at him. "You and me both, sweetheart."

"You know Cheryl's not going to want you in the room, don't you?"

"'Course. And you don't want her there either, so we'll all be equally unhappy."

At that moment, Tom came bustling in. "Sorry I'm a bit late. Slight panic back at the ranch. I've spoken to my opposite number and I think we're ready to start."

They swallowed the rest of their coffee and stood up. "Right," said David. "Let's go."

Tom gestured for them to go first. "Don't forget, try to stay calm and don't let them rile you too much."

Alan kept his hand in the small of David's back as they went along the corridor. They walked into a large room with floor to ceiling windows along one side. In the middle, a large steel-framed meeting table with a high-gloss, dark-wood surface was surrounded by more than a dozen padded leather swivel armchairs.

They were greeted by a florid, ginger-haired man in his early thirties. He shook hands with them both and introduced himself as Kieran Murray, Mona's solicitor. Alan looked past him into the room. On the window side furthest from the door, Mona was flanked by her mother and father. It was more than seven years since he'd seen her but she did not look all that different – same build and similar figure. He could not remember ever having seen

Cheryl Spensley before, but he was struck by the physical resemblance between mother and daughter. They could almost have been sisters as they sat there wearing similar outfits and with identical expressions on their faces: tight-lipped, deliberately keeping their eyes on the table in front of them. It was obvious that they were both under instructions to stay quiet, at least until the meeting was under way.

Tom guided David and Alan to the opposite side of the table and they sat down opposite the Spensleys. There was a moment's silence while Tom retrieved his papers from his briefcase.

Setting a New Course

Chapter 33

David

The meeting room was very impressive, at least to David's eyes. He was unused to this sort of environment and immediately felt even more shaky. He, Alan and Tom had agreed last night that they should try to avoid public displays of affection during the meeting since it would probably exacerbate tensions. He missed the feel of Alan's hand on his back and felt the need for his reassuring touch.

He shook Kieran's hand automatically but did not meet his eyes and hardly took him in at all. Instead he looked across to where his wife and parents-in-law were sitting. They also seemed diminished by the imposing room, somehow less formidable. Judging by their demeanour, they weren't particularly comfortable with the environment either.

Mona did not move but stared fixedly at a point on the meeting table in front of her. Cheryl looked up and gave him a hostile stare. Only David's father-in-law acknowledged his presence properly with a nod and a small smile.

David took his seat opposite the Spensleys, with Alan and Tom on either side of him. He looked across at his wife again. She looked drawn and tired; there were bags under her eyes – and the eyes themselves were dead and spiritless when she looked up briefly. He tried to analyse what he felt in that moment but failed; everything was too jumbled up. There was sorrow for how she was now suffering and what she'd clearly endured since September, but there was also anger for what she'd tried to do to him. Somewhere deep down lay a residual affection for the woman he'd lived with for six years and had once thought he loved enough to marry.

Kieran's voice cut through his reverie. "Right. Let's get started, shall we?"

"Indeed," responded Tom. "I think we all know why we're here, to attempt to reach an agreement on the ending of David and Mona's marriage and future arrangements for the care of their two sons, Tommy and Kevin."

"Quite so," Kieran replied.

David reflected that this fencing around was like a stately dance, using formality and cool tones to keep the lid on strong emotions. After a short pause Kieran opened his mouth to continue, but he was forestalled by Cheryl who suddenly burst forth like a pressure vessel blowing off steam. "Why does *he* have to be here?" she hissed to her husband.

This was much as predicted, David thought.

Cheryl directed a hostile stare at Alan, who shifted uneasily in his seat – not surprisingly, given her venomous tone. "He's the cause of all this, him and his *disgusting* habits," she added.

Brian tried to hush her but without success. She was clearly about to get into her stride when she was cut off by

Tom, who spoke in a cold, calm voice. "Mr Foreshaw is here at my client's request. It was specifically agreed that the principals could be accompanied by up to two people of their own choice without any right of veto from the other side."

David watched his wife's reaction. She stayed silent but glanced sideways at her mother, before closing her eyes and dropping her head in resignation. As Cheryl opened her mouth to speak again, Mona said softly, "Mother, *please*." Miraculously, this had the desired effect and Cheryl subsided.

Tom turned to David. "David, would you like to begin with your opening statement, please?"

David nodded and opened his mouth to speak. He was mortified when nothing came out. Blushing deeply, he turned in desperation to Alan. He smiled back, giving the reassurance David needed, and the moment passed. David cleared his throat and began.

He stuck faithfully to the script they had worked on, using his finger to follow the lines so that nothing got left out. Even so, he managed to put some expression into it: he didn't speak in a monotone or simply read the words in front of him.

At Alan's suggestion, they'd taken David's letter to Mona back in October as their starting point. David made the same points, acknowledging his responsibility for what had happened, but arguing that it was now time to move on and that everybody's first priority should be the boys' welfare.

At that point, Cheryl, who had been snorting softly and moving about in her seat throughout David's statement, could contain herself no longer. "The safety of the boys is already *our* priority," she almost spat out. "And that's why *you're* not getting anywhere near them, polluting their lives with your deviant lifestyle."

Tom intervened, irritated at her interruption. "We emphatically reject any implication that either my client's sexual orientation or his relationship with Mr Foreshaw represent a threat to the boys' safety in any way," he said in a staccato voice that Alan thought indicated the depth of his feelings.

"Well, they would, wouldn't they?" she barked back. "I beg to differ. The vicar at my church…"

She was interrupted by a new voice. Brian Spensley's tone reflected his irritation with his wife. "Cheryl, we don't need to know what your vicar thinks. You've told us often enough but it's not relevant now. Please be quiet and let David finish his statement."

Clearly taken aback by her husband's uncharacteristic intervention, Cheryl subsided. David resumed and managed to get through to the end without further interruption. He glanced at Alan and gave a small smile. Alan responded with a mouthed "well done" as Kieran began to speak.

As he finished reading his statement, David couldn't help but feel slightly pleased with himself. He'd not stumbled too much, had kept his cool during his mother-in-law's interruption and got all the way through without totally freaking out. Nevertheless, it had been one of the most nerve-wracking experiences of his life.

Again at Alan's suggestion, and with Tom's endorsement, he had ended as he had begun on a note of contrition, acknowledging his responsibility for the situation and expressing regret for the distress it had caused. But he would not apologise for who he was, nor for his sexual orientation. He emphasised the need to move on from that August Saturday night and his willingness to do as much as he could to make amends. Then he referred to the proposals that Tom and Kieran had drafted and presented to their respective clients before the meeting.

Now he waited nervously for his wife's response. For a few moments, nothing happened. Mona continued to stare at the table in front of her, whilst her mother cast him such a venomous look that he almost expected to shrivel up and die.

Eventually, Kieran broke the silence. "Thank you, Mr Edgeley. I'm sure that's very helpful. Now, Mrs Edgeley, do you have anything to say?"

Mona finally looked up. She caught David's eye briefly and he thought he could discern the hint of a smile, but it was so fleeting that he immediately concluded that he had been kidding himself. Eventually, her eyes rested on her father, who gave her a small nod and smile of encouragement, and gently jogged her elbow. She took a deep breath and started to speak.

David watched closely, but she did not meet his eyes again.

"I'm not going to go over old ground again. Either from our chats or my letters, you all know what I think about the way my husband behaved last summer. His betrayal hurt me deeply and made me question everything about my life and our marriage. It made me think that I'd been used as some form of camouflage for six years to disguise his homosexuality. He claims that this isn't true, and he's said that repeatedly, so I'm prepared to accept his reassurance."

David experienced a moment of hope; she'd made this accusation right from the start, and the fact that she was now accepting that she might have been wrong must be some form of progress.

"My husband has also said that his betrayal of me with Mr Foreshaw would not, and could not, have happened with anybody else. To be blunt, I didn't believe him then and I'm not sure I do now. But I've come to realise that the fact that he betrayed me with somebody who was his best friend for so many years at school might be significant. You might claim that Al – Mr Foreshaw – was the only person who might have had a prior claim on my husband's affections."

David was puzzled. He didn't quite see the point of making the remark and the language she was using was obviously not her own. It was much too formal and he detected some form of legal drafting. He was prepared to accept the concession, though, which set off another little bloom of hope in his chest. He glanced across at his mother-in-law; she was so tight-lipped that her mouth had almost disappeared completely. Her eyes were downcast and the only clue to her state of mind was the way she was wringing her hands every couple of minutes.

"With Dad's help, I've come to see that my husband's expressions of regret about the course of events are genuine. I accept that his apology for what happened is sincere."

David could hear the strain in her voice as she uttered those words. They sounded so alien coming from her lips but nevertheless the flowering of hope grew a little more.

"In turn, I should apologise for some of what I said both on that Saturday night and in the letters I sent last autumn. I accept that they were said or written out of a desire to hurt rather than being justified by events."

For the first time since she'd begun to speak, she looked straight into David's eyes. He gave her a small nod. "Thank you," he said quietly. He felt Alan's hand land on his thigh under the table and welcomed his touch, glancing quickly to his left and giving him a quick small smile.

After that Kieran took over again, and he and Tom launched into a line-by-line discussion over the terms of the agreement they'd sketched out earlier. David's mind wandered. He looked out of the window and watched the rain making small rivulets on the glass. The building opposite had a flat roof; he could see small puddles rippling every time they were hit by a new raindrop.

He was pleased with the way it had gone so far. The signs were good, especially as the two lawyers were now working their way through the divorce proceedings, the division of property (not that there was much, he reflected) and future financial support. Did this signal an end to the last few months of uncertainty and mental torture? God, he hoped so.

At that moment, he heard the word "custody" and his attention snapped back to the meeting.

Mona was speaking. "With Kieran's help, Dad and

I have studied the proposals you've tabled for the future custody of the children. We're prepared to accept them..." she paused for a moment in response to a sharp intake of breath from her mother, but quickly carried on "...with one or two provisos."

David noticed that Kieran looked slightly uncomfortable whilst Tom's normally rather impassive face registered surprise. David narrowed his eyes as he looked across the table to his wife.

"It's mainly about the access for the children. I want to add two conditions to the arrangements for their monthly visits with their father..."

David's heart sank. He thought he knew what was coming and, if he was right, he wasn't buying it under any circumstances. Cheryl gave the game away by looking up at Alan while her hostile expression to fade into a smirk.

His wife continued. "Firstly, they are to have no contact whatsoever with Mr Foreshaw during the visits. Secondly, any contact between the boys and their father must be supervised at all times by Mr Edgeley's parents."

The meeting that had been so quiet and orderly suddenly erupted into noise as Tom, Kieran and David all spoke at once. The other two broke off when they heard David's uncharacteristically loud voice. "Out of the question," he snapped. "Alan is a part of my life and I won't have him excluded from my relationship with the boys. Not happening, Mona."

"We won't risk them being corrupted by your deviant lifestyle and there's an end of it," replied Cheryl Spensley. Her body was wriggling with delight and there was a gleam of triumph in her eyes.

David realised that the deal was about to founder; this was the outcome she'd wanted all along. In that case, he was going to tell his mother-in-law precisely what he thought of her. He opened his mouth to reply, but Tom intervened.

"Perhaps I can remind Mrs Spensley of what I said at the beginning of the meeting. We will not accept any implication that my client's sexual orientation or his relationship with Mr Foreshaw are in themselves a threat to the boys' safety in any way. It is simply not true."

Kieran nodded. "Understood. Perhaps we might adjourn for a few minutes so that I can consult with my client?"

"Naturally," Tom replied smoothly, rising from his seat and signalling that Alan and David should follow him.

Kieran picked up the phone and asked his assistant to escort them to another room. She came in after a few moments and led them along the corridor to another, much smaller room.

Chapter 34

Alan

As the door shut, Tom grinned at them both. "Well done. That went really well – better than I expected, actually."

Alan was totally thrown by this. As they'd left the room, he'd been convinced that they were back to square one.

David clearly agreed; he was shaking with emotion and looked close to tears. "Glad you think so," he replied. "I thought it was a bloody disaster."

Tom shook his head. "I'll admit that was a disappointment at the end and it threw me for a moment. because I certainly wasn't expecting it. I don't think Kieran was, either."

"So? What now?" David asked.

"We wait and see. We're too close to a deal now to throw it all away."

"But…"

"David, please don't worry. Kieran knows that this won't fly. Since they changed the law a couple of years ago to allow same-sex couples to adopt, there's no way a court would accept that sexual orientation affects somebody's suitability to be a parent. At a guess, that's precisely what

Kieran is telling them now – and not for the first time, I expect."

"But I don't want this to end up in court, Tom!" David replied, his tone growing more agitated.

Alan moved to his side, took his hand and quietly told him to calm down.

Tom smiled. "Trust me, David, neither do I. But I'm sure they'll give way. You'll see."

"I wish I could share your confidence," David replied.

"Hey, Davy." Alan rubbed David's back. "Try to be a bit more positive, love. You got ninety per cent of what you wanted – we're almost there."

"I know, but that last bit is so important. I won't give way on that."

"I should think not," said Tom vehemently. "There's no question of compromise on that – and Kieran knows that as well."

"It's her bloody mother," David observed gloomily. "If I know Cheryl, she'll have gone on and on all weekend like a dripping tap until Mona agreed to try, if for no other reason than to shut her up."

Tom laughed. "God, yes. She's a holy terror, isn't she? Was she always like that?"

"We never got on," David replied. "She always thought I wasn't good enough for her daughter and was never shy about saying so. But a few months ago she got all religious. She started going to a new church with this bloke, the Rev Archie. That made her much worse. He's a noted homophobe, so he's influenced her a lot."

"Well, I certainly wouldn't be keen on letting her near my kids," Tom said. "What a mouth!"

"Me neither," added Alan. "Talk about the mother-in-law from hell."

They lapsed into silence. Alan was still holding David's hand. Some of the tension seemed to have left his body and he seemed more relaxed. but Alan knew that it wouldn't take much for the agitation to ramp up again.

Tom's phone buzzed. "Excuse me, I need to check this message," he said apologetically as he reached for his phone and began to scroll through it. He read the message, huffed and immediately began to type a reply.

Alan was transfixed by the speed at which he was able to work using only his thumbs. "Is that one of those Blackberry phones?" he asked when Tom had finished typing.

Tom nodded. "Yeah, it's fantastic – everything integrated on one device. I love it."

"My boss is thinking about getting them for us but some of the guys are very nervous."

"Tell them not to be. It's a great little machine. I wouldn't be without one."

Silence descended. Tom continued to work on his Blackberry, while Alan and David sat together. Alan rubbed David's knuckles gently with his thumb, trying to keep him calm and to reassure him. It seemed to be working because eventually David looked up, gave him a small smile and squeezed his hand. Alan squeezed back and gave him a wink.

David looked at his watch. "Twenty minutes. Do you think they'll be much longer?"

"I bloody hope not – I'm due back in London for a meeting at four-thirty," Tom replied with a grin. "And

Hugo will have my guts for garters if I'm late home from work, because we're going out tonight."

"That might be tight," Alan said. "You need to be on the 13.05 to King's Cross, don't you?"

"Yes, that's what my PA said. So we've got no more than an hour before I need to be out of here. I'll give them another few minutes. If nothing happens, I'll go and find out what's going on. Ultimately, they're either going to give way or not. If not, there's no point in hanging around. We all need to retire, lick our wounds and work out what's next."

David opened his mouth to protest but at that point the door opened and Kieran's assistant put her head round the door. "They're ready for you, gentlemen."

Chapter 35

David

"They're ready for you, gentlemen."

David felt his stomach drop as Kieran's PA summoned them back into the meeting. Despite Alan's attempts to keep him calm, he couldn't suppress his agitation. All he'd been able to focus on was the thought that an agreement was about to be snatched from him. He could murder bloody Cheryl Spensley.

His feelings were made all the stronger by disappointment. When he'd finished his statement, and particularly when Mona had started hers in a fairly conciliatory tone, he'd actually begun to believe that he'd soon see his boys again. The four months of grief and uncertainty they'd endured were about to end. When Tom spoke about retiring and regrouping, all David could see was a black hole of gloom and despair opening in front of him. Now, as they rose from their seats and left the room, he was reluctant to go back into the meeting because he dreaded the outcome so much,

"Here we go. Keep your fingers crossed," Tom remarked.

"Thank God for that," Alan muttered. He signalled for David to go ahead of him, and once again placed his hand in the small of David's back. David almost arched into the touch, it felt so good. He turned and smiled at Alan, who winked in response.

As they entered the room, the scene had hardly changed: mother, daughter and father sat in a row, staring at the table in front of them. David tried to read their expressions, but it was difficult since their heads remained bowed and they didn't meet anybody's eyes.

Once Tom, David and Alan had resumed their seats, Kieran spoke. He'd lost most of the assurance that he'd exuded earlier and looked distinctly frazzled. "Sorry to have kept you gentlemen for so long. We've discussed the issue of Mrs Edgeley's proposed conditions about access to the children and have come to accept..."

"Well, some of us have," Cheryl interrupted. "Not me, certainly."

Kieran cleared his throat and resumed. "Have come to accept that the proposed conditions are discriminatory and would not be acceptable to the courts."

"Typical," huffed Cheryl.

Kieran snapped. "Mrs Spensley, please! We've been through all this and you've had your say. Now please may we get on with this?"

Brian intervened. "Cheryl, if you can't sit and be quiet, please leave the room. We all know your views and you're not going to change anybody's mind."

She subsided for a moment but then stood up. "Very well. If I'm not allowed to defend the interests of my daughter and grandchildren, I might as well leave." She turned to her husband. "I'll never forgive you for this betrayal, Brian. Never. And you can tell that daughter of yours that there'll be no more unpaid babysitting and drudgery from this granny." With that, she turned and left the room, slamming the door behind her.

"Told you," muttered Tom. "She didn't get her way."

David looked up and noticed the expressions on Mona's and her father's faces. Before they'd said a word, he knew Tom was right. They had a deal and he'd be seeing his sons again very soon. He closed his eyes against the tears of joy and relief that were welling up inside him.

With Cheryl out of the way, Kieran indicated acceptance of the proposed agreement as previously drafted. He acknowledged formally that Mona had accepted that the boys' visits would not require supervision. He and Tom resumed their stately dance, dotting 'I's' and crossing 'T's'.

David tuned out as he tried to get his mind round what was happening. He did not feel quite as elated as he'd expected. He'd missed the boys terribly and had found their absence profoundly disturbing but, on the other hand, he'd had a four-month holiday from parental responsibility. During that time the burden had fallen on his wife and her parents. That break was now over; today's agreement meant that he would have to resume his role as a father to Tommy and Kevin, even if he was only going to see them for one weekend in four.

He did not underestimate the challenges of getting to know them again, giving his version of the events that had led to their separation, introducing Alan to them and explaining his presence in their lives. They were both too young to understand most of the detail, but it was important that they should know that their father was back in their lives and had every intention of staying there. He loved them and would always be there for them.

Tom started to gather his papers together and David realised that the meeting was about to break up. His attention snapped back to the present and he noticed Mona looking at him rather more kindly than she had earlier. He gave a tentative smile in return and cleared his throat. "Mum said to say that she would be happy to help with the boys, if you needed it. I thought I ought to mention it if your mum ... you know, if she meant all that stuff..." He left the sentence unfinished, unsure of its reception.

"Thanks," she replied. "I might take her up on that. Now that this is ... er ... resolved."

David nodded and rose to leave, conscious that Alan and Tom were at the door waiting for him. "Good. I suppose I'll see you soon."

"Yes, I suppose you will." Her expression became guarded again.

David paused to shake Brian Spensley's hand on the way out and offer a nod of thanks to Kieran.

Chapter 36

Alan

Once the formalities of the meeting were over, Alan could hardly wait to get back to Edward Street. The whole thing had lasted no more than a couple of hours but David looked exhausted and rather shocked. In the end it had been comparatively easy to reach a deal, and Alan knew how difficult David had found the burden of uncertainty that had weighed so heavily on his shoulders for the last few months.

It would be a couple of weeks before the formal agreements could be processed and signed, so nothing else would happen that day. They left the lawyers' offices and bade farewell to Tom as he dashed off to catch his train south, promising to meet up with him and Hugo in London very soon. Tom thought the formalities should take no more than ten days, so he suggested that they plan a weekend visit with the boys at the beginning of February.

Meanwhile, they had a refurbishment to plan. They needed to turn a rather fusty house designed for an elderly maiden aunt into a welcoming and attractive home in which two little boys and their dad could spend fun weekends. Alan thought it needed to be somewhere that Tommy and Kevin would look forward to visiting, a happy environment in which they could rebuild their relationship with their dad – and, he hoped, build one with himself.

He did not underestimate the challenges, especially if Mona and her mother were to spend the rest of the time bad-mouthing him and David. Mind you, he wasn't sure what the state of relations between mother and daughter might be after the morning's events.

They sat in the back of the cab back to Sedgethwaite, knees pressed together, holding hands discreetly. It was a saloon car with no partition, so there was little chance of a proper conversation without the driver listening. They passed the journey in virtual silence, occasionally exchanging a smile and a squeeze of the hand. It was constraining, but the ride still felt warm and intimate.

Back at the house, the front door was barely shut when Alan reached out and took David into his arms, hugging him hard and kissing him soundly until they were forced to pause for breath. "I was so proud of you this morning, Davy. You did so well."

"God, I was so fucking terrified, Al – I had no idea what was going to happen. For all I knew, we could have ended up with another shouting match."

"I know – and I suspect you would have done if her mother had had anything to do with it."

"Yeah. There's a storm brewing there, all right. Cheryl isn't used to being defied by her husband and daughter at the same time. There'll be trouble at t'mill, I reckon."

"Couldn't happen to a nicer woman as far as I'm

concerned. God, the hate in those eyes!"

David shifted in Alan's arms. "Enough about Cheryl Spensley, and more about you. Thanks for being there this morning. I couldn't have done it without you."

"It was my pleasure – anything for my Davy."

David look up into Alan's eyes and smirked. "Anything?"

Alan returned his look with a wicked grin and nodded. "Anything."

"Need you, Al," came the throaty reply.

Alan found himself being led upstairs by the hand. Once they were inside his old bedroom, their kissing resumed, though rather more calmly and gently than before. Their bodies came together, their arms wrapped round each other,

As so often when they were together, Alan felt safe and secure in David's arms. He closed his eyes and relaxed, allowing David's tongue to explore his mouth while he revelled in all the sensations that were assailing him – excitement, warmth, joy, comfort and *love*.

He felt David's hands begin to move, pulling his shirt out, breaking their kiss so that he could unbutton it. Alan reached for the button on David's trousers, popping it open and sliding down the zip, immediately aware of the heat of arousal. He pushed David's underwear down, lightly fingering his erection and drawing a hiss of pleasure from him. His own arms were trapped as David pushed his shirt off his shoulders and down. It floated to the floor.

By unspoken consent, their arms swapped places. Alan unfastened David's shirt, while David quickly freed Alan's cock from the constraints of his underwear.

Alan groaned at the touch. "So good, baby. Love you

so much." Suddenly his arms felt empty as David slipped from them and reached into the drawer of the bedside cabinet for a tube of lube.

Alan quickly removed the rest of his clothes. When he looked back, David was star-fished on the bed, looking up at him. When he spoke, his voice was deeper than normal, eyes wide open but his pupils blown. "Need you inside me, Al. Now. Make love to me, please."

Alan beamed down at him. "Never one to refuse an invitation like that, Davy." Within moments, Alan was on the bed with him, preparing him so that his request could be met, pushing in with two fingers and scissoring them to make sure he was ready.

David shivered and groaned as Alan's fingers brushed his prostate. "That's it," he whispered. "I'm ready, Al. Put it in me."

Alan entered his lover, revelling as always in the tight heat that engulfed him. He slid home with one smooth stroke, eliciting another groan of satisfaction. He paused, making sure that his lover could adjust, his hips trembling with anticipation.

"Move, love," David whispered. "Need to feel you so bad."

Alan began to move, slowly at first but gradually increasing the tempo and strength of his thrusts until the room was filled with the sound of their bodies slapping together. They were never going to make this a long session, and Alan felt his orgasm build quickly. He reached for David, pumping him in rhythm with his own thrusts.

David whimpered with pleasure and called Alan's name as he reached the point of no return, shooting all over his stomach and chest. The sudden extra pressure on Alan pushed him over the edge and he released his load deep into David, calling out as he did so, body jerking uncontrollably.

After a few moments, Alan pulled out carefully and lay on his side next to David, who looked across at him and grinned. "Thanks, I needed that." They kissed languidly.

"The pleasure was all mine, Davy. Believe me."

"Love you so much, Al. I'm so glad we're together. I can't imagine my life without you."

"Me neither. It's odd, you know – we've been together for four months, but somehow this morning feels like a new start."

"You feel that too? Funny, isn't it? I suppose it's like Gavin said that night when he gave me the lift – we spend so much of our energies simply steering the ship, keeping everything on course with our lives. Today somehow feels like we've settled on a new course."

"You're right, Davy, it does. Let's hope we can maintain an even keel."

To be continued.

Acknowledgements

My grateful thanks to my editor Karen Holmes, beta reader Kirsten Waite and cover designer Hilary Pitts for their hard work in helping to bring this book to market. My deepest thanks also to my husband Michael Anderson and to all my friends for their help and encouragement over the last couple of years.

About the Author

Chris Cheek was born and brought up in South London. He has strong family ties with northern England and is a graduate of Lancaster University. He and his husband, Michael, have been together for over forty years and moved recently to the Sussex Coast after 25 years in the Yorkshire Dales.

This is Chris's fifth novel. His first book, *The Stamp of Nature*, was published in June 2018. Since then, his writing has focused on two series - *Love in A Changing Climate*, comprising *A Year of Awakening* (October 2018) and *Governing Passions* (June 2020); and *The Navigation Quartet*, of which this is the second volume. The first, *Veering off Course* was published in February 2019.

Chris writes a regular blog which can be found at www.chrischeek.me.

9 781999 647988